LOST HOPE

HOPE LANDING NEW RECRUITS
BOOK ONE

EDIE JAMES

BOOKS BY EDIE JAMES

Hope Landing Romantic Suspense

- Hard Landing
- Fast Landing
- No Landing
- Bad Landing
- Crash Landing
- Last Landing
- Next Landing
- Wild Landing

MacKenzie Cove Romantic Suspense

- Rising Storm
- Rising Seas
- Rising Wind
- Rising Fury
- Rising Hope
- Rising Faith

Redemption Creek Romantic Suspense

- Hidden Sins
- False Sins
- Killer Sins
- Deadly Sins
- Silent Sins

- Deadly Sins
- Lethal Sins
- Final Sins

Hope Landing: New Recruits

- Lost Hope
- Deadly Hope

Copyright 2025 by Edie James

All rights reserved.

No part of this book may be reproduced in any form or by any electronic or mechanical means, including information storage and retrieval systems, without written permission from the author, except for the use of brief quotations in a book review.

∽

Start the HOPE LANDING series FREE. Click HERE to join my newsletter and download HARD LANDING free.

I LOVE hearing from readers! Connect with me at Edie@EdieJamesBooks.com

1

DESERT MIRAGE

The swamp cooler in Desert Mirage Bar fought a losing battle against the Yuma heat. As if there was a cooling system on the planet an August night in Southern Arizona couldn't defeat. Even at 9:00 p.m. the temperature hovered near triple digits, turning the dingy establishment into a sweaty cave of desperation. Ronan Quinn nursed his third Monster of the night.

He and booze had broken up over a year ago.

From his usual corner, he had a clear view of both exits and the parking lot beyond the grimy windows. Old habits die hard, even when you were flying cargo planes of questionable legality for a boss who paid in cash.

In the back, beyond the warped and scuffed dance floor, a pair of Border Patrol Agents racked up another game of pool.

The local news droned on about the illegal immigration crisis, the anchor's voice barely audible over the wheezing air conditioner. Sarah, the owner, cursed softly as she tried to fix the ceiling fan. The ancient thing hadn't worked right in the four months Ronan had been coming in, but she kept trying.

Three years ago, he'd been piloting multi-million-dollar aircraft off carrier decks. Leading ultra-secret ops in shadowy corners of the world. Now he was lucky if the busted-up cargo planes in the boss's fleet started on the first try. The irony wasn't lost on him—a former Navy SEAL reduced to running "agricultural shipments" across the border. He'd earned his discharge, though. No point dwelling on it.

The door swung open, letting in a blast of desert heat. Ronan's heart stopped. For a second, he thought the heat was causing hallucinations. There was no way Axel Reinhardt was standing in the doorway of this dump, looking like he'd just stepped out of a Minneapolis board meeting.

But it was Axel—pressed slacks, button-down shirt with the sleeves rolled up, and that familiar concerned expression that had always made Ronan feel about two inches tall. All six-foot-four of him filled the doorway, his bulk somehow both imposing and comforting. Even wrinkled and road-weary, he carried himself with that particular Midwestern grace that came from a lifetime of making his size work in normal-sized spaces. His usually well-groomed beard was untrimmed, but his eyes still held that same steady warmth that had made him the team's unofficial counselor. The kind of guy who could make a corporate boardroom as comfortable as a NASCAR pit, equally at home in both worlds. Right now though, he looked like a teddy bear that had been through a washing machine—rumpled, exhausted, and somehow more real for it.

The regulars noticed immediately. Outsiders stuck out here, especially ones who looked like they belonged in a Fortune 500 company instead of a border town dive bar. Being a non-drinker now, Ronan wouldn't be there either, if there was any place else in this hellhole to hang out.

Sarah moved closer to Ronan's table, pretending to clean

glasses while eyeing the newcomer. The pool players paused their game, leaving only the drone of the talking heads on the TV news.

Shame and defensiveness warred in Ronan's chest as Axel's eyes found him. He'd pushed the team away after the discharge. Axel hardest of all. Easier to disappear than face their disappointment. Now his past had tracked him down anyway.

"Hey," Axel said, sliding onto the stool next to him.

Up close, Axel looked like he'd been driven over by a John Deere. His normally immaculate clothes were wrinkled. Dark circles shadowed his eyes. Something was seriously wrong. Axel wouldn't have tracked him down—wouldn't have left his comfortable life running his father's car dealership—without a good reason.

"I've been calling you since Sunday." Irritation warred with fear in Axel's voice. "Ten times, Ro. What gives?"

Ronan shifted in his seat. The phone was probably in his truck somewhere, battery long dead. Or maybe he'd left it at his apartment. Hard to say. "Been busy," he muttered.

"Yeah. I can see that." Axel's eyes swept the bar, taking in the peeling paint and ancient desert photographs. His gaze settled on the energy drink. "Seriously? You're really not drinking?"

The question sparked anger in Ronan's gut, but shame doused it quickly. After the discharge, he'd spiraled. Badly. Axel and the guys had scooped him up off the floor of too many base-side bars to count. The man had reason to question him.

He pulled the twelve-month AA chip from his pocket and slid it across the table. "Got it last week." But Axel wouldn't have known that. How could he? After he left San Diego, Ronan had methodically cut every tie to his old life. Eight teammates—family, really—and he'd ghosted them all. Axel had tried the hardest to maintain contact, but eventually even his stubborn persistence had worn thin.

"I'm sorry," Ronan said softly. "About everything."

Relief softened Axel's features. "Glad to hear it." He pushed the chip back across the table. "I mean it, dude. I've been praying for you for ... like forever."

Ronan sighed. Still Axel. Still the faithful, faith-filled SEAL. He'd always envied his friend's unwavering convictions, even if they hadn't worn off on him.

A group of Marines burst through the door, young and loud and full of themselves. The sight made Ronan's chest ache. Had he and Axel ever been that young?

Sarah cranked up the jukebox, drowning out their whooping.

Axel's presence nagged at him. His former teammate looked completely out of place in his business casual wear, but it wasn't just the clothes. Axel had built a good life for himself back in Minneapolis, running his father's dealership. He wouldn't have tracked Ronan down without reason.

"What are you doing here flying freight out of this dump?" Axel asked, his voice barely audible over the din.

Ronan bristled. "It's not easy finding work with a general discharge." He caught himself before adding that it could have been worse. A dishonorable discharge was like a felony conviction in the civilian world. At least he'd avoided that.

"Not easy with a bad attitude, either."

Ronan couldn't argue with that.

A burst of static from the Border Patrol Agents' radios caught his attention. Something about a chase in progress. Behind them, the Marines were getting rowdier by the minute.

"What brought you down here?" Ronan asked, raising his voice over the chaos.

Axel glanced around the crowded bar. "Let's take this outside. Somewhere we can actually hear ourselves think."

Ronan nodded and followed him into the stifling night air. Whatever had brought Axel to this desert hellhole, it couldn't be good.

2

NIGHT FLIGHT

THE DESERT STRETCHED ENDLESSLY in every direction, nothing but scrub brush and sand under a sky dulled by dust and heat and despair. The bar's gravel parking lot was half-empty, Axel's gleaming BMW looking completely out of place next to Ronan's rust-bucket truck.

"When's the last time you heard from Tank?" Axel asked, leaning against his car.

"Not sure." Ronan shifted uncomfortably. "Maybe a year ago?" The defensive note in his voice made him wince.

"He's in trouble."

The words hung in the hot air between them.

Ronan's mind flashed to Copenhagen—the mission that had ended everything. The civilian's face still haunted his dreams, along with the echo of that fatal shot. He'd taken the fall, as a team leader should. Better one career destroyed than eight. The brass had wanted blood after a civilian death on European soil, and he'd given them what they needed—a clean narrative, a single shooter, a clear end to the investigation.

"Don't," he said when he saw the guilt creeping into

Axel's expression. "I was team leader. My shot, my consequences." The lie felt familiar now, worn smooth like river stones after three years of repetition. Griff had been the only other one in position that night, the only one who knew what really happened in that Copenhagen lab.

They'd never spoken of it again—not during the investigation, not during Ronan's discharge, not in the years since. Some secrets were worth protecting, even at the cost of everything you'd built.

He caught Axel studying his face and forced his expression neutral. The big man had always been too perceptive, especially when it came to guilt. But what was done was done. The team had survived, unscathed. That's what mattered.

A black SUV with tinted windows cruised past for the third time. Ronan tracked it in his peripheral vision, noting the driver's furtive glances their direction.

He studied Axel more carefully now—the wrinkled suit, the exhaustion etched in his face. "Did you sleep in that suit or what?"

Axel's jaw tightened. "You think I've slept? Been too busy driving, dude. You might not be aware, but Minneapolis is 1,826 miles from here. That's two days on the road. Nonstop."

The words hit Ronan like a physical blow. "Yikes, Ax. Why didn't you call—" He stopped himself. Right. He had called.

"Tank needs us," Axel said sharply, nodding toward the dilapidated airport on the horizon. "These the only rides you got?"

"Unfortunately." Ronan's stomach tightened. "Why?"

"Because you're flying me to San Diego. Now."

"I've got a run scheduled—" Ronan caught himself. Better not mention where. "We can go after."

"We're already two days late. We're going now."

Ronan opened his mouth to protest again, but as he looked around at his pathetic circumstances—the sketchy bar, the questionable cargo runs—the words died in his throat. "Yeah. Okay."

The BMW's leather seats were cool against his back as they drove to the airfield. His truck sat abandoned at the bar.

"Will it be safe there?" Axel asked.

"I hope not." Ronan directed him toward a storage facility where they could stash the BMW. The luxury car's quiet ride was a stark reminder of how far he'd fallen. His truck leaked exhaust into the cab.

He glanced at his friend. "You doing okay with flying these days?"

"Sure." Axel's attempt at a casual tone failed miserably. "Long as I stay at least ten miles away from an airplane."

Ronan's chest tightened. Axel's PTSD after Kandahar had been brutal—one more reason Ronan had kept his distance. Just being around him seemed to trigger Axel's symptoms. Yet here his friend was, ready to face those demons to help Marcus.

What had their teammate gotten himself into?

The Lockheed Electra waited in the darkness like an aging prizefighter—still powerful despite the patches of bare metal showing through her faded paint. Ronan had grown oddly fond of the old turboprop; she might be past her airline glory days, but the converted cargo hauler could still outperform half the newer freighters in the sky. He ran through his preflight checks, grateful for the empty cargo hold. In this business, you didn't load up until the last possible second.

"Won't your boss miss his plane?" Axel asked, his voice tight as he climbed aboard.

Ronan couldn't suppress his grin. "You bet. I'll consider

this my resignation letter." He started the engines and began taxiing toward the runway.

In the dim cockpit light, Axel's face had taken on an alarming pallor. Ronan searched for a distraction. "Tell me about Marcus. What's he gotten himself into?"

"Not sure exactly." Axel gripped the armrests as they picked up speed. "He wouldn't talk about it over the phone. Just said he needed face-to-face. But he's scared, man. Wanted the whole team together. I figured you and me would be faster though. Whatever this is, it's bad."

Ronan studied his friend's profile. Axel had everything to lose by being here—the dealership, his comfortable life in Minnesota, his father's trust. Yet here he was, white-knuckled but determined, because a teammate had called.

Ronan guided the Electra into position, his mind already jumping ahead to San Diego. Of all places, why had Marcus settled there? The legitimate world felt like a foreign country now—one where he no longer spoke the language. But something about this situation made his old training kick in, instincts he'd tried to bury surfacing like muscle memory.

Hell, even Coast Guard stations made him twitchy these days.

But Marcus? He'd always been the most dedicated of them all. The quintessential SEAL. One of the best operators Ronan had ever known.

He glanced at his friend's white-knuckled grip on the armrests. "You gonna be okay? It's a two-hour flight, minimum, and this old rust bucket doesn't have autopilot. I can't be letting go of the controls if you freak out."

"No freaking out," the big man responded, but the words sounded more like a plea than a reassurance as Axel's murmured prayers filled the cockpit.

Once, Ronan would have joined him, back when he still

believed someone was listening. Now he focused on the instruments instead, trusting in what he could see and touch.

The engines roared as they gathered speed down the runway. Every mile closer to San Diego would bring him that much nearer to everything he'd been running from, but beneath the dread, something else flickered to life. He'd built walls for a reason, constructed a life where no one could get close enough to matter. Where losing someone couldn't break him again. But Marcus needed him, and some loyalties ran deeper than self-preservation.

The wheels left the ground, and they soared into the dark Arizona night, leaving the dust storm and his wasted years behind.

At least for now.

3

CLEAN SCENE

THE FOGHORNS on Coronado made Ronan's teeth ache. He hadn't been this close to a Navy base in three years, and his body was making its objections known. His skin crawled as Axel guided the rental car through the quiet streets of Marcus's neighborhood.

Too close. Way too close to the base.

Through gaps in the buildings, Ronan caught glimpses of the harbor lights, of the massive shapes of ships at anchor. Each sight sent another surge of bitter memories through him. He'd given everything to the teams. Broken bones, spilled blood, lost sleep—none of it had mattered in the end. One bad call, and they'd stripped it all away. The career, the brotherhood, everything.

"This is it." Axel pulled up in front of a modest condo complex.

The middle of the night. Zero one hundred hours and change. Tank's black Jeep sat in its designated spot, a light coating of dew suggesting it hadn't moved in hours.

Ronan pushed away memories of the last time he'd seen

that Jeep—the day he'd cleaned out his locker. "No lights. No response to texts."

"Could be sleeping." But Axel's voice held zero conviction.

They climbed out into the damp night air. Nothing obviously wrong—no broken windows, no kicked-in door—but the hair on Ronan's neck stood at attention. The scene was too perfect, too still. Like a movie set rather than a living space.

His body remembered its training even if his mind wanted to forget. He found himself moving differently, scanning sight lines, checking corners. Beside him, Axel did the same, their old partnership sliding back into place without discussion.

"Something feels wrong." Axel's whisper barely carried over the distant thrum of base activity.

"Copy that."

Ronan studied the building. Second floor corner unit. Good sight lines, decent egress options. Classic Tank. The orange glow of sodium lights cast weird shadows through the palm trees, making the whole scene feel surreal. Like one of those dreams where everything looks normal but feels off.

"Front door or back?" Axel asked.

"Front. If someone's watching, skulking around back will only draw attention."

They approached the stairs, keeping to the shadows. The metal steps felt solid, but Ronan tested each one before putting his full weight down. No sense triggering a booby trap if someone had gotten here first.

At the door, Axel pulled out a set of picks. Despite the tension coiling in Ronan's gut, he had to smile. "Still got it, huh?"

"Like riding a bike." Axel's big hands worked the delicate tools with surprising grace. The lock yielded in seconds.

The deadbolt's click echoed down the empty hallway.

Ronan's pulse hammered in his ears as they entered. The air felt wrong—stale, with an underlying smell that sent his heartrate zooming. Moonlight filtered through vertical blinds, creating bars of light across the floor. In the shadows between, anything could be waiting.

"Tank?" Axel's voice bounced off bare walls. No response.

The silence pressed in, broken only by the soft whisper of the AC. Every instinct screamed danger. Something bad had happened here. Ronan could feel it in his bones, in the way the darkness thickened around them. In the absolute stillness that felt more like absence than peace.

"Taking right," Ronan whispered, falling into their old pattern.

Axel nodded and peeled left.

They cleared the condo room by room, muscle memory taking over. Kitchen first—spotless counters, empty sink. Living room—magazines perfectly aligned on the coffee table. Even the remote controls were arranged with military precision. Too much precision.

"No take-out containers," Axel muttered. "No pizza boxes."

Ronan knew what he meant. Marcus had always survived on delivered food. "No mail either. Nothing personal at all."

The spare bedroom looked like a furniture showroom. Master bath—no towels hung crooked, no toothpaste tube squeezed in the middle like Marcus always did. The wrongness of it made Ronan's skin crawl.

Light spilled from under the office door. Ronan's heart slammed against his ribs as he pushed it open.

"Dear Lord. No." Axel's broken whisper hit harder than a punch.

Axel's prayer wasn't just shock this time—it was raw anguish. Ronan's own throat closed around words he hadn't spoken in years, prayers that died unformed. What kind of God let this happen to good men?

Back to them, their friend slumped at his desk, forehead against the surface, his service weapon still in his right hand. Powder burns to the temple marked the spot of the single shot.

The sight punched the air from Ronan's lungs, but training kicked in, shoving grief into a box to be opened later. Beside him, he felt Axel do the same—that instant shift into operational mode that had kept them alive through countless missions.

"Don't touch anything." Ronan's voice came out rough. He fought the urge to rush to his friend, to check for a pulse they both knew wouldn't be there. The room temperature, the way Marcus's skin had settled, the faint but distinctive odor—all things they'd seen too many times in their line of work.

"He's been gone at least twenty-four hours," Ronan said, his tactical mind cataloging details.

"About the time he sent that last text." Axel's voice was flat.

Ronan nodded grimly. The scene was too perfect, too clean. Like something staged for a photograph. His eyes swept the room again, catching on Marcus's wrist. The watch face gleamed in the dim light, and something in Ronan's gut twisted.

"Axel," he said quietly. "Look at his watch. This isn't right." Ronan forced himself to study the scene clinically, pushing down the grief threatening to choke him. "His watchband is fastened on the wrong hole."

"Could've lost weight." But Axel straightened, professional training overtaking emotion. "Unless ..."

"Tank was obsessive about that watch. Never would have

left it loose." The words tasted bitter. If he'd answered his phone, if he hadn't been so wrapped up in his own misery ...

"Stop it." Axel's voice was sharp. "I see that look. This isn't on you."

"I should've—"

"We all should've. But right now, we need to focus. Something got him killed. Something big enough to bring in cleaners."

Ronan nodded, grateful for Axel's steady presence. His friend was right. They could grieve later. Right now, they needed answers.

The office looked wrong, just like the rest of the condo. Marcus had been methodical, but never pristine. His desk should've been cluttered with coffee cups and protein bar wrappers. Instead, everything was arranged with artificial precision.

They stood in silence, absorbing the implications. Someone had gone to a lot of trouble to sanitize the scene. To make it look like their friend had simply given up and eaten his gun.

The precision reminded him of his SEAL training—analyze, compartmentalize, execute. Skills he'd buried under cargo runs and cheap motels. Skills he'd need again if they were going to find justice for Marcus. The thought should have terrified him. Instead, it felt like coming home.

"We can't leave him like this." Axel's voice cracked.

"No." Ronan squeezed his friend's shoulder. "But we can't call it in yet either. Not until we know what he was working on."

"Something worth killing for." Axel's eyes were wet, but his jaw was set.

They swept through the condo again, this time slower, more methodically. Every surface gleamed. Even the refrigerator had been wiped clean—no obvious smudges, no takeout menus held by magnets, no photos. Tank had always kept photos.

Ronan hesitated at the office doorway, his hand tight on the frame. Marcus's body was still there, still arranged in that unnatural pose, and every instinct screamed at him to stay back. To not look again at what had been done to his friend. But they needed answers.

"I got this," Axel said quietly, moving to stand between Ronan and the desk, partially blocking his view of their friend's body. The simple gesture—pure Axel—helped Ronan focus.

The laptop sat on the corner of the desk, positioned at that precise forty-five-degree angle Tank always used. At first glance, it was his—same model, same subtle scratch near the touchpad. But someone had gone to a lot of trouble to make it look well-used without actually knowing how Tank lived. The wear pattern on the wrist rest was too even, too uniform. Marcus had always favored his right side when typing, should have worn that side down more.

"They studied his habits," Ronan said, fighting to keep his voice steady. "But they didn't get all the details right."

The room itself felt like a military display—everything aligned at perfect angles, pens arranged by size, books alphabetized. But Marcus's organization had been different. Organized chaos, he'd called it. He'd color-coded his files, stacked reference books by frequency of use, kept his favorite coffee mug full of colored markers within arm's reach. None of that personality remained. Someone had stripped away every trace of the man who'd lived here, replacing it with this sterile facsimile of military order.

"They did a thorough job," Axel muttered, running a finger along the dustless windowsill. "Professional clean team."

"Agreed." Ronan's jaw tightened. "But they didn't know him."

"The mail," Axel said suddenly. "There's no mail anywhere. Not even junk mail."

Ronan fought the urge to run. Getting caught here would end badly, but they couldn't leave. Not yet. Not until they figured out what had gotten their teammate killed.

He clapped a hand to the back of his neck, as if he could massage away the fury. The grief. Someone had gone to a lot of trouble to make this look like suicide. Someone professional. Someone meticulous.

Someone who didn't know about the big man's book habit.

The realization hit him like a physical blow. While he'd been running from his past, hiding in desert bars and making illegal cargo runs, Marcus had been fighting something big enough to get him killed.

A flash of red and blue reflected off the window, painting the sterile walls with police lights. Ronan groaned.

"Someone called it in." Axel moved to the window, keeping to the side. "Three patrol cars, and a fourth pulling up."

Ronan's mind raced. Back door? No—they'd be covering it. Fire escape? Too exposed. They were three stories up, and the parking lot below would be filling with law enforcement.

"We're blown." The words tasted like ash. Getting caught here would mean federal charges, minimum. And whoever had cleaned this scene hadn't left Tank like this just to have two ex-SEALs discover the truth.

"Options?" Axel asked, falling into their old pattern.

"None." Ronan heard car doors slam, followed by purposeful footsteps on the stairs. "We'll have to play it straight."

Axel's eyebrows shot up.

"We got worried about our friend. Came to check on him. Found ..." Ronan's voice caught. "Found this."

Axel nodded slowly. "Think they'll buy it?"

"No." Heavy footsteps in the hallway now. "But it'll buy us time."

"Time for what?"

"To figure out who did this. And why they wanted us to find him."

Axel's steady presence at his back felt like absolution he didn't deserve. Three years of silence, yet here they were, falling into old patterns like muscle memory. Whatever Marcus had discovered, whatever had gotten him killed, they'd face it together.

The way it should have been all along.

4

BREAKING PROTOCOL

SAN DIEGO'S newest NCIS Special Agent Maya Chen followed her partner's SUV through the pre-dawn streets, her mind racing through Commander Phillips's urgent briefing. The Commander had just learned that Marcus "Tank" Sullivan—former Navy SEAL who'd somehow accessed classified VA files approximately twenty-four hours ago—was now dead in his condo. Apparent suicide. And two of his old teammates already on scene.

Different city, different badge, but suspicious deaths were universal. She'd worked enough of them in LA to know when things didn't add up. A man breaks into secure files, then conveniently kills himself before anyone can question him? And his SEAL buddies just happen to find the body?

They pulled up to the darkened condo complex, already alive with the red and blue pulse of patrol cars. Her new partner emerged from his agency Explorer clutching gas station coffee like life support, twenty years with NCIS showing in every weary movement. He wasn't anything like her old partner back in LA. Then again, that's exactly why she'd left—to get away from a precinct where every detective had worked with the legendary Lawrence Chen, where every move she made was measured against her father's legacy.

"The locals are containing the scene," Tom Benson said, scanning the collection of patrol cars. "But Phillips wants us to handle everything inside. Says it's sensitive."

Maya checked her weapon with the smooth efficiency that had made her the youngest female detective in LAPD's Pacific Division. "When isn't it sensitive? What else did Command tell you?"

"Sullivan accessed medical records from the VA clinic terminal. Files he shouldn't have been able to see. Then he offs himself? Weird."

"Maybe he knew we were coming."

The sergeant manning the perimeter approached, looking uncomfortable. "Agents. We've got two men upstairs—Quinn and Reinhardt. They were here when we arrived."

Maya exchanged looks with Benson. Command intervention at the local level, this time of night? For a simple suicide?

"What do we know?" she asked the sergeant manning the perimeter.

"Not much. I had a look at the vic. I'm not a coroner, but it's obvious the guy's been dead a while. I'm thinking a day or so." He gestured toward the third floor. "When we arrived, they informed us the body was inside. Apparent suicide. We secured the scene and called it in per protocol."

"And you left them up there?" Benson sounded shocked.

The sergeant shifted uncomfortably. "Got orders from really high up to maintain the perimeter, keep everyone else out, but ... uh ... let those two stay put. Said you folks were coming to handle it."

Maya was already moving, taking in details. A black Jeep with military tags. A rental car that didn't belong. The metal stairs leading to the third floor where two figures stood in the shadows of the doorway. Different jurisdiction, but the fundamentals never changed: observe, analyze, stay ahead of the threat.

She drew her weapon, Benson mirroring her movement with considerably less grace. She gestured for the local officers to hang back—she'd learned that lesson the hard way during a joint FBI-LAPD raid that went sideways when too many badges tried to be heroes.

The door gaped open like a wound in the pre-dawn darkness.

"Federal agents," she called out, voice carrying with practiced authority. "Come out with your hands visible."

Movement inside. Two figures emerged from the shadows, and Maya's threat assessment kicked into overdrive. Back in LA, she'd worked protection details with private military contractors—these men had that same contained lethality. The larger one filled the doorway like a defensive lineman gone corporate in pressed slacks and a button-down, but his casual stance screamed special ops.

She caught the lean one's precise movements, the way he controlled the space. Different from the cocky SWAT guys back in LA who tried to intimidate her. This one had nothing to prove—which made him more dangerous.

From the file she'd scanned, they were Ronan Quinn and Axel Reinhardt. A few years older and a lot more weary-looking than their military ID photos, but clearly the deceased's former SEAL teammates.

"NCIS," Maya announced, keeping her weapon at low ready. "Want to explain why you're contaminating my crime scene?"

"Your crime scene?" Ronan Quinn's voice held a dangerous edge. "Funny. I don't see any crime here. Just two friends checking on another friend who wasn't answering his phone. Now we know why."

Their eyes met in that moment of mutual evaluation, and she saw him catalogue everything about her in seconds. Professional. Dangerous. And definitely hiding something.

"Friends who pick locks past midnight?" She nodded toward the fresh marks on the door.

"He gave me a key." Reinhardt spread his hands slowly. "Look, we can explain—"

"Let me guess," Quinn cut in. "You got here awful fast for local law enforcement. Which means someone important made a call. Which means you're not telling us everything either."

Maya kept her expression neutral. He was fishing for information, and doing it skillfully.

"We'd appreciate it if you'd come back to NCIS with us," Benson said. "Answer some questions about Mr. Sullivan's activities in the past twenty-four hours."

"Not happening." Quinn's stance shifted subtly. "We've got nothing to hide, but we're not going anywhere until we know Tank's body is handled properly."

Quinn checked his phone, a quick glance that seemed rehearsed. Reinhardt murmured what sounded like a prayer, but his eyes stayed sharp, scanning the perimeter. Maya had seen that look before—not prayer, but communication. These men were waiting for something.

The local sergeant approached, holding his radio. "Just got word from dispatch. We're to clear out, leave it to NCIS."

"Perfect timing," Quinn said softly, exchanging another look with Reinhardt. "Actually, you know what? We'll come in. Voluntarily. After your crime scene team processes everything."

The way he emphasized 'voluntarily' made it clear he knew exactly what legal authority they did and didn't have. Maya couldn't shake the feeling they were agreeing because it suited some agenda of their own.

"Wait outside," she told them firmly. "Both of you. You've contaminated this scene enough already."

Quinn's mouth quirked in that dangerous half-smile. Under other circumstances, it would have been breathtaking. "Yes ma'am." He headed down the stairs with fluid grace, Reinhardt following.

Their immediate compliance only heightened her suspicion.

While the local cops packed up, she moved through the condo with measured steps, Benson's camera clicks providing an irregular rhythm behind her. The scene felt wrong in a way that went beyond her training, beyond even her father's meticulous lessons. Something spiritual, her mother would have said. She shoved the thought away. She dealt in evidence, not intuition.

The kitchen gleamed like a showroom display. No dishes in the sink, no takeout containers, not even a coffee mug left out. The living room had the same artificial precision—magazines aligned perfectly on the coffee table, remotes arranged by size.

"When's the last time you saw a guy living alone keep house like this?" she murmured.

Benson grunted, snapping photos. "Military guys can be neat."

"This isn't neat. This is sanitized."

Back in LA, she'd caught three staged suicides where the cleanup crews had done the same thing—stripped away every trace of personality, leaving behind a sterile perfection that screamed cover-up.

Still, none of this would have been noticeable from outside. What had Quinn and Reinhardt seen that made them break in?

She continued searching. The hall bathroom gleamed like a hospital room. No towels hung crooked, no toothpaste residue in the sink. Maya remembered her father drilling into her the importance of personal habits—they told you who someone was, how they lived. And more importantly, how they died. The absence of those habits often spoke louder than their presence.

She paused at the office doorway, that sixth sense she'd developed on the force screaming a warning. The room beyond held answers, but something told her she wouldn't like the questions they raised.

The scene that greeted her confirmed every instinct. The condition of the body suggested he died about twenty-four hours ago, give or take. Probably not long after he broke into that base computer. The body was positioned too perfectly, the weapon placement textbook. She'd worked enough real suicides to know death was rarely this tidy. Her last case with LAPD had been similar—a "suicide" that turned out to be a professional hit meant to silence a whistleblower.

Subtle details hit her. The wear pattern on the chair didn't match how Sullivan was sitting. The angle of the weapon contradicted the blood spatter. Small things, things her father had taught her to notice, things that had made her the youngest detective in Pacific Division.

Car doors slammed outside. While she watched through the window, two NCIS crime scene vans arrived as the last patrol car pulled away. Quinn and Reinhardt waited next to Benson's SUV, their relaxed poses betraying years of tactical training. Every few minutes, Quinn would check his phone, then share some wordless communication with his partner. Reinhardt's lips moved in what looked like prayer, but his eyes never stopped scanning their surroundings.

Van doors opened, the crime scene unit quickly donned Tyvek coveralls. Maya didn't figure there was much else for her to accomplish inside, so she headed down the stairs. The team would need room to work their magic. Benson was just completing his update when she reached the group. After quick nods, the team headed upstairs, leaving her alone with Tom, and the two glowering SEALs.

Tom nodded at his plain wrap SUV. "I'll take them in. You can get preliminaries from the crime scene crew and follow me in."

"Sounds good. Send me those photos. Something about this scene isn't sitting right."

Her partner gestured toward his SUV. "Let's get this done."

"We'll follow you in," Quinn said, nodding toward their Jeep. "Got some sensitive equipment we need to secure first."

Maya caught the look that passed between the two men—something more than just concern about gear. "That's not protocol."

"Your protocol doesn't account for our clearance level." Quinn's voice was calm and reasonable and not-to-be-disobeyed. "Or the nature of our equipment. You can call Commander Phillips if you want verification."

Benson rubbed his tired eyes. "Look, it's almost two-thirty. They're cooperating. Let's just get to base and sort it out there."

Maya didn't like it, but Quinn was right—they had no grounds to force the issue. These men were coming in voluntarily, and Phillips had made it clear this needed to be handled delicately.

"Fine," she said. "But we go straight to base. No stops, no delays."

"Wouldn't dream of it." Quinn's smile didn't reach his eyes. He looked past her, scanning the street with too much intensity for a simple drive to headquarters.

Benson hopped into the driver's seat and fired up the SUV, waving as he backed out of the parking spot. Maya watched Quinn and Reinhardt drive off, eerily calm in the front seat of their rental.

While the vehicles disappeared around the corner, she pulled up Quinn's file on her phone. Former Navy SEAL. Multiple commendations. Then general discharge for killing a civilian. Just him. No one else on his squad charged.

Like the crime scene, it didn't add up.

A dark sedan caught her attention—parked just at the edge of her vision. She shook her head. The job was making her paranoid.

Still, no need to stand outside in the dark. She slipped inside her vehicle, pulling up the terminal logs from base security while she waited for the crime scene team to finish. Might as well study the small details while she had a second.

The files loaded. And her heart stopped. In the hours before his death, Marcus Sullivan had accessed multiple personnel files. Including hers. And Benson's.

She hit speed dial. Straight to voicemail.

"Come on, Tom. Pick up."

She fired up the engine and tried again.

No answer.

Through her windshield, she caught the crime techs' shadows pass back and forth under the harsh portable lights they set up in the apartment.

She tapped the steering wheel, thinking hard. Two ex-SEALs who just happened to find their friend's body. A sanitized scene that screamed professional hit. And now her partner, alone with them, heading toward the base.

According to her father, the difference between paranoid and prepared was about two minutes.

She threw the car into Drive.

5

CHOOSING SIDES

MAYA'S HAND hovered over her phone as she cruised the dark streets, her father's voice echoing in her head: *Trust your gut, baby girl.*

Exactly why she'd left LAPD. Lawrence Chen's shoot-from-the-hip style might have made him a legend, but it had left a trail of chaos in his wake.

And not only for the teenage daughter he'd raised after her mother quietly left them both. Chen, as the entire LAPD called him, had a legendary arrest record. And a disciplinary file only a few pages shorter.

She'd spent her whole career doing things by the book just to prove she wasn't him.

But something about Commander Phillips's tone when he'd called them out here nagged at her. *Handle this quietly, Agent Chen.*

Quietly. She'd heard that enough times in LA to know what it really meant: Someone high up wanted this contained. Dad would already be breaking every rule in the book, charging in without backup. That's what had gotten his first partner killed.

Not a great plan.

Benson should have reached the Thirty-second Street Naval Station by now—it was a straight shot down Harbor Drive. She tried his cell again. Straight to voicemail. The digital clock on her dash read 2:47 a.m. Half an hour since they'd separated. Time enough to process Quinn and Reinhardt through the main gate, start the paperwork ...

Time enough for a lot of other things too.

A black Audi appeared in her rearview mirror, three cars back. Just like the one from the crime scene. Or maybe not—in the pre-dawn darkness every dark sedan looked suspicious. She took the next right. The Audi continued straight.

Paranoid, Chen. Get it together.

Her phone buzzed. Text from an unknown number.

STAY AWAY FROM THE HARBOR.

Seriously? No way she'd stay away now.

She hung a right at the first entrance to the harbor parking lot.

Her pulse quickened. She killed her headlights and turned toward the massive commercial pier. The structure stretched before her, empty and dark. Salty air mixed with diesel fumes and rotting seaweed. The orange glow of ancient sodium vapor lights glinted off chain-link fencing, stacked shipping containers, and abandoned forklifts, throwing long shadows. Everything felt wrong—no security guards, no dock workers, no early-morning fishing boats.

Just Tom's official vehicle, parked at an angle down near the seawall.

From this angle, the vehicle looked empty.

She drew her weapon, using her car door as cover. From here to the SUV—forty feet of exposed concrete. No cover except for a rusted forklift about halfway. The silence pressed against her eardrums, broken only by the soft lap of water against concrete and the distant hum of the city.

Maya swept her tactical light in a slow arc. The beam caught silver threads of fishing line strung between pylons, abandoned nets swaying in the breeze. Perfect place for an ambush.

But why? Killing her would help nothing. If Quinn and Reinhardt wanted to escape, they'd be long gone now.

Unless this was about more than escape. Sullivan had accessed their personnel files right before he died. Now Benson was missing. And someone high enough to contact base security wanted her to stay away.

She knew exactly what would happen if this went sideways. Internal Affairs would crucify her. *Agent Chen demonstrated a pattern of reckless behavior consistent with her father's record...* The comparisons she'd spent her whole career avoiding would finally stick. Everything she'd built at NCIS, all her careful work to establish herself as her own person, would evaporate. And that assumed she survived whatever was waiting down there.

But Tom might be down there, injured.

Three months as partners wasn't long, but it was long enough to know he was a good man. The kind who brought her coffee without being asked. The kind who'd backed her play with the brass twice already, no questions asked. The kind who deserved better than dying alone because his partner was worried about her career.

She eased around her car door, staying low. The forklift threw distorted shadows across her path. Every scrape of her boots against concrete echoed too loud in the stillness.

Standard procedure said wait for backup. But she had no time. If they'd left Tom alive, seconds counted.

Twenty feet to the vehicle now. The driver's door gaped open like a mouth. No movement inside. Her tactical light caught the interior—empty coffee cup in the holder, case files scattered across the passenger seat.

No sign of Quinn or Reinhardt. Or her partner.

Ten feet. Close enough now to see the keys dangling from the ignition, swaying slightly in the pre-dawn breeze.

Maya pressed her back against the car's rear panel, breathing in the familiar scent of leather and gun oil. She reached around carefully, sweeping the back seat with her light. Empty. The tactical gear Benson always kept behind his seat was gone.

The beam of her light caught something else as she moved forward. Dark streaks on the pavement, leading away from the driver's side. Too dark to be oil. Too fresh to be rust.

Her heart hammering against her ribs, she followed the trail toward the edge of the pier. Each step felt like an invitation for a bullet. The streaks grew wider, interrupted by scuff marks. Signs of a struggle. Or something being dragged.

Just before the seawall, the trail ended in a larger stain. Maya forced herself to look over the edge.

Something bobbed in the water. The flashlight beam caught pale flesh, dark fabric. The tide tugged gently at Tom Benson's body, rocking it against the pier's supports. His service weapon was gone. His hands showed defensive wounds.

Her fingers found the small cross at her neck—her mother's parting gift. The same one she'd sworn she'd never take off, even after Maria Chen walked out. "Please, Lord, watch over him," she whispered, the prayer automatic. Like muscle memory. Her father had scoffed at faith, called it a crutch. But right now, staring at her partner's body, Maya needed something to hold onto.

Her phone buzzed in her hand. The same unknown number. This time, she answered.

"I told you to stay away." Quinn's voice, tight with urgency.

Her weapon was already up, scanning rooflines, shadows.

Every exposed position where a shooter might set up. This was exactly the kind of situation her father thrived on—outmanned, outgunned, running on instinct and adrenaline. The thought should have bothered her more than it did. "You and Reinhardt killed him."

"No, we didn't. Why would I be warning you? We'd be halfway to Mexico if we offed him."

Terror for Tom. And for herself, swamped her brain. She couldn't think.

"We need to get you out of here," Quinn continued, his voice low yet commanding.

"I'm not going anywhere with you." That, at least, she knew.

Quinn made a frustrated sound. "The men who shot your partner are still watching. Black Audi, government plates. They're waiting for orders, just like they waited for orders on Marcus. But they won't wait long."

"Why should I believe you?"

"Because if I had killed Benson, there's no way I'd be talking to you right now."

A very good point.

His voice carried that same assured competence she'd sensed at the condo. The kind that came from absolute certainty in one's abilities. The kind her father possessed. The kind that usually preceded someone else getting hurt.

"Agent Chen. Maya. Listen. Please. I wish I had time to draw you a flowchart, but things are about to get insane. In thirty seconds, the men in that Audi are going to get those orders I mentioned. And then you'll be dead too unless you do exactly what I say."

Maya's light caught Tom's face, half-submerged. His empty eyes stared back at her, accusing. All those times she'd ignored her instincts in favor of procedure. All those times she'd refused to be her father's daughter.

She'd built her career on being the anti-Lawrence-Chen. Following rules. Building cases methodically. Being everything her father wasn't. But Tom's dead eyes seemed to ask, "Where did all that careful procedure get you?"

Maybe that had been her real failure. Fighting so hard against becoming him, she'd forgotten why he'd broken all those rules in the first place. Sometimes procedure wasn't enough. Sometimes justice demanded more.

Tom's body bobbed gently against the pier. Another partner lost. Another failure to protect. She squeezed the cross until its edges bit into her palm, remembering all those Sunday mornings her mother had dragged her to church while her father worked cases. All those prayers that hadn't kept their family together.

The harbor stretched dark and still around her. Dad's voice one last time: *Sometimes you have to choose between being right and being alive.*

Time to choose.

Her mother's words came to her: *Sometimes faith means jumping without seeing the landing.*

She had spent years ensuring she always saw exactly where she'd land. But Tom's body in the harbor reminded her that sometimes you ran out of safe choices.

6

PROFESSIONAL COURTESY

Ronan crouched in the shadows of a shipping container, watching the pretty NCIS detective. Thirty yards away, the black Audi idled behind a warehouse.

His jaw clenched. Ten minutes ago, they'd been following Benson's SUV toward the naval base, a compromise that had seemed smart at the time.

Now another man was dead.

Three minutes into the drive, he'd spotted the tail cars. Professional. Military precision. He'd tried to catch Benson's attention by flicking his headlights, but before Benson could react, the black Audis were already boxing in the SUV, forcing it down the road.

Their own pursuers had come fast and hard—three vehicles, classic Special Operations containment formation. The kind designed to trap and extract, not eliminate. He'd reversed the Jeep at full speed, smashing through their attempted roadblock. Two bursts of suppressing fire aimed high—another extraction tactic. Keep the targets down, don't damage them.

Only when they'd broken free did he understand the full

play. The team hadn't really broken off pursuit—they'd herded him and Axel deliberately, trying to separate them from Benson. An NCIS agent would call in armed suspects fleeing the scene. Which meant Benson had to die quickly, buying them time to pursue their real quarry.

Clean. Professional. And now they had another dead body to add to their body count, another good man killed just because he was in the way.

By the time they'd ditched the Jeep and circled back on foot to help, they'd heard the shots. Seen Benson's SUV trapped against the harbor fence, driver's door open.

Too late. Always too late.

"They're moving. North side." Ronan tracked the Audi's headlights as they flicked on. Chen was still standing at the edge of the water, above her partner's body, weapon drawn. Too exposed.

"Ronan." Warning in Axel's tone. "We spook her now, she'll shoot first and—"

"And what? Get dead?" Ronan was already moving. "That worked out great for Benson. We were too slow last time."

"Wasn't our fault. We couldn't have—"

"We could have found a way to warn him. Could have prevented them from separating us." The guilt drove him forward, each step eating up the distance to the woman. He wasn't watching another agent die because he was too cautious, too slow.

Axel muttered what sounded like a prayer but moved to cover him.

The Audi's engine revved softly. Ahead of them, Chen shifted her stance, scanning rooflines. Good instincts; wrong direction. She hadn't spotted the real threat yet, the driver reaching for something on his passenger seat.

"Same goons that dragged the woman's partner out of the SUV and shot him while he and Axel raced to the scene.

He forced the image away. Focus on the target. On the now.

"Ronan crouched behind a stack of pallets. Twenty feet separated him from the detective.

Miraculously, the killers hadn't chosen to shoot Agent Chen. Yet.

"Now," Ronan hissed. "Before they—"

Chen spun, weapon leveled at Ronan's chest. Her hands were rock steady, eyes cold. "That's close enough."

"Agent Chen—"

"On your knees. Hands where I can see them."

The Audi's doors opened with soft clicks. The men emerged. Broad-shouldered. Confident bearing. They raised handguns. Long barrels. Pro equipment.

No time for careful. No time for procedure.

"Get down!" He lunged for her.

Her shot went wide as Ronan slammed into her, pulling her down behind the pallets as the first silenced round cracked past their heads. She fought like someone used to close quarters, all elbows and leverage.

Only he had fifty pounds on her and far more experience. Still, disarming her without hurting her took some doing.

"They're here to kill all of us," he gritted out. "Just like they killed Marcus. And your partner."

Another burst of suppressed fire had them both pressing lower. Axel appeared beside them, keeping his head down. "We need to move. Now."

He caught the distinctive crunch of boots on concrete. They had seconds. Maybe.

"Your choice, Agent Chen," Ronan said. "Trust us enough to get out of here alive, or we all die. Choose fast."

Her eyes locked onto his then shifted to the Audi, to the distinctive professional stance of its shooters.

"Harbor patrol shack," she said finally.

"Move fast and stay low." Ronan kept her Sig trained on the Audi while Axel pulled her behind a row of containers. Seven rounds. Had to make them count. A burst of automatic fire sparked off metal above his head. Three shooters, moving with military precision. No way they could hold position here long.

"The shack's no good," he called to Axel. Too much glass, thin walls. They'd be trapped.

"Working on it." Axel was already moving, dragging Maya with him. His eyes scanned the harbor setup with the practiced eye of someone who saw possibilities in everyday objects. "Got propane tanks on the maintenance dock. Emergency flares in the shack."

Ronan tracked the closest shooter through the Sig's sights. "How long?"

"Two minutes. Maybe less." Axel's voice held the familiar tension that came before he did something insane. "Keep them busy." Then he turned to the woman. "Agent Chen, unless you want to die here, you're coming with me."

Another burst of gunfire forced Ronan lower. He squeezed off one round, making the nearest shooter duck. Six left. The harbor patrol sirens were closer now, but they'd never make it in time.

Through his peripheral vision, he caught Axel's movement—quick and precise, gathering what he needed from the shack's emergency supplies. Maya stayed close to him, whether from trust or necessity wasn't clear.

"Incoming, ten o'clock," he warned as a second shooter tried to flank. Another round from the Sig bought them space. Five to go.

"Ready," Axel called. "Water's our best exit. Can you swim, Agent Chen?"

"Better than I can trust you two," she shot back.

"Fair enough." Axel's grin was razor sharp. "Ronan, on my mark, put two rounds into that tank. Then run."

Ronan nodded. The closest shooter was moving again, confident now. Cocky. Five rounds left would have to be enough.

"Three," Axel began. "Two—"

The explosion ripped through the night, sending a cascade of burning fuel into the air. Ronan grabbed Maya's arm, pulling her toward the pier's edge. She didn't resist, matching his stride. Good. She understood survival trumped procedure.

They hit the water together, the December Pacific shocking the air from his lungs. Maya tensed beside him but kept moving, strong strokes carrying her deeper into the harbor's darkness. The water muffled the sounds of gunfire above, each shot a dull pop through the depths.

Ronan stayed close to her, hyper-aware of her smaller frame in the freezing water. She might be a strong swimmer, but hypothermia wouldn't care about her skills. They needed to find shelter fast. Through the murk, he caught Axel's signal—stay under, stay quiet, fifty yards minimum.

They glided through the black water like seals, letting the current help carry them away from the firefight. Every few strokes, Ronan checked Maya's position, fighting the instinct to pull her closer. She wasn't some civilian to protect—she was a trained federal agent. Still, something about her triggered every protective instinct he'd developed in the teams.

"This way." Axel's voice was barely a whisper. He angled toward the nearest dock, a long stretch of pristine moorings where sleek boats bobbed in the pre-dawn darkness. "B dock. High-end cruisers. Lots of cover."

Maya treaded water beside them, her eyes hard in the darkness. "And if I'm not interested in adding breaking and entering to my night?"

"Then swim for the shore," Ronan said. "If the hostiles don't shoot you, you can try explaining to Harbor Patrol why you're soaking wet near your dead partner. While those professionals back there plant evidence on your hard drive."

"You don't know that's what—"

"Yeah. We do." The image of Benson's body drifting flashed through Ronan's mind. "They're very good at what they do."

Another explosion rolled across the water—secondary charges Axel had rigged. Beyond the pier, voices shouted orders. Red and blue lights painted the smoke. Through the darkness, Ronan tracked movement on the pier—tactical teams pulling back, regrouping. The explosion had drawn too much attention. Local PD would be swarming the area soon.

The black Audi's headlights swept the marina before peeling away, followed by two more sedans. They'd be back, but for now, the heat was too high. These guys might be good, but they weren't stupid. No point risking exposure when their targets were trapped in the harbor.

Ronan wiped saltwater out of his eyes and nodded toward a luxury cruiser. "Over there. There'll be dry clothes, shelter. A chance to figure out our next move."

"Breaking into a million-dollar yacht." Her laugh held no humor. "Perfect."

"Better than floating here waiting to get shot." Axel was already moving, his strokes silent and efficient. "Besides, these guys always hide a key. Part of the maintenance agreement."

They reached the boat's stern platform, keeping low. Axel made quick work of the hidden key box while Ronan kept watch, Maya's wet Sig useless in his waistband. At least the weather was warm. Small favors.

The cabin door clicked open. "Ladies first," Axel whispered.

She hesitated, scanning the docks. More sirens approached.

"Fine," she said finally, and hauled herself up onto the deck with impressive speed.

The yacht's cabin held traces of summer—beach towels, spare clothes in lockers, a lingering mix of sunscreen and salty air. While Ronan crouched on the back deck, keeping watch, Axel moved with practiced efficiency, closing the interior shades, then finding lights, checking spaces.

"All good." He waved Ronan and Maya inside.

Ronan stripped off his wet shirt, used it to wipe down the woman's Sig. Through the windows, emergency lights swept the harbor in steady patterns. They'd have maybe ten minutes before the search expanded to the boats.

"Here." Axel tossed them both clothes from the owner's stash. "I found some women's in the forward berth."

She caught the bundle but didn't move. "Start talking. What did your friend tell you before he died?"

"Nothing specific." Ronan pulled on a dry shirt, thinking fast. "Just that he was onto something big. Asked us to watch his back."

She winced.

"Yeah." The guilt hit fresh. "Whatever trail Tank was following, it was dangerous enough to warrant his death. And your partner's."

Maya's expression didn't change, but her shoulders tensed.

Ronan slumped against the cabin wall, saltwater pouring steadily from his clothes onto the polished teak floor. "Look, I get it. You think we killed Marcus. Maybe even Benson. If I were you, I'd think the same thing." He ran a hand through his wet hair, sending rivulets down his neck. "But we didn't. And the only way we're going to prove that—the only way any of us gets justice for Marcus or your partner—is if we work together. Because right now? We're all running out of time."

"I'm a federal agent," Maya said, voice clipped. She wrapped her arms around herself, suppressing a shiver as her soaked jacket clung to her shoulders. "Once our crime scene unit processes both scenes, we'll have solid evidence. Real proof. Come in with me. We'll do this right."

"We'll be dead before we hit the front doors," Ronan said. "Just like Tank. Just like your partner."

"Or soon after." Axel wrung out his shirt over the sink, water pattering against steel. "Easy to get us into custody, then make us disappear. Wouldn't be the first time."

"Tank called us," Ronan said, his voice tight with urgency. "Said he needed immediate assistance. Something terrified him—a decorated SEAL who'd seen everything. So we showed up to help. Instead, we found him dead."

"Think about it," Axel added. "Who knew we were going to NCIS headquarters? Only your commander. Those weren't random thugs. You saw their tactics. That was military precision. They knew exactly when and where to hit us."

"Someone's already two steps ahead here," Ronan pressed. "They killed Tank before he could talk to us. They separated us from Benson, tried to grab us while their partners killed Benson so he wouldn't call for backup. If we go in now, we're walking right into their kill box. And you know it, or you would've called for backup already."

Maya's hand tightened on her phone, but she didn't dispute it.

"That's not how I operate," she snapped, leaving wet footprints as she paced the narrow cabin. "This isn't some movie. I'm taking you in, and we're doing this by the book. You'll give statements, document whatever evidence you have—"

"You still don't get it, do you?" Ronan straightened, frustration burning through the exhaustion. Water trickled down his back, making him acutely aware of every bruise and scrape from their escape. The woman might be beautiful, with that shining black hair and her delicate features. But she'd be dead soon all the same unless she followed orders.

He stared her down. If facts didn't work, maybe pure intimidation would. "The minute we're in custody, we're dead. And so are you. But not before they frame all of us for whatever Marcus stumbled into. Make it look like we were all part of it."

"Not everything is a conspiracy."

The laugh that escaped him held no humor. "You sure about that? They're thorough. In a couple of hours, you'll be NCIS's most wanted. Right behind us, probably."

Through the cabin windows, a patrol boat's spotlight swept past. Maya's hands tightened on the dry clothes.

Ronan held out her Sig, grip first.

"Oh, wonderful," Axel muttered. "Give the person who shot you their gun back. Because that's how trust-building works in your world? Next time I need a hostage negotiator, remind me not to call you."

Maya's eyes moved from the gun to Ronan's face, the ghost of a smile touching her lips. The spotlight swung back, closer now. Time was running out.

Her Sig felt heavy in his outstretched hand. He was betting their lives on reading her right—that somewhere under that professional mask, she had the same questions about Marcus's death that had been eating at him and Axel.

The woman still hadn't moved. Still watching him with those sharp eyes that missed nothing. Including, he hoped, the fact that he and Axel could have disappeared into the night with her weapon. Could have left her to deal with this alone.

Instead, he was offering her the choice. And the means to shoot them both if she thought they were lying.

"Guys?" Axel's voice held an edge. "Not to rush anyone's trust issues, but we need to move before they start sweeping the docks. Doolittle still has his crash pad. It's less than a mile from here."

Ronan eyed the neighborhood out past the empty parking lot sandwiched between the marina and the homes. "That's the best idea you've had all night, bro."

Maya's face shifted. Something harder settling into place as she reached for her weapon.

Time to find out if he'd bet right.

7

TRUST FALLS

An hour later, finally dry and starting to get warm, at least physically, Maya watched steam curl from the ancient coffeemaker in the corner of the garage apartment, trying to stop her hands from shaking. Exhaustion or cold or shock—maybe all three. Her partner's body was still out there in the bay. And here she sat, in a nondescript apartment less than a mile from the military base with two men who might have killed him.

Axel had picked the lock with a professional's skills, insisting the whole time that this was his friend's crash pad. She had to admit, the lone photo on the half-empty bookshelf did appear to show these two arm in arm with their SEAL squad, Ronan sandwiched in the middle grinning.

Her investigator's mind wouldn't shut off, cataloging details even as she fought the bone-deep chill. Ronan had fired her weapon, contaminating any GSR evidence that might have linked him to Tom's murder. Their clothes were soaked, destroying any other trace evidence.

Her dad's voice echoed in her head: *The system only works*

until someone powerful enough wants it not to. She'd spent her whole career proving him wrong. Now she wasn't so sure.

The space heater hummed, fighting the early morning chill. Their wet clothes hung nearby like dark ghosts—her tactical gear, their civilian clothes. The borrowed sweats draped her frame, making her feel smaller. More vulnerable. She fought the urge to wrap her arms around herself, instead watching the guys' dynamics. The way they communicated without words. Military training, obviously. But there was something else—a rawness to their grief over Marcus Sullivan that felt genuine.

Every instinct screamed that she should be processing the scene of Tom's murder. Collecting evidence. Doing her job. Instead, she'd fled with the suspects. She needed to start thinking three steps ahead. How to verify their story, their whereabouts when Marcus was killed.

Ronan moved quietly around the small kitchen space. He'd found an ancient first aid kit, setting it on the counter near her with deliberate casualness. His eyes flickered to her scraped palms, the cut on her forearm she hadn't even noticed getting. That didn't track with a cold-blooded killer, her mind noted. Unless it was calculated to gain her trust.

"Time for explanations," she said, keeping her voice steady despite chattering teeth.

A beat, then Ronan spoke. "You should clean those cuts. Harbor water's nasty."

Axel was already wrapping himself in what looked like an old moving blanket. He tossed another toward her. The casual kindness almost undid her. These men might have murdered her partner. And Sullivan. She couldn't afford to see them as human. Not until she knew for sure.

The blanket remained untouched beside her. She needed to stay sharp, stay objective. Get access to the evidence being collected at the scene. Contact her office.

How had she forgotten that?

She reached in her pocket for her phone. Gone. But she'd had it on the dock, hadn't she? She couldn't recall.

Unless ... She crossed to her wet clothes and patted them down. Nothing.

"Have either of you seen my phone?" she asked.

"It's probably at the bottom of the marina," Axel said.

"Or one of you took it."

"That's not how we roll," Axel chided. "At all."

Ronan didn't say a word, the tightening of his jaw the only sign that he'd heard her. Finally, he shrugged, turning back to the coffeemaker. "Sugar's there, if you want it. Might help with the shock."

She almost laughed. Trust a potential killer to diagnose shock before she'd admitted it to herself. But her hands reached for the first aid kit anyway. One problem at a time. Clean the cuts. Warm up. Then figure out how she'd ended up here—and whether these men were killers or allies.

As for her phone, Axel was probably right. She couldn't recall securing it anywhere before they hit the water.

"I've read both your files," she said once she finished, wrapping her hands around the coffee mug again for warmth. "SEAL Team Eight. Retired two years ago." She watched Ronan's face. "Three for you, given your General Discharge."

He met her eyes steadily. "Yup."

When he didn't elaborate, his friend broke the tension by rattling through kitchen cabinets. "Anyone else starving? There's ... ah ... expired protein bars and some questionable peanut butter."

"Marcus tried contacting us last week," Ronan said. He couldn't seem to stay still, moving from window to door, checking sight lines, running through what Maya recognized as tactical assessment patterns. A man used to action, not sitting in safe houses. "Said he needed help. Wouldn't explain over the phone."

"And you just came running?" She kept her tone skeptical.

"He was our friend." Simple. Direct. Ronan paused his prowling to lean against the counter, fingers drumming against the worn Formica. "You read our files. Marcus's, too. You probably have way more current info than we do. Tell us what you know," he ordered, then caught himself. Softened his tone. "Please."

Maya weighed her options, then decided there was nothing to be gained by hiding what she knew. They'd figure most of it out anyway. "Tom and I got orders to pick Marcus up last night. Base security found security footage of him entering the base and accessing restricted files after hours twenty-four hours previously. Including personnel files. Mine and Benson's."

Ronan and Axel exchanged looks.

"That doesn't track," Axel said. "Whatever he was searching for, Tank was too careful to get caught that easily."

Ronan's dark brows narrowed. "Who called the local cops?"

"My supervisor. Said we should have backup in case Sullivan resisted arrest." Her heart thumped against her chest. "Turned out that wasn't necessary."

"Why send investigators in the middle of the night?" Axel asked.

She shrugged. "Commander Phillips didn't say. I assumed it was because someone on base had just discovered the break-in."

"Or someone wanted us to get caught in his apartment," Ronan said to his friend.

Axel snorted. "Not a coincidence."

"What about Benson?" Ronan made the question more of an accusation. "How do you know he was on the level?"

"Tom wasn't involved in any of this." Her voice caught. "The only thing he was guilty of was following orders to show up at Sullivan's house. He wouldn't—" She broke off, steadied herself. "There's no reason anyone would want him dead."

Probably. When it came down to it, how well did she really know her partner of less than three months?

"Your partner was between us and them," Axel added, abandoning his search for food. "Wrong place, wrong time. These guys don't leave loose ends."

"Professional cleanup," Ronan agreed. "They eliminate anyone who might have seen something. Heard something." He met her eyes. "Or anyone who might ask questions about what happened to their partner."

The implication hung heavy in the pre-dawn air. Maya felt the walls of her normal, ordered world crumbling. "You really think they'll come after me next?"

"They already have," Axel said quietly. "You just got lucky we showed up first."

Maya paced the small apartment, her mind racing. The protein bar sat untouched on the counter. Tom's face kept flashing through her thoughts—coaching his daughter's soccer team, bringing donuts to the office, laughing at her terrible coffee. No way he'd been involved in anything illegal. Which meant she was hiding out with the only two suspects in his murder.

She considered her pitiful options. No way she'd be able to force these men anywhere. But heading to headquarters alone seemed increasingly dangerous. She'd seen how quickly evidence could be manufactured, careers destroyed.

Ronan tracked her movement, his expression knowing. "Whatever you're planning—don't."

"There are procedures," she snapped. "Protocols. Ways to handle this through proper channels."

"Like the proper channels that just branded you a traitor?" His voice was gentle but firm. "Sometimes the rules don't work."

"That's not—"

Axel's phone buzzed. He pulled it out automatically, blinking hard at the screen. "Well, this is about what I'd expected." He turned the screen toward her and Ronan.

BOLO ALERT: NCIS AGENT MAYA CHEN IDENTIFIED IN CLASSIFIED INTELLIGENCE BREACH AND MURDER OF A SPECIAL AGENT. CHEN CONSIDERED ARMED AND DANGEROUS. POSSIBLY IN COMPANY OF SUSPECTS RONAN QUINN AND AXEL REINHARDT. BOTH MEN HAVE BLACK OPS MILITARY TRAINING. APPROACH WITH EXTREME CAUTION.

She exhaled hard, clutching her stomach. "Is this some kind of joke?"

"I wish," Ronan muttered. He was doing something with peanut butter and protein bars that looked dubiously edible.

"Welcome to the club," Axel said grimly. "Time to assess our situation?"

"No resources," Ronan started. "No weapons except Maya's Sig."

"No cash, no transport." Axel said as Ronan handed them each a protein bar sandwich. "Can't use credit cards or phones—they'll track us instantly."

"We've got burners," Ronan added. "But we need help."

"Knight Tactical," Axel said immediately.

"No." Ronan's voice went flat.

"They're literally perfect for this. Top tier private security, all former special ops—"

"And Bible-thumping true believers," Ronan cut in, jaw tight. "Everything's God's plan with them. Even the wetwork."

"They get results," Axel countered. "And they have resources we need."

"They have an agenda," Ronan said. "Just like everyone else who claims to be fighting for something bigger than themselves. They're not an option."

"Your brother—"

"Half-brother," Ronan cut in. "Who I've never even met."

Maya looked between them, momentarily distracted from her own spiraling thoughts. "Someone want to explain?"

"Christian Murphy," Axel said. "Founded Knight Tactical. Also happens to be—"

"Nothing to me," Ronan finished.

"They haven't actually met," Axel told her, rolling his eyes. "About time you two got acquainted, don't you think?"

"We need a plan," Maya interrupted. "A real one. I have contacts in the LAPD—"

"Who'll arrest us on sight," Ronan said.

"Better than whatever you're suggesting."

Axel's phone buzzed again. "Friend of a friend keeps me in the loop on any intel about me or my team," he explained and turned the screen toward her.

She didn't have to look to realize it was bad. His stony expression made that clear. She looked anyway. New images filled the screen—surveillance photos of her with Marcus, timestamps altered to put them together at classified sites she'd never visited. The evidence trail was already being laid.

"We need pros on this, dude," Axel said quietly.

Maya stared at his phone, at the fabricated evidence of her betrayal appearing in real time. Her world had shifted in the space of a few hours, leaving her with nothing but instinct to guide her. And right now, instinct was screaming that whatever was coming, she wasn't going to survive it alone.

She recognized the tactical precision in Ronan's movements, the way he positioned himself between the windows and her without seeming to think about it. Everything in her training said not to trust him. Everything in her instincts said he was the only thing standing between her and whoever had killed Tom.

Her father's voice again: *Trust your gut, little dragon. It's the only thing they can't take from you.*

She watched Ronan check sight lines for the third time in as many minutes, his shoulders tense with the need to move, to act. To protect, her mind supplied unhelpfully. She pushed the thoughts away. She couldn't afford to see him as anything but a potential threat.

No matter what her instincts were trying to tell her.

8

ESCAPE VELOCITY

They did not need help. Well, okay. Yeah, they did. But not from some lame boutique personal protection company run by a stranger who happened to share fifty-percent of Ronan's DNA.

They could call up the rest of the old squad. Zara, Deke, Kenji, and the rest of the team would be there in an instant. In the meantime, they'd hide out. Gather whatever intel they could get their hands on without risking detection.

Ronan leaned against the wall, watching Maya process what was happening. His body ached from the night's exertions, but his mind was sharp, cataloging details, mapping scenarios.

She was even smaller without her tactical gear, but he wasn't fooled. Those chocolate-colored eyes missed nothing, and her hand never strayed far from her weapon. Smart. Stunning. And ready to bolt at any second.

He shifted slightly, ensuring he had a clear path to the door. She wasn't getting past him. Not when running meant certain death.

"Let's walk through this again," he said, keeping his voice

neutral. "According to your supervisor, Tank supposedly accessed classified systems at 2300 hours Tuesday. Then nothing until almost twenty-four hours later when someone catches his little breaking and entering act on security footage and sends you and Benson after him. Only he's already been dead since right after he broke in."

"How'd the call come in?" he asked her.

His question obviously puzzled her.

"It couldn't have been a neighbor hearing a gunshot," he explained. "Tank was long dead before any of us arrived."

She bowed her head. A small sign of defeat that hit him in the chest. "My supervisor got the call about your friend breaking into the computer system and told Tom and I to bring him in for questioning ASAP. He ordered up the local law to hang out in case we needed help persuading him to come in. You know the rest. The first officers on scene called in the death before we reached you."

That made a horrible kind of sense. NCIS obviously hadn't known Tank was already dead.

"We need documentation," she insisted. "Surveillance footage from the base, access logs, witness statements—"

"Which I guarantee have already been erased." Ronan couldn't keep the edge from his voice. "We need to move fast. Find who did this and—"

"And what? Take the law into our own hands?" She straightened, all five-foot-nothing of righteous authority. "That's not how justice works."

"No? How's it working so far?" He gestured at Tank's phone. "They're three steps ahead of us, fabricating evidence that'll have every law enforcement agent in the state gunning for us, while you want to file paperwork."

"Following procedure keeps innocent people from getting hurt. Keeps investigations from being compromised—"

He pushed off the wall. "They killed your partner. Framed you for treason. There's no procedure for this."

"There's always procedure." But uncertainty flickered in her eyes. "We gather evidence. Build a case. Present it to—"

"To whom?" He stepped closer. "The same people who just branded you a traitor? The ones who'll shoot first and delete the bodycam footage later?"

"That's not—"

"That's exactly how it works. Not the sanitized version they teach at FLETC. The real world, where good men die and bad men edit the security tapes." He forced himself to soften his tone. "Look. I'm sure you're good at your job. But this isn't a normal investigation. These people operate outside the rules."

"So your solution is to do the same?"

"My solution is to stay alive long enough to expose them." He held her gaze. "Sometimes you have to break the rules to serve justice."

She looked away first, but not before he caught the flash of recognition in her eyes. Part of her knew he was right. The question was whether the dedicated agent could override the lifetime of training that said otherwise.

"If Tank really did access those files, he had a good reason," Axel added quietly. "Whatever he was onto, it was big enough to get him killed. Big enough to authorize the killing of two federal agents and"—he gestured between himself and Ronan—"whatever we're called these days."

Ronan watched her process that. "This goes deeper than any official investigation will reach. You know that."

She didn't answer, but her silence felt less hostile. Progress?

Maybe.

They needed her sharp mind, her insider knowledge. But first, they had to keep her alive long enough to use it.

"Sullivan was working as a clinic aid at the VA facility on base," Maya said. "But you wouldn't know that, would you? Since you walked away three years ago."

The acid in Ronan's stomach burned hotter. She wasn't wrong. He'd cut all ties, burned every bridge. What else had he missed? What had Tank been into that was worth killing for?

"Sounds about right," Axel said into the tension. "Tank always did have a big heart."

Maya's laugh held no humor. "Right. Because you two know him so well." She swung her gaze to Ronan. "Tell me again how your good friend didn't contact you for three years, then suddenly needed help?" She grabbed her jacket. "I'm done playing games. There are killers out there, and I'm not finding them hiding in some garage apartment with two former-SEALs who can't even keep their stories straight."

"Maya—" Axel started.

"No. I'm doing this my way." She yanked the door open. "Stay out of my way, or I'll arrest you both myself."

The door slammed hard enough to rattle the windows.

Axel blinked at Ronan. "What now?"

Ronan pressed a fist to his churning stomach. Stress always triggered the acid reflux these days. Another souvenir of his last mission. "We follow her. Jump in when her stupid plan falls apart."

"Ride to the rescue, you mean." Axel's voice was dry. "Sure. Whatever. I guarantee you Special Agent Chen isn't gonna see it that way."

"Don't care how she sees it. Long as she's alive to be mad about it."

"A fair point," Axel agreed, already moving toward the door. "Though for the record? I'm fairly sure she's right about one thing—we're missing something big about Tank."

The acid burned harder. Because that was the real question, wasn't it? How well had they really known Marcus Sullivan? And what secrets had he taken to his grave?

9

FIGHT OR FLIGHT

MAYA PULLED her borrowed jacket tighter as she walked away from the garage apartment, her mind churning through facts like case evidence. Her initial certainty about Ronan and Axel's guilt had crumbled with each passing hour. Their handling of Marcus's death scene replayed in her mind—the raw grief in Axel's prayer, the way Ronan's hands had shaken before he'd forced them still.

Killers didn't react like that.

And they'd had multiple chances to eliminate her. Instead, Ronan had handed back her weapon—a move that still baffled her. Murderers didn't arm potential witnesses. Their tactical movements were too clean, too professional. The way they cleared rooms, maintained sight lines, communicated without words—that kind of training ran bone-deep.

No, whatever was happening here, Ronan and Axel weren't the killers. Which left her with a dead partner, no resources, and a desperate need for help.

The apartment complex sprawled around her, a maze of identical beige buildings showing their age. Half-empty parking spaces held a collection of well-worn Hondas and ancient pickup trucks. The morning air hung heavy with marine layer, not yet burned off by San Diego's familiar sun. The gray light gave everything a film noir quality that matched her situation perfectly.

Twenty-four hours ago, she'd been a federal agent. Now her partner was dead, and she was somehow a suspect. The absurdity of it made her want to laugh, but she was afraid if she started, she might not stop.

In movies, this would be where the hero appeared. Maya scanned the empty courtyard, the silent windows. Nothing moved except a stray paper bag tumbling across cracked concrete. No dramatic music swelled. No cavalry charged in. No broad-shouldered former SEAL appeared to watch her six.

"Please, Lord. Is this the way forward?" she whispered. The words disappeared into the fog.

She pressed her fingers against her temples. Think. No ID. No credit cards. No phone. But across the street, the sprawling bulk of Plaza Del Mar Mall loomed against the brightening sky. The once-proud shopping center had seen better days. Half the store signs had been removed from its faux stone exterior, leaving ghostly rectangles of unfaded stucco. Only the county library branch and a scattered handful of mom-and-pop shops still advertised their presence. The kind of place that had once hummed with teenagers and holiday shoppers, now clinging to life with discount stores and government offices.

But it had computers. And if her rental car account from Andrea's wedding was still active, with her credit card data on file ... It wasn't much of a plan, but it was something. Better than admitting she'd made a mistake walking out. Better than going back and seeing the knowing look in Ronan's eyes.

Anyone good enough to stage two murders would track her eventually, but she'd be long gone by then. The sun was finally starting to break through, burning away the marine layer. Time to move.

But something made her pause before crossing the street.

The man at the coffee shop window. Dressed casually, in chinos and a rumpled button down, he was reading a paper like any other bro on a coffee break, but his posture was wrong—too alert, too controlled. Another by the dry cleaner's, phone in hand but never looking at the screen. They moved like professionals, checking corners, maintaining distance.

Not Ronan and Axel. These men were different. Hunting.

Maya's throat tightened. Through the mall's grimy glass doors, she could see the library branch's familiar blue sign hanging above a first-floor storefront. What choice did she have?

Ten minutes. That's all it would take to run back. She could picture Ronan's face—no judgment, just that careful assessment as he adjusted plans to include her again. Axel would probably make some smart comment about women changing their minds, trying to break the tension. They'd be angry, but they'd take her back. Protect her.

The thought made her jaw clench. She didn't need protection. She was a federal agent, trained and capable. Even if right now her heart was hammering against her ribs and her palms were slick with sweat.

But these men hunting her ... they moved like Ronan did. Like people trained to eliminate threats. And she was alone, armed with two rounds and borrowed clothes.

She took one step back toward the apartment. Then another. Then forced herself to stop.

No way she'd make it back to their hiding place before these men caught her.

It would have to be the mall. The empty corridors and abandoned shops would give her plenty of cover to lose a tail. She'd worked enough undercover ops to know how to use a building's layout against pursuers. Get inside, lose them in the maze of service corridors and empty retail spaces, then double back to the library. One step at a time. Just like tracking a suspect, only now she was the one being hunted.

She squared her shoulders and started walking. Time to see if seven years of LAPD experience could outmaneuver whatever professionals were on her tail.

Maya pushed through the mall's heavy glass doors, hit by the familiar mix of stale popcorn, cleaning products, and decay that seemed universal to dying malls. Her footsteps echoed off dated terracotta tiles. Most of the first-floor storefronts were dark, their security gates permanently drawn. A lonely kiosk seller scrolled through his phone, not even bothering to look up.

The library branch beckoned from the far end, past the defunct fountain where copper-green pennies still gleamed through murky water. An elderly couple power-walked the perimeter, their shuffling steps marking time like a metronome. Near the food court, a young mother wrestled with a stroller while her toddler wailed. Civilians. Potential casualties if this went wrong.

Maya kept her hand away from her weapon, though every instinct screamed for its reassurance. No need to start a panic. She forced herself to browse the window of a dusty gift shop, using the reflection to track her pursuers. They'd split up—one by the entrance, one drifting toward the escalator, a third moving parallel to her position. Professional. Coordinated. They were boxing her in.

The second floor might offer better options. Maya took the still-functioning escalator, nodding casually to a mall maintenance worker heading down. Now only a dollar store and a tax preparation office showed signs of life among the empty shopfronts. A cluster of teenagers lounged outside the dollar store, sharing a bag of chips. She needed to get clear of the public areas before this turned ugly.

She passed a shuttered Foot Locker, then a boarded-up Victoria's Secret. The men adjusted their positions smoothly, one taking the escalator, one the stairs, the third maintaining line of sight from below. They were herding her, she realized. Using standard tactical containment to force her toward ... what?

A service corridor caught her eye, its "Employees Only" sign hanging askew. Too narrow for vehicles, but it might let her double back downstairs through the old service areas. More importantly, it was away from innocent bystanders. She took it at an easy pace, not running. Running attracted attention.

The corridor stretched ahead, emergency lights casting sickly fluorescent shadows. Past empty stockrooms and abandoned break areas, the smell of mildew growing stronger. Twenty yards in, she realized her mistake. The far exit was blocked by fallen ceiling tiles and debris, and footsteps echoed behind her.

Two new figures appeared at each end of the corridor. Black tactical gear, weapons holstered but ready. Not law enforcement—their movement was too predatory, too unleashed.

That made five, at least. The narrow walls suddenly felt like a trap.

Maya drew her weapon, knowing two rounds weren't nearly enough. All she had was bluster. She held up her badge. "Federal agent! Stand down!"

The men kept coming. No badges shown, no commands

given. Just the steady advance of professionals who knew they had their target cornered. The scent of old food court grease and cleaning products gave way to something metallic. Fear.

The first attacker moved faster than she'd expected. She fired once, catching him in the shoulder. He barely flinched. The second round went wide as another attacker slammed into her from behind, sending her weapon skittering across the stained linoleum.

Then the world exploded into violence.

Two shadows dropped from above—Ronan and Axel moving with liquid grace. The fluorescent lights caught the flash of a blade as Ronan swept the first attacker's legs, while Axel drove an elbow into another's throat with brutal precision. No shouts, no warnings. Just the muffled sounds of hand-to-hand combat from men who'd learned their trade in the world's deadliest places.

Maya managed to break her attacker's hold, even landed a solid combination that would have dropped most opponents. But these men were different. Professional. Trained. He shrugged off her best shots like they were love taps.

Then Ronan was there, moving past her with deadly efficiency. His attack was nothing like the controlled takedowns she'd learned at the academy. This was something else—swift, brutal, final. The kind of fighting that belonged to shadowy operations, not shopping malls in San Diego.

The fight ended as abruptly as it began. Five attackers down, Ronan and Axel barely winded. Maya retrieved her weapon, hands steady now despite everything. Beyond the service corridor, she could hear the normal sounds of mall life—muzak, distant conversations, the hum of escalators.

"We need to call this in," she said, already reaching for her badge. "There could be civilians—"

"No time." Ronan was already searching the first unconscious man, his movements quick and practiced. No wallet. No ID. Not even a phone. He moved to the second while Axel checked the others. "Nothing. Not even unit patches or manufacturer's labels in their gear."

"Pros," Axel confirmed, holding up a jacket liner where the tags had been carefully removed. "The kind who don't leave breadcrumbs." He pulled a single phone from one man's pocket, thumbed through it. "But they left us this."

The screen showed surveillance photos of her father's condo complex. Time-stamped that morning.

"They were waiting for you to run," Ronan said quietly. He was doing something to ensure the attackers stayed down—Maya decided not to look too closely. "Probably have teams at every transit point between here and LA."

A child's laughter echoed from the main concourse, making Maya flinch. "We can't just leave them here. The mall opens properly in an hour—"

"Already called it in." Axel's voice was grim as he handed the cell phone to Ronan. "Anonymous tip about suspicious activity. Local PD will find them, but we'll be long gone."

"The sort of professionals who can make a murder look like suicide," Ronan added, pocketing the phone. "Ghost teams. No ID, no trace." His meaning was clear—the same kind who could frame federal agents and erase evidence trails.

Distant sirens made the decision for them. "Move," Ronan ordered, already heading for what looked like a maintenance exit. "Unless you'd rather explain to responding officers why a supposedly corrupt federal agent is standing over four unconscious men in tactical gear."

Maya's hands trembled as she stared at the fallen men. Her lungs felt too small, each breath shorter than the last.

Four years working gangs in LA, three years in violent crimes, barely three months with NCIS—none of it had prepared her for this. These men had moved like machines, had shrugged off her best defensive techniques like she was a rookie. If Ronan and Axel hadn't shown up ...

Her father had always said there were predators, and then there were apex predators. She'd thought she understood. But watching Ronan and Axel fight—that liquid grace, that lethal efficiency—she realized she'd been playing in a completely different league. These weren't street thugs or even hardened criminals. They were something else entirely.

They'd known exactly where she'd run. Which meant every plan she'd made, every option she'd considered, had already been anticipated. She was a cop playing soldier, and she was hopelessly outmatched.

"Fine," she said, hating the slight quaver in her voice as she fell into step behind them. "But this doesn't mean I trust you."

"Good." Ronan eased the door open, checking sight lines with a precision that made her own tactical training feel like child's play. "Trust gets people killed. Right now, I'll settle for you staying alive long enough to help us find who murdered our friends."

Maya followed, her cop's mind struggling to catalog details through the fog of adrenaline crash. The mall's muzak played on, something upbeat and forgettable, while somewhere above them early morning shoppers went about their normal lives, unaware of the violence that had just played out beneath their feet. She might not trust them, but Ronan was right about one thing—she needed their help to solve this case.

She'd trained her whole life to protect others, to serve justice. Now she couldn't even protect herself.

The thought burned like acid in her throat.

LOST HOPE

Maya followed them through the service exit, leaving behind the cheerful muzak and oblivious shoppers. Her body ached, her confidence shaken, but something deeper than training or instinct steadied her steps. Whatever darkness lay ahead, she had to trust that God had placed these warriors in her path for a purpose.

10

FALL BACK POSITION

Ronan kept them moving through the mall's service corridors, his mind mapping exit routes while cataloging threats. Through the walls, they could hear the controlled chaos of first responders—radio chatter, boots on tile, the clipped tones of officers establishing a perimeter around their recent battle zone.

Maya moved well for someone without his training—staying low, checking corners, maintaining spacing. But she kept leading with her left, favoring the shoulder that had taken that hit back in the corridor. That'd get her killed if they ran into another team.

He caught Axel's eye, got a slight nod. His partner had noticed too.

They paused at a junction as a pair of uniforms hustled past the corridor entrance, weapons drawn. The local PD's response time was better than expected. They'd have the main concourse locked down by now, probably reviewing security footage.

"We need resources," Axel said quietly. "Intelligence. Transport."

"The library branch," Maya whispered. "It's why I came here. I can access federal databases, check our options." She hesitated. "But we'll have to circle around. That section of the mall will be crawling with cops."

Ronan didn't like it. Going back inside meant limiting their escape routes, exposing themselves to security cameras, civilian witnesses. And now they'd have to evade both tactical teams and local law enforcement. But they needed intel.

"Two minutes," he conceded. "We'll use the service tunnel that runs behind the old department store. Axel, watch our six. Those cops are going to expand their search pattern soon."

They ghosted through the maintenance tunnels, pausing whenever voices echoed too close. Above them, the mall's PA system crackled to life, announcing the facility would be temporarily closed due to a "security incident." That would clear most civilians, but it also meant every remaining person would be either law enforcement or hostile.

The library entrance was down a secondary corridor, past the defunct fountain. An elderly couple power-walking the perimeter stopped mid-stride as mall security directed them toward the exits. Each shuffling step sounded like a countdown timer.

"Hold," Ronan whispered, pulling Maya back as two officers swept past, checking shop entrances. Through the glass walls of the library, he could see a drowsy clerk gathering her things, responding to the evacuation order.

They waited until she left, then slipped inside. Maya went straight to a computer station, and logged into the secure federal systems she could access.

"Knight Tactical," Axel whispered, positioned where he could watch both entrance and escalator. "We gotta contact them. They've got resources, international reach, specialized extraction teams—"

"No." The word came out harder than Ronan intended.

"Found them," Maya interrupted, scanning through database entries. Her eyebrows rose. "Multiple government contracts ... specialized training programs ... Your brother's outfit is serious business."

"He's not my brother. I mean, he is technically, but—"

"Did you know they just pulled off that impossible hostage situation in Buenos Aires?" Axel interrupted. "Full tactical support, clean exfil, zero civilian casualties—"

"Enough." Ronan stepped closer to his partner. "Since when are you such an expert on Murphy's company?"

Another radio squawked nearby. Maya tensed, but kept typing.

"Did my homework after Buenos Aires hit the news," Axel said, adjusting his position to better cover the entrance. "They're impressive, Ro. And we need help."

Maya kept scrolling. "They've got better resources than most federal agencies. Why wouldn't we contact them?"

"The lady's right. You got a better plan?" Axel pressed. "Because right now we've got no resources, no backup, and a federal agent with a target on her back. Plus about fifty cops who'd love to question us about those unconscious operators downstairs."

Ronan turned away, running tactical scenarios that all led to the same conclusion. They needed help. Real help. The kind that came with clean paperwork and official credentials, not the under-the-table favors he usually traded in.

"Fine." The word tasted like ash. "I'll make the call."

But when he turned back, Maya was already typing into the secure contact form on Knight Tactical's government portal.

"She moved fast while you were brooding," Axel said. "Already reaching out to them."

Ronan stared at the computer screen, remembering those long nights flying questionable cargo across borders. He'd thought that was rock bottom. Now he was facing both Maya's independent streak and having to work with Christian Murphy.

"You know what the worst part is?" he said finally.

"That you're being a dramatic child about working with your brother?"

"Half-brother. And no." Ronan checked his weapon, an old habit when stressed. "The worst part is you're actually excited about this."

"Did you know they have their own tactical training facility in Dubai?"

"I hate you."

"Love you too, partner." Axel grinned, then tensed as footsteps approached. "Now let's get our fed out of here before her login attracts the wrong kind of attention. Or before those cops decide to check the library."

Ronan's phone vibrated. He checked the display, jaw tightening. "It's him. My b—" He caught himself. "It's Murphy."

"So answer it. Duh." Axel kept watch on the entrance.

Ronan connected. "Murphy."

"Status?" Christian's voice was pure operator.

"Mobile. Three-man element. One minor injury."

"Threat assessment?"

"Multiple hostiles. Professional. Agency-grade gear and training."

A pause. "Golden State Bank building. It's five clicks from your present position. Be there at thirteen hundred."

"What, we making a withdrawal?"

"You're getting on a helo." The line went dead.

Ronan stared at his phone. No questions about why his half-brother, a virtual stranger, suddenly needed an extraction. Just coordinates and a timeline, delivered in the clipped cadence of a SEAL commander.

"Well?" Maya asked.

"We've got a ride." Ronan checked his watch. Four hours to make it across town without getting caught by local LEOs or whoever had sent that tactical team. And then ... he'd have to face Christian Murphy.

He'd fought his way out of hot zones on three continents, survived two helicopter crashes, and spent a couple years now flying rust buckets for operators who made cartels look legitimate. But somehow, this felt worse.

What had he gotten himself into?

11

AIR SUPPORT

Twenty stories above downtown San Diego, Maya Chen tried not to feel like a target. The August sun beat down mercilessly on the bank building's roof, offering no shelter, no place to hide. Though she knew they were alone up here, every shadow, every glint of sunlight off surrounding windows made her pulse jump.

Since answering Commander Phillips's dispatch last night, she'd broken every rule she believed in. Now, standing exposed on this rooftop just before 1 p.m., she waited for what felt like judgment.

Rules had been her armor since police academy. Training at Quantico only cemented her love of procedure. Follow protocol. Maintain the chain of command. Trust the system.

Those rules had gotten her partner killed.

Please Lord, she prayed silently, *let me be doing the right thing. Show me the path through this darkness.*

A subtle movement caught her attention. Ronan adjusted his position against the utility shed wall, his stillness speaking of years of combat experience. Even in repose, tension radiated from his powerful frame. His dark hair was slightly tousled from the earlier fight, and those haunted eyes never stopped scanning their surroundings. The hard planes of his face spoke of battles fought alone, of wounds that went soul-deep. Everything about him was controlled, contained. A man used to operating alone.

She wondered how many of his own rules he'd broken by helping her.

"Five minutes," Axel said quietly from his lookout position. His usual humor was absent, replaced by a calm but watchful tension. His gaze kept returning to Ronan, worry evident in the set of his shoulders.

Maya forced her hands to stay steady. She was risking everything by running, but staying clearly meant death. They'd proven that with Tom. Once they got somewhere safe, once she and Ronan and Axel could separate the good guys from the bad, she'd turn herself in. Get this sorted out properly. Whether that permanently destroyed her career in law enforcement ... well, she'd leave that in God's hands. Right now, staying alive long enough to expose the truth had to be enough.

The thwack of helicopter blades cut through her thoughts.

Ronan went absolutely still. His fingers flexed once before going motionless.

The aircraft appeared over the building's edge, sleek and blue, the Knight Tactical logo understated but professional. Everything about it spoke of money, of success, of power.

The pilot set the bright blue helo in the center of the pad. Two men emerged from the cockpit as the rotors slowed. Neither was Christian Murphy. The slender one had to be Jack Reese. The big man would be Austin Daggett.

"Should have known."

The words were barely audible, but the bitterness in Ronan's voice made Maya flinch. She saw Axel shoot his friend a worried glance.

"Gentlemen, Agent Chen." Jack's approach was carefully diplomatic. "Let's get you somewhere secure."

"Sweet ride," Axel offered, clearly trying for casual.

Ronan's only response was silence. But Maya caught how his eyes cataloged every detail of the machine. She knew nothing about aircraft, but this one screamed money.

The interior was immaculate, better equipped than any federal aircraft she'd ever seen. Maya watched Ronan take it all in, his expression growing more closed with each second.

"Weather's perfect for flying," Austin tried again from the cockpit. "Clear skies all the way to—"

"How long?" Ronan cut him off.

"A buck twenty to the compound," Jack answered smoothly. "Get yourselves buckled in and we'll hit it."

Maya studied Ronan's profile in the dim light. The military precision in his bearing couldn't quite hide the tension underneath. This man had saved her life today, yet something about approaching his brother's domain seemed to cost him more than facing armed killers.

The helicopter lifted off smoothly, banking east toward the mountains. Maya watched the city lights recede below them, each mile taking her farther from everything familiar. She'd crossed a line, burned bridges she likely could never rebuild.

Looking at Ronan's carefully controlled expression, she wondered what lines he was crossing, asking for help from a stranger who should have been family.

The helicopter banked again, gentler this time. Axel's knuckles went white on his armrest.

"Looking a little pale there, partner." Ronan's voice held the first hint of humor Maya had heard from him in hours. Since she contacted Knight Tactical, actually. "Need a bag?"

"Bite me, Quinn." Axel flexed his big hand. "Some of us prefer our feet on solid ground."

"Could be worse," Ronan said, clearly enjoying himself. "Could be like that time in Paraguay—"

"We don't talk about Paraguay," Axel ground out.

Jack chuckled. "Sounds like someone else we know."

"Christian hates flying too," Austin said. "Gets green around the gills every time."

Maya caught Ronan's startled blink. Such a small detail about his brother, but clearly news to him. His expression shifted, processing this unexpected frailty.

"Speaking of flying," Axel said suddenly, his grin showing he'd found a way to get back at Ronan for the teasing, "what are we doing about the Lockheed?"

Ronan's curse was creative. "Forgot about that."

"The what now?" Jack's tone sharpened with interest.

"Had to find a way to get here from Yuma ASAP," Ronan answered. Maya heard the defensive note in his voice, saw how his shoulders tensed for criticism. "Grabbed what I had available. A Lockheed Electra outfitted for cargo. Parked it at an airfield east of town. Should be good for a while."

"You might want to let your employer know where it is," Axel suggested helpfully.

"You mean former employer," Ronan corrected grimly.

"That's ... probably a good point."

To Maya's surprise, Jack and Austin exchanged knowing grins in the cockpit.

"Been there, done that," Jack said easily. "Sometimes you gotta do what you gotta do, right?"

The tension in Ronan's shoulders eased slightly. Something resembling a smile touched his eyes. "Right."

"Though next time," Austin added, "maybe go for something smaller than a Lockheed. Those things drink fuel like Christian drinks coffee."

Another fragment of information about his brother. Maya

watched Ronan file it away, saw how each casual mention simultaneously drew him in and pushed him back.

Axel's next white-knuckled grab at the edge of his seat broke the moment. "Speaking of drinking, anyone else notice we're flying through mountains? Can we maybe focus on that?"

"Be not afraid," Maya quoted softly. "For I am with you."

"Amen to that," Jack called back.

Austin nodded, adding his own "Amen."

Maya caught the flicker of something in Ronan's expression—not quite discomfort, more like longing. A man who'd lost not just his career, but maybe his faith too.

"Relax," Austin said to Axel. "Jack here's the best pilot we've got. Though speaking of the best ..." He grinned. "You should see Christian on overwatch. Man can hit a target at fifteen hundred yards in high winds. Never seen anything like it."

The almost-smile vanished from Ronan's face.

How many conversations in the compound would end like this—casual mentions of Christian Murphy's accomplishments leaving new bruises on old wounds?

Below them, the vast San Joaquin Valley stretched to the horizon, an endless patchwork of farmland shimmering in the summer heat. The megalopolis that was So Cal had disappeared behind them, leaving only scattered buildings and roads cutting through the agricultural expanse. Somewhere ahead, Christian Murphy's world waited.

Maya watched Ronan's reflection in the window, saw how his jaw set as a compound appeared in the distance. Whatever came next would test them both.

She just hoped they were strong enough to face it.

12

BETTER BROTHER

Knight Tactical's compound came into view as they crested the mountain pass, anchoring one end of Hope Landing's small commercial airport. The facility looked like something from a military recruitment video—four modern buildings arranged in tactical formation around a central courtyard. High-tech security systems were subtly integrated into the architecture, and two Sikorsky helicopters sat in precise alignment near the main structure. Everything about the operation screamed success, legitimacy, and the kind of operational excellence Ronan had once lived for.

Perfect. Just perfect.

He caught Maya studying him and forced his expression neutral. She was already dealing with enough without watching him process meeting his biological brother for the first time. A brother whose career he'd followed through news clips and mission citations, each achievement a reminder of what the only legitimate Murphy son could accomplish.

"Welcome to Hope Landing," Austin called from the cockpit as they began their descent. The helicopter touched down smoothly on the pad, rotors slowing to a stop in the bright afternoon sun. "Christian and the team will meet up with you inside."

Of course they would. Ronan had memorized enough about Christian Murphy to know he never did anything without precise tactical consideration. Including, apparently, meeting his stranger of a brother.

Once the engines had fully shut down, Jack released his harness. "I'll take point," he said easily, but Ronan caught the careful assessment in his gaze. "Agent Chen, if you'll follow me. Quinn, Austin will—"

"I've got him," a new voice cut in.

Ronan turned to find a stunning woman in tactical gear approaching the helicopter. Her bearing screamed special operations, but her smile was genuine.

"Angie Michaelson," she said.

Her handshake was firm, professional. No hint of curiosity about meeting her teammate's long-lost brother. These people had discipline.

Maya stiffened beside him. "The CIA's already involved?"

Angie shook her head. "I am with the Company, but I consult with Knight Tactical on the side. I'm not here in an official capacity. Just more brainpower if you need me."

Ronan shot Maya a look. How would she know Angela Michaelson was CIA?

"I read their files. What I could find, anyway." She shrugged. "Guess you didn't."

Wrong. He read everything he could find on Christian Murphy. And Knight Tactical. He just wasn't going to admit it.

"This way." Angie gestured toward the main building. "Team's gathering in the conference room. Christian's finishing up a call with the DOD."

Of course he was. According to every file Ronan had

quietly acquired over the years, Christian Murphy and his friends had more connections in the Pentagon than most generals. The medals alone ...

The massive hangar door stood open, releasing a wave of familiar scents—aviation fuel, gun oil, fresh coffee. It hit something deep in Ronan's muscle memory, a visceral reminder of everything he'd lost. The space could have housed a small airline. Instead, it held a collection of aircraft that made Ronan's chest tight with envy. A sleek Pilatus PC-24 dominated the center, its pristine paint job probably worth more than everything Ronan owned. He couldn't even afford a single prop for that beauty. Or one tire.

The far corner had been transformed into what looked like a professional training facility—weight stations, climbing walls, and equipment Ronan recognized from his Special Forces days. Plus some he didn't.

"No way," Axel breathed, staring at the workout area. "Is that a hypoxic chamber? And look at that obstacle course setup ..." He trailed off, practically drooling.

"Quite an operation," Maya said quietly beside Ronan. He caught the unspoken question in her tone.

"Knight Tactical specializes in high-risk private security and extraction," Austin explained as they walked. "Best in the business."

The pride in his voice was genuine. Ronan cataloged details as they moved through the facility—cutting-edge equipment, veteran operators moving with purpose, everything running like clockwork. The kind of setup he'd once dreamed of building. Back when he still wore a uniform.

They passed through the hangar area and up the metal stairs to the third floor. Angie squared her shoulders slightly —a tell that gave away more than she probably intended.

"Ready?" she asked.

No. But Ronan nodded anyway.

The command center could have been lifted straight from any top-tier military installation. Gleaming screens covered one wall, and cutting-edge tactical displays another. But someone had put thought into making it feel less sterile—comfortable leather chairs, custom wood desks, even some tasteful art on the walls. Everything spoke of unlimited resources applied with tactical precision.

And at the center ...

Christian Murphy turned from a communication console. The air whooshed out of Ronan's lungs. The room's carefully controlled temperature suddenly felt too cold against his skin, raising gooseflesh along his arms. Even the recycled air seemed to carry his brother's expensive cologne—something subtle and refined that made Ronan intensely aware of his own sweat-dried clothes and the lingering gunpowder residue clinging to his skin. It was like looking in a mirror with the settings slightly altered. Same build, same features, but refined where Ronan was rough. There was government money in top-of-the line tech wear. Pentagon polish in that posture.

Their eyes met. Ronan caught the microscopic flinch before Christian's expression went professionally neutral.

"You all look like hell." Christian gestured toward a bright hallway. "Rooms are ready. Get cleaned up, grab some food. Team meeting in sixty."

The dismissal was clear, but Austin jumped in. "I hope you guys are okay with DreamBurger for lunch. My wife's—"

Axel groaned with pleasure. "Company. We know. And the flagship restaurant's right here in the terminal. I am totally down with that. Any chance I can get my fries extra crispy?"

A grin transformed Austin's craggy face. "I do have some pull. I'll see what I can do."

Ronan looked away. This might be his buddy's dreamland, but it was fast becoming his nightmare. Exactly as he expected.

"We've got the best coffee this side of Baghdad," Jack added.

"And actual hot water," Angie said with a pointed look at their rumpled state.

"Sounds great." Ronan kept his own voice even. "Appreciate the extraction."

He and Christian faced each other, two strangers, neither sure what came next. Ronan had a couple inches on his older brother, but that was about all he could claim in the plus column. Where Ronan's build spoke of endless ground ops and basic military gyms, Christian had the lean, precise muscle of someone with access to elite training facilities. His clothes probably cost more than Ronan's monthly rent. Even his bearing screamed success—relaxed confidence instead of Ronan's perpetual combat-ready tension. Looking at Christian Murphy was like seeing an optimized version of himself, one that hadn't screwed up every opportunity that came his way.

Maya stepped forward. "Thank you all for offering your help. I know this is an unusual situation—"

"Of course," Christian said, his attention shifting to her with practiced diplomacy. "Knight Tactical specializes in unusual situations." He glanced at Ronan, a dry note entering his voice. "Though my little brother seems to have dropped you in a particularly complex one. Let's see if we can't get you out."

Something in his tone made Ronan look closer. There was steel under that casual manner, and genuine concern. This wasn't just professional courtesy.

"Tehran," Christian said suddenly, his eyes finding Ronan's. "That extraction you ran for the Resistance. Four civilians, zero casualties, middle of a riot. That was solid work."

The words hit Ronan like a punch to the solar plexus. Tehran.

His mouth went dry, pulse hammering in his throat. That op wasn't even in his official record—he'd made sure of that. The details were buried under three layers of classified reports and enough redacted documents to choke an admiral. The fact that Christian knew about it, had been watching him ... Something warm and unwanted unfurled in his chest. Pride. Recognition. He crushed it immediately, angry at himself for caring what this stranger thought, brother or not.

"We keep tabs on operations in that region," the man said simply. "That was some of the cleanest work I've seen. Even by SEAL standards."

The words hung between them, heavy with unspoken meaning. How long had Christian been watching? Why hadn't he reached out before? Ronan pushed the questions away. He wasn't here for family reunion time.

Twenty minutes later, Ronan stood in the guest suite's bathroom, staring at his reflection while steam filled the space. Behind him, Axel was already monopolizing the enormous shower, making obscene noises of pleasure.

"Sweet summer sunshine, this shower has sixteen jets. SIXTEEN! I'm never leaving. Tell Christian I live here now," Axel called out, turning off the water. He emerged from the vast enclosure, wrapping a bath towel the size of New York around his hips. "It's all yours."

Axel cleared his throat. "Earth to Quinn. You gonna stand there doing your brooding supermodel pose all day, or are you gonna check this baby out? Because I gotta tell you, my man, you're a little ripe for that meeting."

Ronan didn't answer. He'd come here prepared—or

thought he had. Ready to face the successful brother, the golden boy who had everything he'd never had a chance to hold. He'd steeled himself for envy, for bitterness, for the awkward dance of strangers who shared blood but not history.

What he hadn't prepared for was the man's quiet competence, so reminiscent of the best commanders Ronan had served under. The respect the other Knight Tactical operatives showed him wasn't forced—they genuinely trusted him.

Most unsettling of all were the glimpses of the brother he might have had. The dry humor. The straightforward praise about Tehran. The way he'd noticed Ronan's tension and cleared the room without making it obvious.

The kicker wasn't that Christian had everything Ronan didn't—it was that he was exactly the kind of man Ronan would want to serve with. To trust. To call brother.

The realization hit harder than any resentment could.

He braced his hands on the sink, letting his head drop. He'd come here for Maya's sake, expecting to hate asking his stranger of a brother for help. Now he was facing a truth he never expected: He didn't just want Christian's help with Maya's situation.

He wanted his respect.

And that made him more vulnerable than he'd been since the day they stripped his rank.

"Seriously, dude," Axel said softer now, catching his mood. "The water's fine. And we've got work to do."

Ronan straightened, squaring his shoulders. Right. Focus on the mission. Deal with everything else later.

If later ever came.

13

FAMILY FORCES

Maya stood at the guest room window, working her fingers through hair that still dripped on the shoulders of her borrowed tactical gear. The clothes fit perfectly—of course they did. Everything about Knight Tactical's setup screamed precision and deep pockets, from the spa-worthy shampoo to the rack of color-coordinated workout wear. Like some fantasy boutique hotel where retired operators dropped platinum cards instead of brass shell casings.

In another world, she'd have time to actually appreciate the amenities. Right now, she needed to get this mess sorted. So far, it looked like she was in the right place to get that done. Knight Tactical had resources that made her NCIS clearance look pathetic. Between their connections and her knowledge of internal procedures, they could tear through the fabricated evidence, trace those deepfake images and videos, and get her world righted again. A day or two of their help and she'd be back at headquarters, hunting down Marcus Sullivan's real killers. The ones who'd murdered Tom.

But first, she'd have to get Ronan Quinn to stand down.

The man switched from brilliant strategist to tactical loose cannon without warning. His past haunted every decision, every interaction, and that issue with his brother ...

Lots of future therapy bills there.

Having grown up with her passionate, hard-driving father who lived to bend rules for justice, Maya understood exactly how things with a man like Ronan Quinn would play out. Dad's intensity had driven Mom away before Maya turned twelve. His dedication to the job had shaped her childhood into a series of missed events and broken promises—all for good reasons, but still. She'd sworn she wouldn't live that way herself.

Even if Ronan was on the right side of the law, he was exactly the kind of complication she didn't need.

The memory hit without warning—Tom, floating face-up in that murky water at the boat ramp.

Her hands clenched. She shouldn't have left him there. Her partner, her friend, deserved better than to be abandoned like evidence in a crime scene.

Her father.

The realization jolted through her like electricity. The BOLOs would have hit his desk hours ago. Those deepfake videos ...

She hit the hallway at a run, banging on Ronan and Axel's door.

Axel swung it open immediately.

She didn't bother with niceties. "I need a phone. Now."

"Whoa, easy." Ronan emerged from the bathroom in utility pants and a black tech shirt, hair still wet. "What's wrong?"

"My father's probably got half the LAPD looking for me already. He'll have seen everything—the BOLOs, the videos, Tom's murder. He's probably calling in every favor he's got."

"No one outside law enforcement will have seen those

alerts yet," Axel added. "We should probably check with the team before—"

"You don't understand." Maya fought to keep her voice steady. "My father—"

"Will be fine until we talk this through with the Knight Tactical crew," Ronan assured her. "What he doesn't know won't hurt—" He stopped, finally taking in her expression. "What?"

Axel shrugged.

She stared at them. "You really didn't do your research, did you?"

Axel was already typing on his phone. His eyebrows shot up. "Yikes."

"Yeah." Maya ran a hand through her hair. "Twenty-eight years with the LAPD. Currently Captain of Northwest Detective Division. Trust me, he's seen the BOLOs. And he knows literally everyone in law enforcement on the West Coast. How long do you think it'll take him to trace us here?"

Without another word, Ronan tossed her his phone.

Maya's fingers trembled as she dialed, muscle memory taking over. The familiar number felt like touching a live wire.

Twenty-eight years of commanding officers, organizing task forces, and moving heaven and earth to protect his only child had honed Lawrence Chen into a force of nature. He'd take over, reorganize everything, call in every favor from San Diego to Seattle. The full tsunami of Captain Chen's protective instincts was about to be unleashed.

And she needed to stop him before he destroyed both their careers trying to save her.

Her throat tightened. How many times had she sworn she'd never need rescuing? That she'd learned from his mistakes, would never put either of them in that position again? Yet here she was, about to drag him into the mess she'd made.

Her father answered on the first ring. "I've got three task forces running scenarios. Where are you? I'm sending a team. I've already talked to the DA and—"

"Dad—"

"—called in markers with the FBI's forensics lab. Those videos are obvious fakes. Just need forty-eight hours to prove it. You sit tight and let me—"

"They killed my partner." Her voice cracked, stopping his flow of words. "They knew we were called out to the scene—or they called it in themselves—and then they killed Tom. These people have reach inside NCIS. Maybe the Navy itself."

"I'm not Benson, sweetie. I've got three decades on the force and connections he didn't have. I can protect you."

"That's exactly why I can't come in. They'll use you to get to me." She swallowed hard. "I'm safe. Hidden. I've got ... resources."

"What resources? Maya, honey, you don't know who to trust right now—"

She gritted her teeth. Time to bargain. "Give me twenty-four hours. If I stall out, you're in."

Silence for a heartbeat. Then two. Finally, a sigh. "Deal."

"I love you, Dad. I'll contact you when I can."

"Maya, wait—"

She ended the call before her voice could betray her. Her father's fear and frustration hung in the air like smoke. The silence after she ended the call seemed to ring in her ears, mixing with the soft hum of the room's air conditioning and the distant thrum of helicopter blades. Even the metallic taste of adrenaline in her mouth reminded her of countless stakeouts with her father, waiting for his signal.

She stared at Ronan's phone, hearing the echo of her

father's desperation. Behind her, Ronan and Axel made a show of examining the room's high-tech security system.

"Nice panic buttons," Axel commented way too casually. "Very *Mission Impossible*."

"Motion sensors in the windows," Ronan added. "Top of the line."

She almost smiled at their awkward attempt to give her privacy. "You can stop pretending you weren't listening."

She handed Ronan's phone back, pacing the length of the room. "I need these charges cleared. Now. Every hour I'm stuck here is another hour I'm not tracking down who killed Marcus Sullivan and Tom."

"What exactly do you think we're doing?" Ronan's frustration matched hers. "Knight Tactical has resources that—"

"I'll give your team twenty-four hours." She spun to face him. "That's all the time we have."

"Twenty-four hours? To untangle a conspiracy this deep? That's not—"

"That's all we've got. My father won't wait longer than that. He'll dive into this investigation himself, start pulling threads, asking questions ..." Her voice cracked. "These people killed my partner. They won't hesitate to take out a police captain who gets too close, no matter how well-connected—or overconfident—he is."

"Maya—"

"Team's ready." Christian's voice cut through their argument as he appeared in the doorway. "Conference room."

They followed him down the hall, their footsteps echoing off polished floors in a rhythm that reminded her of precinct corridors. The taste of Knight Tactical's premium coffee still lingered on her tongue—worlds away from the bitter breakroom brew she usually survived on. Even here, surrounded by elite operators and high-tech security, her senses stayed sharp, cataloging sounds: the subtle click of door locks engaging, the whisper of tactical gear as operators moved, the almost silent communications system broadcasting status updates in controlled tones.

Christian glanced at Ronan. "Your mom called. She expects a full update ASAP."

Ronan's groan was heartfelt.

Axel winced. "Mama Quinn is a handful and a half."

"Tell me about it," Ronan huffed.

Despite everything, Maya smiled. Maybe she wasn't the only one with complicated family dynamics.

14

TRUST CIRCLE

Ronan followed Maya and Christian into the briefing room, his boots silent on polished concrete. The space carried that distinct mix of smells he remembered from command centers—fresh coffee, gun oil, and that peculiar scent of electronics running hot. But underneath was something unexpected—fresh-cut flowers from a vase near the windows. A domestic touch that felt jarringly out of place. And yet totally fitting. Reassuring, even.

Clean. Professional. Expensive.

But it was the team that caught his attention. Everyone displayed the casual confidence of operators who'd survived enough disasters together to become family. Austin dropped into a chair, boots on the table until Jack Reese smacked them off. He'd never admit it, but he'd read up on the Knight Tactical team to know Star and Ethan Hernandez by sight. The two cyber-security specialists were already deep in their own world of algorithms and data streams, finishing each other's sentences.

The easy flow of people who trusted each other completely.

Christian stood apart, his expression distant. Probably going over every ugly detail of Ronan's General Discharge in his mind. His perfect, polished brother who'd never made a wrong move in his life would have memorized every line of that report. Would have analyzed exactly how Ronan had managed to throw away a promising military career with one catastrophic decision.

Or so it looked.

Who was he kidding? These people had distinguished service records, successful civilian transitions, legitimate operations. And here he was, the guy with a General Discharge that might as well have been stamped "Suspected Traitor" in red ink. They had to be wondering if he was involved in whatever had gotten Marcus killed.

His gaze shifted to Axel, who looked like Christmas had come early. His friend was practically bouncing on his toes, drinking in the tech, the gear, the whole setup with unrestrained enthusiasm. Trust Axel to see this place as his version of Disney World, complete with innovative toys.

Then to Maya. He'd known her less than twenty-four hours, but her laser focus and fierce determination already impressed him. The Knight Tactical team would see it too—her quick mind, her unwavering sense of justice. The kind of federal agent who'd never compromise, never back down. Who'd earned every commendation in her spotless record.

At least their credibility might keep the team from assuming he was dirty. The black sheep of the group, sure, but not a threat.

He almost smiled at that thought. Black sheep. Story of his life. At least he knew the role by heart.

Old habits die hard. Ronan found himself analyzing the room dynamics, reading the team like he would've done before a mission. Jack stood at the head of the conference table, loose but alert, the kind of natural leader people followed without question. No surprise Admiral Knight had picked him to run operations.

The double doors swung open. Two women breezed in—both beautiful enough to stop traffic, one blonde, one dark-haired—juggling DreamBurger coffee carriers. Civilians, by their casual summer dress. A pair of towheaded toddlers clung to the blonde's legs like determined koalas.

One of the twin boys broke free, making a wobbly sprint for Austin, who scooped him up without missing a beat in his conversation with Angie, the CIA officer.

The other twin zeroed in on Christian. The tiny man ran so fast he did a header straight into Christian's leg, but his bio bro scooped the baby up before any damage was done.

Ronan's breath caught as his stern-faced brother's expression transformed, softening into a wide grin. Christian swung the little boy up onto his lap, accepting a sticky kiss.

At the head of the table, Jack smiled, shaking his head as he snagged a coffee and watched. "As usual, I'm chopped liver."

Christian looked up from tickling the squirming kid in his lap. "Sorry. Not sorry."

"Don't worry. I still love you." The stunning blonde brushed back Jack's hair and bussed him on the cheek.

The man's cheeks pinked. "Kelli, meet Ronan, Maya, and Axel. Guys, my wife. And the Twin Terrors."

Maya wrinkled her nose. "You have a daughter, too, right?"

Pride shone in the man's eyes. "Amelia. She's at preschool."

Smiling, the woman acknowledged them with a wave. "Sorry to break up the meeting, but the kids insisted on seeing Daddy."

"And by that, you mean their uncles," Jack corrected, laughing.

Axel turned his attention to the dark-haired woman. "So great to meet you, Mrs. Daggett. DreamBurger is ... Wow."

"His favorite. By a million miles." Ronan stepped in as Axel's voice sputtered out. You'd think he was meeting the Beatles.

The cyber-guy, Ethan, patted his six-pack abs. "And the main reason we maintain that fancy gym downstairs."

Nobody even blinked at having toddlers in a high-level tactical briefing. These people were more than a team—the casual touches, the inside jokes, the way they anticipated each other's movements.

The fabric of Ronan's tactical shirt suddenly felt rough against his skin, a physical reminder of how out of place he was. Even the air felt different here—warmer, softer somehow, carrying traces of baby powder and Lauren's expensive perfume mixed with the lingering scent of weapons and tactical gear. A combination that shouldn't work, but somehow did.

Jack's twins were just part of their strange, deadly family.

So Bio Bro had managed to break the Murphy family curse. From what Ronan's mother had told him, the Murphy men were, as far as she knew, completely allergic to emotion. And interpersonal ties.

Or at least that was his excuse.

Jack waited until Kelli and Lauren had corralled the twins out of the room before he took a seat and leaned forward. "Before we get into details, let's be clear about what you need and what we can offer."

"We need to clear our names," Maya said immediately. "So I can get back to investigating two murders."

"While staying alive," Axel added. "That would be my vote."

LOST HOPE

Jack nodded. "Knight Tactical specializes in complex operations requiring multiple skillsets. Investigation, protection, cyber intelligence, tactical response." He gestured around the room. "Everyone here has an extensive military or law enforcement background. We're licensed, bonded, and have connections throughout the intelligence community. Plus, we've been through this kind of deal ourselves."

"More than once," Star added.

"And what's the cost?" Ronan asked bluntly. No point dancing around it.

Christian's jaw tightened, but Jack held up a hand. "You're family. Literally. And even if you weren't, you're SEAL brothers. No charge. But first, we need complete transparency from all three of you. Everything you know. Everything you suspect. No holding back."

"That works both ways," Maya said, her tone careful. "We need to know what you find. All of it. No sanitized briefings."

"Agreed." Jack looked at each of them in turn. "But understand what you're buying into. We're a team. We work together, or not at all."

Ronan felt the weight of Christian's stare. "And if we don't like how you operate?"

"Then we part ways. But right now, you're fugitives with limited options and powerful enemies. We can help. If you let us."

Axel's eyes were bright with possibility—or maybe just the thought of access to Knight Tactical's impressive tech and unlimited DreamBurger meals. But beneath his eager expression, Ronan saw the tactical assessment running. His friend was convinced they needed backup.

Ronan met Maya's questioning look. Much as he hated involving Christian's team—hated giving his bio bro a front-row seat to his messed-up life—they were out of options. Tank was dead. Maya's partner, too. Whoever was behind this had the resources to make three more people dead just as easily.

Not like they had any other choice. He gave Maya a tight nod.

She turned back to Jack. "We're in."

15

HARD CALLS

THE COMMAND CENTER hummed with contained energy. At the far end of the polished conference table, Star and Ethan moved in perfect sync, their rapid-fire tech discussion flowing in the kind of shorthand that came from years of partnership. She'd point at something on her screen, he'd nod and type, completing her thought without a word.

Jack cleared his throat and the room snapped to attention. Crime scene photos materialized on the main screen, and Ronan's stomach lurched. He'd seen plenty of death in his years as a SEAL, had caused more than his share. But this was Tank. Marcus Sullivan. The man who'd saved his life in Kandahar, who'd carried wounded teammates on his back through firefights. Now he looked wrong—small somehow, crumpled against his desk like a discarded uniform.

"Timeline," Christian said quietly. "From the beginning."

Ronan started to speak, but Maya cut in, her voice clipped and professional. "Base Commander Phillips contacted NCIS at zero one hundred hours yesterday. Marcus Sullivan had accessed classified Naval Intelligence files just before zero hundred hours Tuesday from a terminal on base."

"A terminal he shouldn't have had access to," Star murmured, hands gliding over the keys.

"Exactly." Maya nodded. "He'd been out of the service for two years. Phillips wanted Tom and me to bring Sullivan in immediately. Said it couldn't wait till morning."

"How about this Phillips guy?" Austin asked, eyeing Maya.

Maya shrugged. "Don't really know him. I've only been at NCIS San Diego for three months."

"No worries. I'm running Phillips now," Ethan said, his screen reflecting in his glasses. "Star, you want to trace Marcus's movements?"

"Already on it."

"Tell us about the ambush." Jack's eyes locked onto Ronan and Axel. "Walk us through it." He pulled up a tactical display.

"We were following Benson's SUV toward the naval base," Ronan said. "Three minutes in, I spotted the tail cars."

"How many?" Christian asked.

"Three vehicles on us, two on Benson. Professional. Military precision." Ronan's jaw tightened. "They split into two teams—one to separate us from Benson, one to take him down."

"Classic Special Operations containment formation," Christian noted.

"Yeah. Suppressing fire aimed high, herding tactics. They weren't trying to kill us." Ronan marked positions on the display. "They wanted us alive."

"We managed to break through their roadblock," Axel added. "But that was probably their plan all along—separate us from Benson."

Ronan nodded grimly. "By the time we ditched our vehicle and circled back to help ..."

"They'd already forced his SUV down to the boat ramp," Axel finished. "Two shots, close range."

"They killed him to keep him from calling reinforcements," Maya said quietly. "While their main team went after you two."

"Question is—why do they want you alive?" Christian asked.

The room went quiet. Finally, Jack spoke. "How long had you been investigating Sullivan?"

"We weren't." Maya shook her head. "No active investigation until Phillips's call."

"Marcus contacted me last week," Axel said suddenly. All eyes turned to him. "Said he was in trouble. Needed help from people he could trust."

"What kind of trouble?" Christian's voice was sharp.

Ronan shifted uncomfortably. "I've been ... out of touch since leaving the service. But Marcus was solid. Best heavy weapons specialist I ever worked with. Built like a linebacker, but he'd give you the shirt off his back."

"He was an outstanding SEAL. No one better with heavy explosives," Axel added. "Always looking out for the team."

Christian shot Axel a sharp look. "So why didn't he come to you directly with whatever he found?"

Ronan shifted in his chair. "I haven't ... exactly been too social since—" Since taking the fall. Since watching his entire team's careers flash before his eyes and making the call to shoulder all of it. "Since leaving the teams."

"I've pulled up Sullivan's file," Star announced, saving him from fumbling through that explanation. "The classified one."

Axel whistled softly, exchanging a look with Ronan. Yeah. He felt it too. The power these people had at their fingertips to pull up whatever intel they needed. Must be nice.

Star's frown deepened as she read. "This doesn't track.

Your friend wasn't intelligence. Not even close. He was pure combat operations. And since leaving the teams, he's been working at a local VA hospital. Strictly civilian-level stuff."

"Yet he accessed Naval Intelligence files," Christian said, leaning forward. Ronan identified with the posture—the same tension in the shoulders, same way of bracing an elbow on the table.

He moved his hands into his lap. "Not hard to conclude something in those files got him killed."

"Fair to assume that's what the people who offed him thought," Jack added, glancing between the brothers. Ronan caught the slight raise of Jack's eyebrow—he'd noticed their mirrored positions too.

"We need to trace his—" Christian and Ronan spoke simultaneously, then stopped, glaring at each other.

"His recent contacts," Austin jumped in smoothly, diffusing the tension.

Across the table, Angie silently slid her coffee toward Maya, who looked ready to vibrate out of her skin with contained energy. Maya's quick nod of thanks spoke volumes.

"Star, you're amazing," Axel breathed, leaning over her shoulder to study the screens. "Is that real-time satellite tracking? I didn't know civilians could access—"

"We're not exactly civilians," Star's husband squeezed her shoulder as he passed, a casual gesture that spoke of years of partnership.

Ronan watched Christian with his team, the easy flow of information, the trust in every interaction. His brother had built something real here. Something Ronan had thrown away when he'd stepped up to take the blame for that final mission.

"Focus," Jack's voice cut through his thoughts. "We need to figure out what Sullivan was investigating. Before anyone else dies."

"I appreciate the help," Maya cut in, her voice steady but strained. "But I've got twenty-four hours. Then I'm heading back to San Diego."

The room erupted in protests. Jack raised his hand for silence, but Maya pushed on.

"My father won't stay on the sidelines. The longer I'm gone, the more likely he is to start his own investigation."

"Maya—" Christian started.

"Here's his LAPD file," Star interrupted, exchanging glances with Ethan. "Captain Lawrence Chen. And ... she's right."

Ethan nodded grimly. "Multiple commendations. And an equal number of official reprimands for creative interpretation of regulations. Known for, quote, 'aggressive pursuit of justice regardless of jurisdictional boundaries.'"

Maya gestured impatiently. "Exactly my point. He's going to come after me. And then bad things are going to happen. I have to head back. Sooner than later."

"Not advisable," Christian said flatly, his frustration evident. "These people got the drop on a SEAL team operator—"

"Staged an elaborate suicide," Jack continued.

"And killed a federal agent," Axel added.

"While trying to take out two more SEALs, and another special agent," Ronan finished. "This isn't a twenty-four-hour fix, Maya. You go back now, you'll die."

The room fell silent. Maya's jaw clenched, but Ronan could see the fear behind her anger. Not for herself, most likely. But for her father.

That's when the idea hit him. This problem they could eliminate. "So let's get your dad out of the line of fire."

Maya's eyes narrowed. "What exactly are you thinking?"

"Bring him here," Ronan and Christian said simultaneously.

Maya's jaw dropped. "My father. Here?" She glanced around the high-tech room, at the tactical gear, at the team's focused faces. "You'll hate that."

Yeah. Ronan knew the feeling.

He watched Maya's face cycle through a familiar range of emotions—horror, resignation, grim defeat.

Her dad sounded intense. But at least the man was a fellow professional.

If Victoria Quinn caught wind of this, she'd descend on Knight Tactical like a perfectly coiffed tsunami, armed with passive-aggressive concerns about her son's life choices and suggestions for redecorating the tactical operations center.

He'd rather face down a raging terrorist. With a toothbrush.

"I'm not concerned." Jack shrugged.

That drew a bitter laugh from Maya. "You should be."

"Fair enough. We'll consider ourselves warned. So how do we extract your father?" Jack persisted.

"I could call him," Maya said slowly. "Try to explain—"

Christian made a face. "And give him time to dig in his heels? Not a great plan. We need to move fast."

"A direct approach might work," Ronan countered, deliberately not looking at his brother. "The man's law enforcement, he might appreciate—"

"Straight talk won't cut it," Christian interrupted. "Not with someone this connected. He'll start making calls, demanding answers—"

"Because treating a decorated police captain like a hostile target is so much better?" Ronan's voice had an edge now.

"Stop." Maya's command cut through their brewing argument. "You're both right, and you're both wrong." She rubbed her temples. "My father ... he's stubborn. Protective. The minute he suspects something's wrong, he'll launch his own investigation. And he won't stop until he gets answers or gets killed."

"So what's your call?" Jack asked quietly.

Maya met his eyes. She looked like she wanted to throw up. "Black ops style grab. Quick and clean. No warning. No discussion." She glanced around the room. "I'll reason with him once he's safe."

"You sure about this?" Ronan had to ask.

"No." Maya's laugh was hollow. "But I'd rather have him hate me than have him dead."

Ronan caught Christian watching him, an unreadable expression on his face. For once, they were both thinking the same thing: sometimes protecting family meant making the hard calls.

Or so he imagined.

16

BREADCRUMBS

Ten p.m. in Marina Del Rey. Maya crouched in the shadows between two luxury SUVs, the familiar tang of salty air mixing with exhaust fumes from the nearby freeway. Through tactical binoculars, she watched her childhood home—the condo in the fifteen-story glass and steel tower where she'd spent countless nights listening to her father's tread in the hall, the quiet clink of his service weapon being stored, the rustle of case files. Now the building's bright facade loomed against the Los Angeles skyline, its usual nighttime symphony of distant traffic and marina bells replaced by an unnatural silence that set her teeth on edge.

She shouldn't be here. The Knight Tactical team had fought hard against bringing her, arguing that her emotional connection to the target would compromise the operation. But Maya had dug in her heels, the words burning in her throat: "He's my father. I'm coming." She'd stared them down, federal agent to private operators, until Jack had finally nodded.

Now, six hours after that tense standoff, she was helping

a private military team kidnap her father. The irony wasn't lost on her.

"Infrared scan complete," Star's voice purred through their earpieces. "Twelfth floor's reading cold. No heat signatures."

Maya's stomach dropped. "That's impossible. His phone—"

"Cell signal's still active in the unit," Star confirmed, "but thermal imaging shows no one's home. Hasn't been for hours, based on residual readings."

"He left his phone deliberately," Ronan said beside her, voice tight. "It's a diversion."

"Confirmed empty," Jack's voice cut in. "Building's security feeds show Captain Chen leaving three hours ago with a briefcase. No return entry."

Maya's hand clenched around her binoculars. Her father never went anywhere without his phone. Never broke routine without reason. He was meticulous, calculated. He wouldn't just abandon his phone unless— "He knew we were coming."

"Someone warned him," Axel whispered, fingers tracing his earpiece. "The encryption on these comms is military-grade, but if someone knew we were mobilizing—"

"Focus," Christian's voice cut through the night. "Star, run thermal sweeps on all surrounding buildings. Austin, extend perimeter scan to two blocks. Someone tipped him off, which means—"

"We're being watched," Maya finished, her gaze sweeping the rooflines with new urgency. Her father wasn't just missing. He was three steps ahead of them.

And they'd just walked into his territory blind.

"This gear is insane," Axel whispered beside her, fingers tracing his earpiece. "The encryption alone must be—"

"Focus, puppies." Christian's voice cut through the night. "We know it's empty, but we still do this by the book. Three-man team clearing the apartment. You three maintain perimeter watch. Look for any surveillance, any sign of who tipped him off."

Maya bit back a protest. She understood the logic, but watching others search her father's home felt wrong.

Ronan shifted on her other side, radiating tension. She recognized that stillness—the forced inaction of a trained operator regulated to the sidelines. His gaze swept the roofline, the surrounding buildings, the street access points. "You're right, Maya. Someone's watching. Has to be."

"Moving to entry point," Jack murmured through comms. "Austin, maintain exit route alpha. Star, keep scanning for any new heat signatures in the surrounding buildings."

"Copy that," came the calm responses.

Christian's team melted into the shadows. Through her binoculars, Maya studied the familiar twelfth-floor windows. The darkness felt deliberate now, a message rather than an absence.

"Apartment secured," Christian's voice was clipped. "But you need to see this. Bring them up."

"Moving to your position," Ronan replied, already in motion. "Watch our six."

Maya and Axel fell in behind him as they crossed the street, staying tight to the shadows. The service entrance yielded to Knight Tactical's electronic skeleton key, and they took the stairs two at a time to the twelfth floor.

Christian met them at the apartment door, his team maintaining a defensive perimeter in the hallway. His expression was grim. "It's not just empty. It's staged."

Maya stepped into her father's apartment, the familiar scents of coffee and leather hitting her like a physical blow. The space felt wrong—too still, too quiet. Around her, Knight Tactical's team moved with practiced efficiency, but as she took in the scene, her detective's training kicked in.

This wasn't just her father's home. It was a message, carefully crafted and waiting just for them.

She moved to her father's reading chair, noting the angle. Wrong. He was meticulous about keeping it positioned for optimal light. Lawrence Chen might be a maverick when it came to his job, but in his personal life, the man was as OCD as it got. Everything in its place. Always. "He knew they were coming."

Christian paused his sweep. "How can you tell?"

"Everything's slightly off." She gestured to the military biography on the side table. "This book isn't straight. Dad always lines things up." Her eyes tracked across the room. "Coffee cup left out—he never does that. And his reading glasses ..."

She moved to his desk, mind clicking through the evidence. "His backup weapon's gone. So is his go-bag—he keeps it in the bottom drawer." A detective's habits, passed down to his daughter. "But he left his phone." Something they could track.

"How long?" Jack asked.

"Hours. Maybe less." She touched the coffee cup. "Still has a ring of moisture under it."

He would have left more clues. She crossed to his closet. "His old patrolman uniform is gone." She pointed to the garment bag hook, conspicuously empty. "And his medal case is shifted." Moving to the case, she carefully lifted it. A business card lay beneath—Phil's Boat Service. Something he knew she'd check if she'd read his other clues right. "He's not running scared. He's hunting."

The tactical teams exchanged looks. This wasn't their world—stakeouts and informant networks, piecing together clues from displaced objects and deliberate signs.

"Your father's good," Jack said quietly.

"The best." Pride mixed with fear in her chest. "And he

just laid out a trail of breadcrumbs. Question is—for us, or for them?"

"Direction?" Christian pressed.

For the first time since the pursuit began, Maya felt solid ground under her feet. This she understood. "He'll start with his old CI network. There's a diner in Venice ..." She stopped, detective's instincts screaming. "No. That's too obvious."

She scanned the room again, seeing it through her father's eyes. Career police officer. Master investigator. Man who'd taught her to read a scene.

"Multiple vehicles approaching," Star's voice crackled through comms. "Professional formation. Time to go."

"Copy." Jack's response was instant. "Alpha team, cover our exit. Beta team—"

"Windows," Ronan cut in. "They'll have the stairs and elevator covered."

"Bingo." His brother responded instantly. "Abort."

The night erupted into motion. Maya caught glimpses of Christian's team emerging fast but controlled, just as unmarked sedans began sliding out of side streets.

"Company," Austin announced. "Multiple vehicles, tactical approach pattern."

"Run." Christian's command galvanized them into action.

Maya sprinted for the lead SUV, Ronan right behind her, Axel already yanking open the rear door. She dove in as Austin gunned the engine.

"Four vehicles in pursuit," Star reported from Hope Landing. "Taking you off main streets. Right at the next corner, then immediate left into the alley."

Maya grabbed the overhead handle as Austin took the turn at speed. In the darkness behind them, engines roared.

"They're not law enforcement," Ronan said grimly. "They're too good."

Her heart hammered against her ribs. They'd been too late to save her father ... and now maybe even themselves.

"Second vehicle, maintain parallel course," Jack ordered through comms. "We'll split their focus."

Streetlights strobed in her eyes as Austin threaded through Marina Del Rey's back streets. Each turn brought them deeper into the maze of storage facilities and boat repair shops.

"LAPD units responding to calls about suspicious vehicles," Star reported. "Austin, hang right at the marina. Christian's team will draw the pursuit north."

Maya's stomach lurched as Austin swung the SUV around a corner, tires screaming. Behind them, two of the pursuit vehicles peeled off after Christian's team.

"Two still on us," Axel reported, twisted around in his seat. "Gaining."

"Warehouse district coming up," Star said. "Cut through the loading yard at Fuller Marine. Security gate's disabled."

Austin didn't hesitate, taking them through a gap barely wider than the SUV. Metal scraped metal as they squeezed past abandoned shipping containers.

"They're boxing us in," Ronan warned, voice tight. "Classic tactical containment."

"Not for long." Austin's smile was fierce in the rearview mirror. He yanked the wheel hard, sending them through a shower of sparks as they scraped between two buildings. "Star, we need that safe house location now."

"Uploading coordinates. Apartment complex two klicks to your west. Underground garage access. Security systems are already looped."

The pursuit vehicles matched them turn for turn, their drivers showing the kind of skill that only came from professional training. Austin wove through a construction site, sending barricades flying. Maya's knuckles went white on the handle as they burst through a chain-link fence.

"They're not even trying to disable us," Axel noted, tension in his voice. "Just keeping pace."

As if his words triggered something, the pursuit vehicles suddenly dropped back. No dramatic moves, no last-ditch efforts. They simply ... withdrew.

"Christian, report," Jack barked through comms.

"Same here. They just broke off. Clean."

"That's not normal," Maya said, the hair on her neck rising.

"We'll take the win," Austin replied, but his expression was wary. "Star, local LEOs?"

"Three units converging. Two minutes out."

Austin guided them into a twenty-four-hour grocery parking lot, killing the lights. They watched two patrol cars scream past, sirens wailing.

"Loading dock behind the store," Star directed. "Delivery trucks provide cover. Wait three minutes, then take surface streets to the safe house. They're looking for vehicles in motion."

Maya held her breath as a third patrol car crawled past their position. The delivery trucks screened them perfectly – just another dark SUV making a late-night grocery run.

Maya's world narrowed to flashing lights, squealing tires, and the pulse pounding in her ears. Ten minutes that felt like hours until Star finally announced, "Clear. No pursuit vehicles within ten blocks."

The garage door rolled shut behind them with a final-sounding clang. Maya stumbled out of the SUV, legs shaking. Her father was gone. They'd been too late.

"Maya." Ronan's hand settled on her shoulder, steady and warm. "We'll find him."

She turned, meeting his eyes in the dim garage lighting. "They knew we were coming. They were waiting for us."

"Good." His voice was steel. "Because they just showed their hand." He squeezed her shoulder gently. "Now we show ours."

Maya drew a deep breath, straightening her spine. He was right. This wasn't over.

Frozen to her core, she did the only thing she could: pray to her Lord and Savior.

17

HIDDEN IN PLAIN SIGHT

One a.m. in Culver City hit Ronan like a fist to the gut. His body remembered this hour, even if three years of civilian life had softened his edges. The witching hour, they'd called it in spec ops. When fatigue made you stupid. Made you slow. Made you dead.

The stale taste of too many energy drinks coated his tongue as he braced one shoulder against the floor-to-ceiling windows of the safe house, using the cold glass to keep himself alert. Below, Los Angeles sprawled like a circuit board gone wrong, all scattered lights and dark spaces where anything could hide. The city that never slept was lying—everything slept eventually. Everything except people running for their lives.

Behind him, Knight Tactical's team fought their own battles with exhaustion. Ethan worked his laptop, but his usual steady rhythm had developed hitches. The familiar scents of gun oil and coffee drifted from across the room where Christian cleaned his weapons for the third time, the repetitive motion as much about staying awake as maintenance. Austin's perimeter checks had grown more frequent—

a veteran's response to fatigue-dulled senses. Jack, the guy with twin babies at home, flat out gave in, stretching out on the floor, eyes closed, snoring softly.

Only Maya seemed immune, her nervous energy carrying her back and forth across the modern space like a caged tiger. But Ronan caught the slight tremor in her hands, the way she blinked too hard, too often. The crash would come soon. He just hoped they found her father before it did.

His chest tightened as he watched Maya pace the length of the open-plan living room, arms wrapped around herself like she was keeping something vital from spilling out. Twenty-four hours ago, she'd been a rising star at NCIS. Now her partner was dead, her father hiding, and she was on the run with a guy whose service record screamed traitor.

"Stop it," Axel murmured, appearing at his shoulder. "This isn't on you. Whatever Tank was mixed up in, whatever conspiracy he stumbled into—not your fault. All we can do now is fix it."

Ronan's laugh was bitter. "Right. Because trouble doesn't follow me everywhere I go."

"Got a signal," Ethan announced. "Star's accessing traffic cams from the marina area."

Maya turned sharply, and the streetlight caught her face. Ronan moved without thinking, closing the distance between them. "You're bleeding."

She touched her cheek, looking surprised at the smear of red on her fingers. "Must have caught something during the chase."

His calloused fingers caught slightly on the zipper of the med kit in his thigh pocket.

The antiseptic's sharp bite cut through the room's coffee-tinged air as he cleaned the small cut.

Her skin was warm under his touch, and she held

perfectly still, eyes locked on his. "Thank you," she whispered.

The empty feeling in his gut intensified. He wanted to pull her close, tell her everything would be okay. Promise her they'd find her father. Make it right.

But they barely knew each other. And what she did know—his General Discharge, the classified reports, the whispers of betrayal—none of it inspired confidence. On paper, he looked like the last person she should trust.

Yeah. On paper, he didn't look good at all.

Maya suddenly stiffened. "Wait. Show me that video sweep again. The security camera from the stairwell."

Everyone crowded around Ethan's laptop. The footage showed the emergency stairwell, grainy but clear enough. Maya jabbed a finger at the screen. "There. That Snickers wrapper."

"Could be anyone's trash," Blair said gently.

"No." Maya leaned closer. "Look how it's placed. Perfectly flat, wrapper facing up. Right in the camera's line of sight." Her voice gained strength. "My father eats Snickers all the time. Has since I was a kid. He says sugar helps him think."

Ronan studied the image. The wrapper wasn't crumpled or torn. It had been deliberately positioned. "Nice." The excitement in his voice matched Maya's expression.

"Hold on," Christian cautioned. "Star, can you access any other cameras from the area? Before the system went down?"

"Already on it." Star acknowledged. "Got something. Four tangos approaching the complex two hours before we arrived. Two front, two back. Full tactical gear."

"Russian-made AS Val rifles," Axel noted, studying the grainy figures. "Suppressed. High-end stuff."

"Wait." Ethan zoomed in on footage from a boutique's security camera half a block away. "There. In the window reflection."

The image was brief—just a flash of movement caught in plate glass—but unmistakable. Lawrence Chen, moving fast but controlled, disappeared into the shadows. "He caught sight of them in time to leave you clues and get out. How'd he have time to respond so quickly?"

Maya's eyes were glued to the image. "After the BOLOs went out, he would have anticipated this. Go, Dad." Her whisper held equal parts relief and fear. "Now where's our next clue?"

The room fell silent as they all considered the impossible task ahead: tracking a highly trained LAPD detective who didn't want to be found, while staying ahead of professional hunters who clearly had significant resources.

Ronan watched Maya pace the length of the safe house, the soft whisper of her boots against hardwood matching his own restless energy. The recycled air from the building's ventilation system raised goosebumps on his arms as he studied her movements.

Then she stopped, like a bloodhound catching a scent. She turned to face them, something like hope lighting her face. "Seven years ago, missing girl case. Dad had this whole system worked out." The words tumbled out faster now. "He was famous in the department for his gas station coffee addiction—used to say fancy coffee was for people who'd forgotten how to be real cops. He worked out this entire communication network with his CIs using coffee cups and newspaper stands."

Ronan watched her expression shift as she explained—the mix of exasperation and admiration in her voice painting a picture of her father that no personnel file could capture.

"The position of the cup, the brand, whether it was empty or full—it all meant something different." She shook her head. "I gave him such grief about it. Told him it was terrible tradecraft, that he needed to follow proper CI protocols. He just laughed and said sometimes the best hiding place was in plain sight."

Ronan stepped closer to the screen, studying the Snickers wrapper with new eyes. "So this is what—a marker?"

"More like the start of a trail." Maya's eyes were bright now, that sharp intelligence he'd noticed from their first meeting focused like a laser. "Star, can you pull footage from any newspaper stands within a six-block radius of the condo?"

"On it," Star responded. "Sending feeds now."

"There." Maya jabbed a finger at the screen. "Seven-Eleven coffee cup, left corner. That was his signal for 'follow me' to his CIs."

"Got another," Ethan announced. "Three blocks east. Different cup, right side of the stand."

"'Danger, go to ground,'" Maya translated, and Ronan could hear the years of experience behind her understanding —how many times had she watched her father work his unorthodox system? "He's leaving us directions."

She straightened, certainty replacing her earlier fear. "I know where this trail ends. The old Morton's Coffee Shop on Sixth. It's where he first showed me this system. Said if I ever needed to find him ..." She swallowed hard. "It's been closed for years, but the building's still there."

"Could be a trap," Christian warned.

"No." Maya's voice held the kind of conviction that came from bone-deep knowledge of another person. "This is pure Dad. He's thinking like a street cop, not a tactical operator. The people after him will be watching official channels, looking for high-tech communication. They'd never expect ..." She trailed off, staring at the screen.

"He's brilliant," Ronan said softly, studying Maya's face. Admiration twisted with something darker in his gut—here was a man who'd built his career on pure instinct and street smarts, while Ronan had thrown away years of elite training with one catastrophic judgment call.

"And buying time," Christian added. "Star, how many cameras have eyes on Morton's?"

"Two traffic cams, one ATM. All clear so far. No tactical vehicles, no suspicious movement."

"What if we're wrong?" Maya's voice caught, and Ronan fought the urge to reach for her. "What if they figured it out, what if—"

"They didn't," he cut in, certainty hardening his voice. "Men with Russian weapons and high-tech gear? They're looking for digital trails, electronic signals. Not coffee cups and candy wrappers." Like him, they'd be expecting military precision, not street cop ingenuity.

"He's right," Axel said. "These guys are pros, but they're thinking like pros. Your dad's thinking like a cop."

Christian was already moving. "Blair, you and Austin take up positions here and here." He marked points on Ethan's street map. "Jack, coordinate with Star on surveillance. Ronan—"

"I go with Maya." The words came out before he could stop them. She might only know him as the disgraced operator with a file full of redactions, but he'd be damned if he'd let her face this alone.

Christian studied him for a long moment, then nodded. "Stay on comms. First sign of trouble—"

"We're gone," Maya promised. She reached for her jacket, then hesitated. "The coffee shop ... there's a back entrance through the kitchen. Dad used to joke it was the best escape route in LA. It connects to the old service tunnels. Prohibition-era smuggling routes. He used to say only old beat cops remember they exist." A ghost of a smile touched Maya's lips. "He's really doing this. Playing their own assumptions against them."

"Your father," Ronan said as they headed for the door, "is going to be an interesting man to meet." If the man lived up to even half of what he'd seen so far, Lawrence Chen would take one look at Ronan's record and want him nowhere near his daughter.

The thought shouldn't have hurt as much as it did.

18

NIGHT ECHOES

MAYA'S EARS strained against the unnatural quiet of downtown LA at 2:00 a.m., catching fragments of sound—a distant siren, the metallic rattle of a shopping cart, the soft whisper of Ronan's tactical gear against brick. She pressed herself flatter against Morton's facade, the lingering heat of the August night radiating through her shirt. The acrid taste of adrenaline coated her tongue, mixing with memories of burnt diner coffee and early morning stakeout conversations.

She fought the urge to check her watch again. The empty street stretched before her like a scene from one of those post-apocalyptic movies her father loved—all shadows and silence and waiting.

Seven years ago, she'd stood in this same spot, clutching her carefully organized case notes while her father chatted with a homeless man about the missing Hancock Park girl. She'd wanted to scream at him to focus on real evidence, not waste time with his "street sources." Twenty minutes later, that same homeless man had given them the breakthrough that saved the girl's life.

Now she forced her breathing to stay steady, hyperaware

of Ronan's solid presence beside her, of Christian's team positioned strategically around the block. Her father's coffee cup markers had led them here, but doubt gnawed at her certainty. What if she'd read the signs wrong? What if someone else had decoded his system?

"Movement," Star's voice whispered through their comms. "Southeast corner. Single male, staying in the shadows."

Maya's heart hammered. The figure moved like her father —that distinctive rolling gait from an old motorcycle accident. But it could be a trap, could be someone who'd studied him ...

"Second signal," Jack reported. "All clear on perimeter scan."

This was the part her father had tried to teach her—that moment when procedure had to yield to instinct. When you either trusted your gut or lost everything.

The figure reached the edge of Morton's stubborn pool of streetlight. Maya caught a glimpse of silver hair, a familiar stance. Then he stepped into the light.

His usually immaculate chinos were wrinkled, his left hand curled like it did when his old shooting injury acted up. But his eyes were sharp as ever as they swept over her, then locked onto Ronan with laser focus.

"Baby girl," he said softly, using the nickname she'd outgrown decades ago. "Want to tell me why you're running with this crowd?"

Ronan tensed beside her.

"Who are you?" Her dad's voice held the edge she recognized from interrogation rooms. "And how did you get my daughter into this mess?"

"Dad—"

"It's a long story, sir." Ronan's voice remained steady,

professional despite the hostility. "One we should discuss somewhere secure. Right now, we need to move."

"They killed Tom." Maya's voice caught on her partner's name. "And probably the victim Tom and I were called out to question." She swallowed hard. "And now they're after you."

Her father's expression flickered—too brief for anyone else to catch, but she had thirty-four years of practice reading Lawrence Chen's micro-expressions. Fear. Not for himself.

"You need to walk away from this, Maya. No matter what your partner might have been involved in." He shifted his weight, and she recognized his tell. He was about to disappear into the shadows again. "Forget you found me. Go back to—"

"That's not happening." The steel in her voice surprised even her. "Those men at your condo weren't amateurs, Dad. Russian weapons, tactical gear—"

"Which is exactly why you need to—"

"Tom wasn't dirty." The words came out raw. "He was in the wrong place at the wrong time. But our victim, Marcus Sullivan, was onto something big enough to kill for. To destroy my life for. And now I think they're going after you to get to me."

Her father went still. That dangerous stillness she remembered from stakeouts, from moments before everything exploded into action. His gaze shifted back to Ronan, reassessing.

"Are you really military?"

"Former SEAL." Ronan kept his tone neutral. "And I brought help. Operatives with Knight Tactical Protection. All former special forces. They're a professional team with a secure facility and plenty of resources. And they have a common interest in finding out who's behind this."

"Common interest?" Her father's laugh held no humor. "Son, you have no idea what you're stepping into."

Maya fought back a hard eye roll. "Like you do? Tell me why you're out here alone instead of utilizing department resources."

The silence stretched. She watched her father's face, seeing the war between his instinct to protect her and his need for help. She knew that war intimately—had fought it herself every time she'd had to choose between procedure and what was right.

"This Knight Tactical team," her dad asked Ronan sharply, "they any good?"

"We're still alive." Ronan kept it simple.

Her father nodded once, a decade of street cop instinct weighing their options. Then he looked at Maya, and for the first time she saw real fear in his eyes. "You sure about this?"

"You raised me to finish what I start."

A ghost of a smile touched his lips. "Yeah. Sometimes I think I did too good a job." The smile faded. "But baby girl, you've been federal for all of three months. I've dealt with these alphabet agencies for thirty years. When the feds get involved ..." He shook his head. "You better know what you're getting us into. Because once we start down this road, there's no turning back."

"Yeah, about that." Ronan interrupted. "We need to hit it."

Then Dad was moving, that familiar purposeful stride that meant decisions had been made.

The small group moved fast and tight through the shadows, Maya hyperaware of her father analyzing every movement, every formation position. Ronan took point while Axel materialized from the darkness to cover their six. Her father's eyebrows rose slightly at their silent efficiency.

Two black SUVs idled in the adjacent alley, engines purring with quiet German engineering.

"Thirty seconds," Star warned through comms. "Bogey vehicle approaching from the north."

Christian stood ready at the lead vehicle's passenger door. "Lieutenant Chen." His nod was respectful but urgent. "Welcome to the party. Maya, you're with your father in the lead car. Ronan, Axel—"

"Second vehicle," Ronan finished, already moving.

Her father paused before getting in, his cop's eyes taking in the team's smooth choreography, the high-end gear, the practiced precision.

"Nice setup," he murmured as he climbed in and they pulled away from the curb. "Not exactly standard NCIS resources."

"No," Maya agreed, watching the city blur past. "It's not."

The pursuit vehicle's headlights flashed in their rearview, but Christian's driving was subtle, professional—nothing to draw attention. Just two expensive SUVs gliding through the LA night, headed for the private airfield where their plane waited.

Her father sat back, his expression unreadable. "You've gotten yourself mixed up with some interesting people, baby girl."

Maya thought of the initial victim, Ronan's friend. "Yeah," she said quietly. "I really have."

The SUVs purred through LA's empty streets, Christian taking a deliberately meandering route through the city. Maya watched her father's posture shift as he studied the vehicle's tactical displays, the secure comms, the advanced surveillance setup. Thirty years of cop instincts kicking in.

"Your pursuit vehicle dropped back," he said suddenly. "They're parallel tracking now, probably called in backup." His fingers drummed against his knee—his old tell when piecing together a pattern. "You said airfield?"

"Van Nuys," Christian confirmed. "Private hangar."

"They'll be watching the main approaches." Her father leaned forward, all business now. "But there's a service road off Hayvenhurst. Old construction access. Most maps don't show it."

"Star?" Christian asked.

"Satellite confirms. Looks clear."

Just like that, Maya became invisible—the familiar sensation from a hundred operations with her father. He and Christian fell into a rapid tactical discussion, years of experience meshing seamlessly. Alternative routes, counter-surveillance measures, airfield security patterns.

Maya caught Ronan's voice through the comms, coordinating with the follow vehicle, but her focus stayed on her father. The way his voice had shifted to that familiar command tone, the one that had directed countless operations. The one that had always made her feel simultaneously proud and overshadowed.

Some things never changed. Somehow she was right back to being Lawrence Chen's kid, watching from the sidelines while the grown-ups handled things.

She sank deeper into the leather seat, exhaustion hitting her like a physical wave. Her body felt hollow, wrung out from too many hours running on adrenaline and coffee. Even keeping her eyes open had become a conscious effort.

The familiar cadence of her father's voice washed over her as he and Christian discussed approach vectors. She'd been an NCIS agent for all of three months, determined to forge her own path, to step out of Lawrence Chen's long shadow. And here she was, pulled right back into his orbit like some huge, cosmic joke.

Through the comms, she heard Ronan's voice continue—steady, confident, adapting instantly to her father's suggestions. The similarity struck her then: that same quiet competence, that instinctive grasp of tactical thinking. But where her father was all contained energy and sharp edges, Ronan moved with the fluid grace of a predator. A younger, more dangerous version of Lawrence Chen.

And significantly better looking, whispered a traitorous part of her mind.

She pushed that thought away, but couldn't help noticing how naturally the two men had fallen into sync, even through their initial antagonism. Like recognizing like. Her father might have started as a beat cop and Ronan as spec ops, but at their core, they operated on the same wavelength—thinking three moves ahead while trusting their gut.

What was her Savior trying to teach her, letting her get tangled up with two such hard-driving, reckless men?

19

FALSE FIT

Late morning light crept through the high windows of Knight Tactical's guest quarters as Ronan eased the borrowed t-shirt over his head. Six hours ago, they'd touched down in the company's private jet—a luxury he'd been too exhausted to appreciate. The expensive fabric settled against his ribs like muscle memory, a reminder of everything he wasn't. He was going to miss these clothes. Whatever wonder fabric it was the stuff was way out of his price league.

Across the room, Axel's soft snores provided a steady counterpoint to the distant hum of early morning aircraft.

He slipped out of bed. His thoughts and emotions tumbled like clothes in a dryer, refusing to sort themselves into anything coherent. Lawrence Chen had proven to be exactly as his daughter described—smart, intense, running on seemingly limitless energy even after their early morning arrival back at headquarters. The man's wariness of Ronan and Knight Tactical was palpable. Understandable, really. What father wouldn't be suspicious of a guy with a record like his? A guy who'd dragged his daughter into a deadly game of shadows?

Because that's exactly what Ronan had done. If he and Axel hadn't shown up at Tank's house, Maya wouldn't be in the crosshairs of killers who clearly had massive resources at their disposal. And Tom Benson would still be alive.

His gaze drifted toward Maya's room two doors down. It was probably a blessing that they were polar opposites—her the rule-follower, him ... decidedly not. Because otherwise, he'd find her impossible to resist. Her energy, her dedication, even her faith—though he'd never admit that last part aloud. He wasn't religious, but he envied that kind of unwavering devotion.

Just like he envied Christian Murphy's team and their rock-solid belief. Add that to the growing list of ways his half-brother had beaten him at life: growing up with a real father instead of a rotating cast of nannies and a celebrity journalist mother who was never home. Getting the structure and discipline to succeed in the teams. Building this impressive second life as a civilian.

"Ugh." The frustrated gesture escaped before he could stop it.

Axel groaned, lifting his head off the pillow. "Time?"

"Early. Go back to sleep."

But his friend was already sitting up, reading Ronan's mood with a decade of practice. "You're thinking too loud."

"Yeah." He needed to get over himself. And get out of Hope Landing. As soon as this manhunt ended. "Gonna hit the gym. Need to move."

Mostly, he needed to stop thinking about Maya Chen, about her father's suspicious glares, about all the ways this could go sideways. Needed to focus on finding Marcus's killer before anyone else died because of his mistakes.

Blankets rustled and Axel sighed deeply. "Roger that. I'll meet you down there."

Ronan slipped into the quiet hallway, his boots silent on

the plush material. The rich aroma of freshly ground coffee pulled him forward, probably some fancy single-origin roast knowing Christian's operation. No standard military sludge here at Knight Tactical. They probably had a professional barista on staff.

He rolled his shoulders, trying to ease the tension that had nothing to do with last night's poor sleep. Too many people here. Too many eyes watching, judging. Axel was solid —his friend was as committed to finding Tank's killers as he was, to uncovering whatever shadow players had ordered the hit. But Knight Tactical …

Anger flared, hot and sudden. Anger for Marcus, executed in his own home. For Maya's partner Tom, caught in the crossfire of something he never saw coming. And yeah, if he was honest, anger at Christian Murphy and his perfectly ordered world.

Irrational? Absolutely. His half-brother only knew what the Navy and Ronan himself had allowed him to know—that Ronan was a screw-up who'd earned his General Discharge. Christian had no idea that Ronan had fallen on his sword to protect a teammate.

Hard to fault Christian for looking down on him when he didn't know the truth. And never would.

The coffee scent grew stronger, drawing him straight into the modern kitchen. He needed space, air, distance from all these people with their assumptions and their order and their … rightness. But first, caffeine. And a good, hard workout.

The French roast's rich aroma curled around him as he leaned against the railing, steam rising from the matte black mug like morning fog. Two stories below, the hangar sprawled in industrial vastness, all gleaming equipment and precision-placed gear. His stomach clenched as he spotted movement in the gym area.

So much for a solitary workout.

Jack's lithe frame was easy to spot, along with a massive guy who had to be the one Knight Tactical partner he hadn't yet met: Patrick Olivetti and—of course—Christian. Perfect. The coffee's warmth turned bitter on his tongue.

Jack's wave and shouted invitation echoed off the metal walls. Ronan hesitated, but then Lawrence Chen emerged from the shadows of the weight room, calling up something about young guys getting soft. Christian's answering smirk was all it took. Ronan was down the stairs before he'd even set down his coffee.

The next thirty minutes were a blur of sweat and controlled violence. Chen might be thirty years their senior, and half Ronan's size, but he moved like a far younger man, all economy and precision. Christian had the technical perfection you'd expect, but Ronan ... Ronan had something else. That raw edge that had made him a state wrestling champion, that animal instinct that kept him alive in places where rules didn't exist.

He could feel Axel watching from the sidelines, heard his friend telling Christian, "Best fighter I've ever seen, bar none."

Pride surged through Ronan's chest—until Christian's voice cut through his concentration. "Raw talent only gets you so far without discipline."

That split-second of distraction was all Chen needed. The mat slammed hard against Ronan's back, driving the air from his lungs. Above him, Christian's expression shifted to something that looked a whole lot like disappointment.

"Mad skills," his half-brother said quietly. "But you don't have the head game to keep up. Not yet."

The words burned worse than the takedown. Ronan's jaw clenched as he watched them walk away, already planning how quickly he could wrap this mission and get clear of Hope

Landing, of Knight Tactical, of Christian's perfectly ordered world.

Then Maya's face appeared above him, hands on hips, head shaking slowly. She turned without a word, following the others.

Ronan groaned, letting his head fall back against the mat. It was going to be that kind of day.

20

CHAIN OF COMMAND

Maya leaned against the conference room window, the morning sun warm on her back but doing nothing to ease the chill in her gut. Her father paced nearby, that familiar contained energy that had driven her crazy growing up. Now it was oddly comforting. He was here. He was safe. And watching him work the room—already directing traffic like he owned the place—almost made her smile.

Until she remembered that by now, every law enforcement agency in Southern California thought Lawrence Chen's daughter was a traitor and a murderer. Her stomach twisted. Everything she'd worked for, destroyed in less than forty-eight hours.

"Stop it." Her father's voice, low enough for only her to hear. "I can see you spiraling."

"I'm not—"

"You're doing that thing with your jaw. Same thing you did before every spelling bee."

"Dad." The familiar exasperation felt almost normal. "I'm not twelve anymore."

"No." His eyes softened. "You're a federal agent being framed for murder. But we're going to fix that."

"Exactly." Jack stepped forward, all professional courtesy. "That's where we come in. Knight Tactical has access to intelligence channels that local law enforcement can't touch."

Christian cleared his throat. "Before we start—team, if you'll join me?" He bowed his head without fanfare, the others immediately following suit. Maya felt her father's surprised glance but closed her eyes, finding unexpected comfort in the familiar ritual.

"Lord, guide our steps and clear our minds. Protect those in harm's way and lead us to truth. Amen."

"Amen," the team echoed quietly.

Ronan shifted his weight, carefully studying the tactical display on the wall. The simple prayer had lasted perhaps fifteen seconds, but Maya caught the tension in his shoulders, the way his fingers drummed against his thigh.

Her father, ever observant, simply folded his hands and waited respectfully. A veteran cop's instinct for reading the room.

From the look, he liked what he saw.

"We should begin with this," Star said before exchanging a grim look with Ethan. "It's not good. These people are doubling down on the fake evidence."

The displays flickered, new images forming. Maya's heart sank as more deepfake videos appeared—her, Ronan, and Axel supposedly meeting Marcus Sullivan at various times. Then security footage from the marina, showing Ronan and Axel rushing from Tom's SUV, weapons clearly visible.

Ronan jabbed a finger at the monitor. "That never happened."

"We know," Star cut him off. "But there's more. They found a handgun in a harbor trash can. Your prints were on it."

"Prints aren't hard to get," Maya said. "We're all in the system."

Austin nodded. "And they're easy enough to fake. Basic 3D printing tech could do it."

"So we're no better off than we were last night." Ronan's frustration was palpable.

"We need to work backward," her father said, that familiar commanding tone making Maya's spine straighten automatically. "Find Sullivan's killer—"

"And we find who's framing us," Maya finished. "I know how to investigate, Dad."

"Baby girl, I've been doing this since—"

"Since before I was born. I know." She caught Christian trying to hide a smile. "But I'm not your rookie anymore."

Her father's expression softened. "No. You're not." He turned to the group. "So where do we start?"

Maya met Ronan's eyes across the room. They needed a lead. Fast. Before anyone else died because of whatever Ronan's friend had stumbled into.

Star pulled up thermal imaging from her father's condo. "The team was top-tier. Four-man stack, synchronized breach tactics."

Ronan turned to her dad. "How'd you give yourself time to leave clues and get out?"

"Planned it that way," her father responded, pulling out his phone. "Set up a network of cheap wireless cameras at strategic points—coffee shops, convenience stores. Places people don't look twice at some guy fiddling with his phone." He swiped through several feeds. "Piggybacked off public Wi-Fi, nothing traceable. When their vehicles hit my first marker six blocks out, I had five minutes. More than enough time."

Maya shook her head, remembering all the times she'd teased him about being paranoid. "Let me guess—you've had this setup for months?"

"Years." He didn't look apologetic. "Street cop's version of a surveillance network. Sometimes the best tech is the stuff nobody thinks to look for."

Christian and Ronan shot her identical looks. "Your dad's no joke," Ronan said, while Christian nodded his agreement.

Her dad folded his arms across his chest. "Old dogs have the best tricks, boys. What can I say?"

"Hold up." Star studied the infrared footage. "There's something ..." She enhanced a section, the ghostly thermal image sharpening. "See that signature around their comms? That's not standard gear."

Christian was already moving closer to the screen, tension visible in his shoulders. "Can you isolate that heat pattern?"

Star attacked the keyboard. A distinctive thermal signature filled the screen—a unique radiation pattern around the operators' communication equipment.

"Well look at that." Christian exchanged a look with Jack. "That's a modified Knight Industries XR-7 setup. Custom job."

"You're sure?" Ronan asked.

"Yeah." His brother's jaw tightened. "Sentinel's the only outfit running that config. They modify the thermal dispersal to—"

"To minimize detection by opposing force IR," Axel finished, earning surprised looks. "What? I keep up."

Maya watched the interplay, noting how her father had positioned himself—unconsciously or not—between her and the screen. Some habits die hard.

"Sentinel's good," Axel added quietly.

She wrinkled her nose. "So a rival personal protection firm is trying to kidnap my father? That literally makes zero sense."

Ronan's features softened. "It does if they want to get to you."

"Something bigger is at play here," Christian mused. "Sentinel Security's on the level. Like us. And they don't do wetwork unless—"

"Unless someone with serious pull is calling the shots," Jack finished, reaching for his phone. "I think it's time we interrupt the admiral's vacation." He pulled out his phone. "Sentinel Security's owner Buck Richardson and the admiral go way back. All the way to Annapolis."

"The admiral?" her dad asked.

"Admiral Knight. Our founder." Christian's voice held equal parts respect and affection. "He and Richardson have been friendly rivals for decades. Navy, private sector, you name it."

The wall screen flickered to life, revealing a man at the helm of a huge motor yacht. Sun glinted off silver hair and the kind of deeply tanned face that spoke of a lifetime at sea. But Maya caught the sharp intelligence behind his grandfatherly smile—this was a man who'd commanded carrier groups and sat in rooms where nations' fates were decided.

"Jack! Christian!" The admiral adjusted his course with practiced ease. "To what do I owe the—hold on." He peered at the screen. "Why do you all look like someone kicked over a hornet's nest?"

"We've got a bit of a situation brewing here, sir. It involves Sentinel Security." Jack made quick introductions.

"Buck Richardson's outfit?" The admiral's jovial expression sharpened to laser focus. He glanced over his shoulder before lowering his voice. "Give me the rundown."

As Jack explained, Maya watched the admiral's face. Decades of command experience showed in how quickly he processed the information, asking precise questions that cut straight to the heart of the matter.

"Well now." He grinned suddenly, looking like a kid offered an unexpected treat. "This beats shuffleboard."

Another furtive glance behind him. "Minerva insisted on two weeks in the Med. I'm going stark raving mad here, but don't you dare—"

"John?" A woman's voice called from off-screen. "Who are you talking to?"

"Just checking the weather, dear!" He turned back, dropping his voice to a conspiratorial whisper. "Let me make some calls. I owe Buck a call anyway. Gotta catch up on the grandkids. I'll get back to you as soon as I can shake loose from—"

"Are you working?" The voice was closer now.

"Gotta go!" The admiral's hasty wink was the last thing they saw before the screen went dark.

"Well," Chen said into the silence. "That was ..."

"The admiral," Christian finished with a fond smile. "Give him an hour. He'll have intel that would take us weeks to dig up."

Maya caught Ronan fighting a grin. Even her father looked impressed, which was saying something.

"So," Christian continued, "while the admiral works his magic, let's break down what else we know."

"Right." Ethan pulled up multiple screens, intelligence flowing across them. "We've got three major events in the past thirty-six hours—Marcus Sullivan's death, Tom Benson's murder, and the attempt on Captain Chen."

Maya felt her father shift beside her, that familiar protective energy radiating off him. She forced herself to focus on the data, not the raw ache of Tom's loss.

"Tank—Marcus," Ronan corrected himself, "was targeted first. Professional hit, made to look like a suicide." His voice held barely controlled anger. "Right after he accessed restricted files."

"Which means they were watching him," Chen observed. "Probably watching you too."

"And Agent Benson?" Christian asked carefully, his eyes on Maya.

"Wrong place, wrong time," Christian answered before Ronan could.

Her father's expression darkened. "The question is, what did Sullivan know that was worth all this?"

The screens flickered, Admiral Knight's face appearing suddenly. He wasn't smiling now.

"You'll want to hear this," he said grimly. "Richardson just called me back. This goes deeper than we thought."

21

CALL SIGNS

Ronan shifted his weight, trying to quell the restless energy coursing through him as Admiral Knight's face reappeared on screen. The yacht's steering station was visible in front of him, crystal waters stretching to the horizon.

"Sentinel was hired to protect Captain Chen. Extract him to a secure location," Knight said without preamble.

"Then why'd they chase us?" The words were out before Ronan could stop them. He felt Christian's disapproving glare but kept his eyes on the screen.

"Fair question, son." The admiral adjusted his course slightly. "Richardson says his team followed because they assumed you were hostiles who'd grabbed the captain before they could extract him."

Ronan caught Axel's subtle head tilt—his friend was thinking the same thing. It made a weird kind of sense, but ...

"They won't disclose the client," Admiral Knight continued. "But between us? Smells like Navy brass trying to contain—"

"John Knight!" An elegant woman in resort wear appeared behind him. "Oh, hello everyone!" She waved, then smacked her husband's shoulder. "I love seeing you all, but my husband is supposed to be resting. Doctor's orders after that heart incident."

"Minerva, I'm fine—"

"That's what you said right before you collapsed at the Kennedy Center."

The team's gentle ribbing was respectful but swift, and they signed off leaving Ronan with a knot in his gut. Something wasn't adding up. The pieces were there—Marcus's death, Tom Benson, the frame job, Sentinel's involvement—but the picture they formed made his skin crawl.

"We need to figure out what Tank died for." His voice came out harder than intended, but he couldn't soften it. Not when his friend's killer was still out there. Not when Maya's partner was dead because of whatever Marcus had stumbled into.

Christian nodded slowly. "Star's been analyzing your friend's movements. He spent significant time at VA clinics across Southern California."

"His medical records show nothing," Star added. "No personal appointments, no treatment. Man was healthy as a horse."

"So why the medical visits?" Maya asked.

"A great question." Ronan met Axel's eyes. Finally, a place to begin their investigation.

"I'll dig deeper into those VA visits," Ethan said, already typing. "Cross-reference with staff schedules, security footage, anything that shows who Tank was meeting."

"I'll reach out to some contacts at the DOD," Jack added. "See if anyone's heard whispers about brass trying to contain something."

Christian outlined the rest of the assignments. "Patrick and Austin, start mapping Sentinel's recent operations. Look for patterns. Star, keep mining those traffic cams around Sullivan's usual routes."

Axel caught Ronan's eye, tilting his head toward the door. Ronan followed him to a quiet corner, already tensing at his friend's expression.

"We need to call them in," Axel said without preamble.

The mere thought made Ronan's chest tight. "No. I can't ... not now." Not when he had no idea if they'd even welcome his presence after three years of silence.

"Listen." Axel's voice dropped lower. "First off, Tank was their friend too. They deserve to know what's going on." When Ronan started to protest, he pressed on. "Second, what if whoever's behind this starts digging? They'll be in danger too, whether they know it or not."

Ronan ran a hand through his hair. "And?"

"And these Knight Tactical guys?" Axel gestured at the room. "They're ridiculously competent. But more brains in the room can't hurt. Tank deserves the best. From all of us."

The logic was rock-solid, unfortunately.

Ronan drew a deep breath, then turned back to the group. "Axel and I have one other task," he announced, the words coming fast. "We're bringing in the rest of our team." He braced himself for arguments, questions, resistance. Not that any of them would matter.

Instead, Jack just shrugged like it was the most obvious thing in the world. Christian's expression was almost comical. "About time, dude."

The team dispersed, leaving Ronan, Axel, Maya, and her father in the conference room. Chen's measured pacing reminded Ronan of a tiger he'd once seen in a Mumbai zoo—all contained power and frustration.

"We'll help you contact your team," the man offered, pausing mid-stride.

Maya nodded eagerly. "I can—"

"No." Axel's voice was gentle but firm. "These folks ... they're particular about contact. Especially now."

"They're family," Ronan added, seeing Maya's expression darken. "But they're also special ops. Paranoid is their default setting."

"He's right, baby girl." Chen's tone made Maya's eyes narrow. "Why don't you come down to the range with your old man? Work on that stance of yours."

"Dad, my stance is fine—"

"Is that what you call that paper target I saw yesterday? Looking like it was hit by a drunk marksman in an earthquake?"

"That was ... I was distracted!"

"Exactly." Chen steered her toward the door with practiced ease. "Range time. Now. Show me you can still shoot like I taught you."

Maya's expression suggested she'd rather have dental surgery without anesthesia, but she allowed herself to be guided out, throwing one last frustrated look over her shoulder. She paused at the door. "You don't have to do this alone anymore."

Ronan met her eyes, caught between gratitude and that familiar urge to protect her from his mess. "I know."

Ronan waited until they were gone before turning to Axel. "Where do we start?"

Ronan's stomach churned as he stared at the list of names on his phone. Three years of silence stretched between him and each one like a chasm. He wouldn't blame them if they told him to go to hell. Or worse, just didn't answer.

"Maybe you should make the calls." He glanced at Axel. "I should be ... checking the VA security protocols. Or—"

"Hiding?" Axel's voice was sharp but kind. "That's over, brother. Time to put the past behind you."

The fear hit harder than anger now. What could he

possibly say to them? Sorry I ghosted you all when things got rough? Sorry I couldn't handle being around anyone who reminded me of ...

"This is for Tank," Axel said quietly, reading him like always. "They'll help. They loved him too."

Ronan exhaled slowly, nodding. "Okay. How do we split this?"

"I'll take Deke and Kenji. You handle Zara and Izzy."

"What about Ghost?"

Axel's expression tightened. "Last known number's disconnected. But I've got a few back channels we can try. Let's start with the others."

Ronan looked down at his phone again. Zara would be awake—she kept vampire hours. And Izzy's shop would be open. His finger hovered over Zara's number, stomach twisting again.

"Stop overthinking it," Axel said. "Just dial."

Ronan's thumb trembled slightly over Zara's number. He forced himself to hit dial before he could chicken out, half-hoping it would go to voicemail.

It rang once. Twice.

"This is a secured line." Zara's voice, crisp and professional, hit him like a physical blow. "State your business."

"Z ... it's Ronan."

The silence stretched so long he thought she'd hung up. Then, "Well. King Ronan Quinn himself. Must be the apocalypse."

He deserved that. "Z, I—"

"Save it. What do you need?" Her tone wasn't angry, exactly. Just flat. Controlled.

"Tank's dead." The words felt like ground glass in his throat. "Murdered. And we need ... I need ..."

Another pause, shorter this time. "Give me a sec to secure this call properly."

Ronan caught Axel watching him, nodded slightly to show he was okay. While they waited, he could hear Zara's rapid typing, imagined her in her dark office, screens glowing around her like always.

"Okay," she said finally. "Tell me everything."

As Ronan laid out the situation, he heard the subtle changes in her breathing, the tiny sounds she made when pieces clicked together in her mind. Same old Zara, building a puzzle in her head.

"I'll start digging," she said when he finished. "And Ro? Next time you disappear for three years, I will hack every electronic device you own and make them play nothing but ABBA. On repeat."

He actually smiled. "Copy that."

After disconnecting, he looked at Izzy's number. One down, one to go. Across the room, he could hear Axel talking quietly to Deke.

"Your turn," Axel mouthed, pointing at the phone.

Ronan nodded, dialing before he could lose his nerve. The shop's phone rang three times before a familiar voice barked, "Reyes Custom. Make it quick."

"Iz." His voice cracked slightly. "It's Ronan."

The clang of a dropped wrench echoed through the line. "As in Lieutenant Commander Ronan Quinn? You kidding me?" Her tone could have stripped paint. "What, you drunk? Lost? Dying?"

"Tank's dead."

Another clang, softer this time. Like she'd sat down hard. "¿Qué? What are you talking about?"

"Someone murdered him. Made it look like a robbery." His free hand clenched into a fist. "Iz, we need—"

"Address. Now." The sound of keys jingling. "I'll close the shop—"

"No, wait. We need intel first. Tank was investigating something. Something big enough to get him killed."

A stream of creative Spanish filled his ear. Then, "Talk."

He outlined the situation, hearing her pace, the rhythmic sound of her boots on concrete. When he finished, the silence stretched.

"You know," she said finally, "my kid asks about her Uncle Ro sometimes."

The words hit him like a punch to the gut. "Iz—"

"Don't. Just ... don't." She took a breath. "I'll make some calls. Got a few clients who might know something about private security operations in SoCal. And Ro?"

"Yeah?"

"You ever go dark on us again, I'm tracking you down and replacing your brake fluid with maple syrup."

Despite everything, he felt his lips twitch. "Understood."

He ended the call, looking up to find Axel watching him. His friend raised an eyebrow.

"They're in?" Axel asked.

Ronan nodded. "They're in. And apparently going to torture me with ABBA and maple syrup if I disappear again."

"Sounds fair." Axel checked his phone. "Deke's already praying and making calls. Kenji's pulling hospital records." He paused. "Still no luck with Ghost's back channels."

"He'll surface," Ronan said, hoping he was right. "He always does."

Hearing Deke was already praying brought a familiar twist of ... something. Envy? These people, his old team, had held onto their faith through everything. Even Tank had never lost that quiet certainty. While Ronan ... well, he'd lost more than just his team that day.

"Yeah." Axel didn't sound convinced. "Team meeting at eighteen hundred. Want to hit the range? Work off some of that tension?"

He shot his friend a weak smile. "Nah. I'm good. Thanks."

Axel headed for the stairs. "You're smarter than I am. I'm sure I'm gonna regret sharing range space with a legend like Lawrence Chen." He stilled, gaze far away. "I think I'll opt for plan B."

"Which is?"

The man grinned hard. "The range is in the far hangar, right? Looks like I've got to head straight past the airport terminal to get there."

Understanding dawned. "DreamBurger."

"Exactamundo. You want me to bring you something back?"

A tempting offer, under other circumstances. Right now, Ronan knew he wouldn't be able to choke down a thing. He waved his friend off.

Once alone, he stared at his phone, the echoes of those conversations still ringing in his head. The anger he'd expected—deserved—had been there, but underneath it was something else. Something that felt like family. Like the fine group he'd walked away from three years ago.

He thought of everything he'd missed, everything he'd hidden from. And now Tank was gone. Tank, who'd tried to reach out so many times, who'd never given up on him even when he'd given up on himself.

The weight of his failure pressed against his chest, but this time, instead of crushing him, it strengthened his resolve. Tank had died trying to expose something. Something big enough, dangerous enough, that someone had decided to silence him permanently. But they hadn't counted on this—on a team coming back together, on bonds that ran deeper than time or distance or silence.

Maybe there was something to be said for faith in something bigger than yourself—whether it was God, or family, or justice. Tank had believed that. Maybe it was time Ronan started believing in something too.

He pictured his friend's easy smile, his solid presence, his unfailing loyalty. Whatever his friend had discovered, whatever had gotten him killed—they would find it. All of them. Together.

For Tank.

Re-energized, and ready to flee the ghost of his dead friend, Ronan headed for the stairs. Thrashing himself in the gym might be just the thing he needed to sharpen his brain for the upcoming fight.

22

DIGITAL GHOSTS

RONAN STARED at the data spread across the command center's displays, his mind working to connect the dots. In the six hours since Star and Ethan had broken into Tank's private cloud storage, the picture had only gotten darker. Fifteen veterans dead in eight months. All recently treated at VA facilities in Southern California. None with life-threatening conditions.

Tank must have contacted Griffin—Ghost—for help investigating. Those two had always been close.

Marcus had tagged them all. The accountant who'd driven off a cliff on Mulholland Drive. The retired Marine who'd supposedly shot himself cleaning his gun. The Army nurse who'd drowned in her pool. The Air Force tech who'd had a "heart attack" while hiking. The rest, all seemingly healthy vets, who simply ... disappeared.

Too many coincidences.

But where to go from here? He paced the floor, trying to channel Griffin's mind. *Think*.

The lights flickered. Security cameras cycled through random feeds. Somewhere, an alarm started wailing.

"Breach!" Star called out. "Someone's in our—"

Every screen in the command center went black.

Boots thundered up the stairs. Christian burst through the door, Austin and Jack on his heels, weapons ready.

"Got a ghost in the system," Ethan announced, his usual calm cracking. "They're playing with—"

A digitally distorted voice filled the room: "Aww, professional branding. How cute."

The main screen lit up with a spinning Knight Tactical logo. Then it shattered, pixels scattering like broken glass.

"Multiple system breaches," Star reported. "They're everywhere."

"Not everywhere," the modulated voice taunted. "Just wherever I want to be."

New images flashed across the screens.

"How are they seeing these angles?" Austin demanded. "We don't even have cameras there."

"Nothing's impossible," the metallic voice sang. "Just improbable."

Ronan felt the corner of his mouth lift. He knew that pattern, that style.

A shadow detached itself from the corner behind them. Ronan wasn't surprised to see Zara hadn't changed—same tactical black, same coiled grace, same knowing smirk. His team's ghost, their digital phantom, looking exactly as she had the last time he'd seen her three years ago. Even her dark hair was still cut in that precise chin-length bob that never seemed to move, no matter what she was doing.

"Your system's good," she said, her natural voice replacing the digital distortion as she materialized like smoke. "Mine's better."

Maya had her weapon half-drawn before Ronan caught her wrist. "She's one of us."

"Was wondering when you'd call," Zara dropped into the

chair next to Star, who was staring at her with equal parts horror and admiration. Zara narrowed her eyes at Ronan. "Though technically, you didn't."

"How did you—" Star started.

"The same way I knew you ordered Thai food last Thursday, have a dinner date tomorrow night with the hubs here, and really need to change your personal banking password." Zara whipped out her phone, studied the screen, and grinned. "Also, FYI, you've got three more bogies about to breach your perimeter. But don't worry. They're with me."

Movement near the back wall caught Ronan's attention. Axel emerged from behind a desk, his face too pale, hands slightly trembling.

Ronan could have kicked himself. And Zara. Two years out, Ax was doing better, but it still didn't take much to activate his PTSD.

Zara's smirk vanished. "Ax, I'm so sorry. I didn't think—"

"I'm good," Axel cut her off, but his voice was rough. "Just ... maybe text next time?"

Ronan shifted closer to his friend, not touching, just present. The Knight Tactical team politely found other things to look at, but Ronan caught Maya's concerned glance. She'd read the signs, but she wasn't asking. Good.

The tension broke as heavy footsteps approached—two sets, moving in sync. Deke appeared first, his six-foot-four frame filling the doorway, looking every bit like the former NFL linebacker he was. Even in tactical gear, his athletic build was impossible to miss.

"Deke Williams," Jack said, impressed. "Raiders defense never recovered after you left."

"That touchdown in the Cleveland game?" Austin added. "Legendary."

Deke's laugh rumbled through the room. "That was a lifetime ago, boys."

Ronan caught Maya watching as Deke quietly bowed his head before speaking, noticed her small smile of recognition. She'd grown up with that same quiet certainty he'd always envied in others.

Right behind him came Kenji, moving with the fluid grace of a martial artist. Six feet of lean muscle and focused intensity, his Japanese-American features set in their usual careful neutrality. But those dark, observant eyes missed nothing—especially not Axel's state.

"Dr. Marshall," Christian nodded respectfully. "Your paper on battlefield trauma response protocols changed how we train."

"Just Kenji," he corrected quietly, still watching Axel. "And I hear your team's implementation of those protocols is exemplary." They'd talk later, away from curious eyes.

Star was still glaring at Zara. "You completely bypassed our quantum encryption. How did you—"

"Trade secret," Zara winked. "But I left you some notes. Check your second backup server."

An engine roared in the parking lot—custom headers, triple exhaust.

"That would be Izzy," Kenji grinned. "Still running that souped-up Raptor?"

"The one she rebuilt after that explosion in Kandahar," Ethan added. "What did you do to the engine management system? The specs are insane."

Isabella Reyes sauntered in—their mechanical genius, all five-foot-two of her, wearing her usual cargo pants and tank top that showed off impressively muscled arms. Her black hair was still pulled back in that messy bun, streaked with engine grease despite the gold hoop earrings she refused to give up.

"Still driving that monstrosity?" Ronan asked.

"Still being a killjoy?" she shot back, dark eyes flashing.

There was an edge under the banter, a hint of the hurt they'd all been carrying these past three years. "And my 'monstrosity' could outrun anything in your fancy garage."

"Is that a challenge?" Austin perked up.

"Focus, people," Axel cut in smoothly, drawing attention away from the growing tension. "Now that Zara's done showing off"—a grateful look from Zara—"maybe we should talk about why we're all here."

Ronan had forgotten how good Axel was at managing the team's dynamics. Or maybe he'd just tried to forget everything about those days.

"Yeah," Ronan said, forcing himself to meet their eyes. His team. His responsibility. "We should talk about Tank."

The room went quiet. Deke leaned forward, elbows on his knees. "We lost touch. I shouldn't have let that happen. I have no idea what he was working on."

"He was looking into something big," Zara said quietly. "Week before he died, he asked me to run background on a list of names. All military contractors."

Kenji's fingers tightened around his coffee cup. "He called me too. Wanted to know about certain medication trials. Combat enhancement protocols."

"He reached out to all of us," Axel said, his voice carefully neutral. "Scattered pieces of intel, like he was building a puzzle but didn't want any of us to see the whole picture."

"Protecting us," Ronan muttered. "Stupid guy was always trying to protect everyone else."

"That's what got him killed," Deke growled. "Whatever he found, whoever he was investigating—"

"They got to him first," Zara finished. The edge in her voice was razor-sharp now. "Maybe Griff, too."

Silence fell again, heavy with three years of unanswered questions and unspoken guilt. They'd all been busy with their own lives, their own missions. None of them had seen the danger until it was too late.

After the teams settled into an uneasy rhythm of introductions and shop talk, Christian caught Ronan's eye and jerked his head toward the hallway. Ronan bristled at the summons—he wasn't some rookie who could be called out for a lecture. But he followed anyway, if only to keep Christian from making a scene. He noted how his brother positioned himself where he could still see into the command center. Old habits.

"About Axel," Christian said quietly.

Ronan's shoulders tensed. Here it came—the big brother routine. Like Christian had any right to question how Ronan handled his team. "He's fine."

"Yeah. Like I was fine." Christian's voice was neutral, but his meaning clear. "Took me three years to admit I needed help. Would've been four, but Jack and the team ... they knew. Didn't push, just had my back."

The unexpected confession knocked the defensive anger right out of Ronan. He studied his brother's face, seeing past the hard exterior to something unexpected—understanding.

"It's better now," Christian continued. "Not gone, but better. Your boy in there? He's got good people watching out for him." A ghost of a smile. "Even if they're a bunch of dramatic show-offs who like terrorizing our security system."

The tension in Ronan's chest eased slightly. "Christian—"

"If you ever tell anyone I admitted to having feelings," his brother literally from another mother cut him off, "I will break your neck." He pushed off the wall. "Okay. Enough family bonding."

But there was something almost like approval in his eyes as he walked away, leaving Ronan to process this new piece of the puzzle that was his bio bro.

23

INSIDE LANGUAGE

MAYA LEANED against the command center wall, watching the two teams settle into a rhythm as natural as breathing. The soft symphony of typing from multiple keyboards mixed with the gentle hum of cooling fans from overworked computers. Even after two years apart, Ronan's people moved around each other like dancers in a well-rehearsed ballet. And the Knight Tactical crew was no different—each person anticipating the others' needs, finishing sentences, sharing looks that spoke volumes.

Seven years in law enforcement, and what did she have? A dead partner and a father who thought helping meant taking over.

Lord, what are you trying to show me here?

Zara worked three keyboards simultaneously. "Got something on Griffin. Digital signature, forty-eight hours old. He accessed a terminal at the Santa Monica Public Library."

"Finally, the ghost made a mistake," Austin said.

"Griff Hawkins doesn't make mistakes," Kenji and Izzy said in perfect unison.

Deke nodded. "Man's been off-grid for two years. If he left a trace—"

"He wanted us to find it," Axel finished.

"I've got a visual," Ethan announced. "It's fuzzy, but—"

Ronan leaned over his shoulder. "That's our boy." He pulled back, face contorting as if he'd been slapped.

Maya touched his arm. The man vibrated tension in waves. "What?"

He pointed at the reflection in the tiny reading glasses perched on his friend, Griffin's wide face. "The mermaid. It's the Hans Christian Andersen Mermaid statue. In Copenhagen."

The temperature in the room plummeted. The subtle change in breathing patterns rippled through the room like a wave. Quick glances exchanged between team members like a silent morse code.

"You're talking about Copenhagen. Why?" Axel's voice was carefully neutral.

Ronan nodded. "Griff's telling us this has to do with Copenhagen."

"Copenhagen." Axel repeated the word, as if it tasted like ash. "As in the Copenhagen Op? Just want to be clear here."

Ronan met his friend's gaze. "'Fraid so." He stepped away from the group and shoved his hands in his pants pockets, staring at the ground.

The op where he'd killed a civilian. Whatever Ronan was about to say, it was bad.

"The facility we compromised?" Kenji's voice held old pain. "The one where you—"

"The one where I violated ROE. Yup." The bleak look in Ronan's eyes made her tear up. "I think they found a connection," Ronan said. "Between Copenhagen and these deaths. Griffin was trying to tell me without tipping off anyone watching him."

The room fell silent again as implications sank in.

"Why didn't he come to us directly?" Izzy asked finally.

"That's what we need to find out," Ronan said. "Before they find him first."

He eyed the Knight Tactical crew who were watching all this, faces carefully blank. "Look, guys, I can take the time to explain the op to you, but it's probably quicker if you just access the files. There'll be details there I probably don't remember. And background that might lead us to our next clue."

"On it," Ethan said and jumped back onto his computer. "I'll check all the way up the chain of command."

"I'll check State and the CIA," Star added.

Ethan grinned, waggling his eyebrows. "See why I love her?"

His glaring attempt to lighten the mood fell flat, but Maya could have hugged him for trying.

Clearly oblivious to the subtext in the room, her dad clapped his hands together, shifting into his familiar "teaching stance"—shoulders back, chin lifted. "Good. So we're moving now. Let's dig into this guy's message and move forward, people."

She gritted her teeth, biting back a sarcastic remark. Adding more fuel to the emotional fire raging between Ronan and his team wouldn't help.

Her father clapped again, that familiar gleam in his eye. "When I worked Narcotics, we used to leave signs for deep cover agents. Special codes—"

The sharp contrast between her father's too-cheerful voice and the room's tension made Maya wince.

"Dad, this isn't 1992. We can't just—"

"Actually," he pressed on, "there was this one time in Hancock Park—"

"When you single-handedly saved the city?" she muttered.

Ronan caught her eye across the room, his lips twitching despite looking like he'd just been punched in the gut.

But there was something else happening—something in the way his team watched him. Worry in Kenji's careful observation. Anger in Izzy's sharp retorts. Some undefined debt in the way Deke positioned himself, always between Ronan and the door. Like they were all carrying something heavy. Something that had to do with why their leader had let them down and then walked away three years ago.

Another mystery, she thought. But right now, they had to figure out how to answer Griffin's breadcrumb trail before it went cold.

Maya watched Ronan trying to clear a wave of emotion from his face, saw the weight settle on his shoulders. And saw how his team—both teams—shifted subtly closer, holding him up without touching him.

"We need to be smart about this," Ronan said. "Griffin won't respond well to a tactical team descending on Santa Monica."

Their eyes locked. Maya felt that now-familiar spark of attraction, tangled with irritation. "And waiting around while we debate this is better?"

"The Ghost spooks easy," Izzy added, glancing between them with interest. "Trust me, you don't want to see him riled."

Maya stepped closer to Ronan. "My case, remember? My jurisdiction."

They were almost toe to toe now, Ronan giving no ground. "And Griff isn't some suspect you can just—"

The soft squeak of tactical boots on polished floors echoed as people shifted positions, tension building in the room.

"Children," Lawrence interrupted cheerfully. "If I might suggest—"

"Dad, not now."

"Lawrence, please."

They'd spoken in unison. Maya felt heat climb her neck as Deke poorly disguised a laugh with a cough.

"The library's public," Star offered diplomatically. "We could set up surveillance—"

"And scare him off completely," Axel said. "Griffin's not going back there anyway."

"But he'll be watching it," Zara mused. "He'll want to know who responds to his message."

Maya could feel Ronan's warmth, smell that hint of soap and gunpowder. It was distracting. Irritating. "So we leave our own message."

"Using your dad's old undercover codes?" The corner of Ronan's mouth lifted.

She wanted to kiss him. Or punch him.

"Actually," her dad said, "I was thinking something more modern. Something that would look innocent to anyone else, but Griffin would recognize ..."

Maya watched understanding dawn in Ronan's eyes. She might not like it, but the man was sharp.

"A job posting," they said together.

This time, the heat in her cheeks had nothing to do with embarrassment.

"A help wanted ad," her dad suggested, warming to his topic. "For a security consultant position. With extremely specific requirements."

Maya caught on. "Requirements only your friend would recognize as significant."

"I hear you." Deke grinned. "Like the dates of certain ops."

"Or locations that mean something to the team," Kenji added.

Ronan nodded slowly. "Posted from an IP address he'd recognize."

"I can make it look like it came from Marcus's old terminal," Zara offered. "He'll be monitoring that."

Maya felt her frustration building. They were all so in sync, finishing each other's thoughts while she stood on the outside. And Ronan ... he'd shifted seamlessly into team mode, that wall going up between them again.

"And what if someone on the other team recognizes those codes?" she challenged.

Ronan turned those intense eyes on her. "That's why we need to be precise. Choose markers only Griffin would know."

"Mission protocols from the Copenhagen op," Axel said quietly.

The team went still. Maya watched emotions flash across their faces—pain, guilt, something darker.

"He'd recognize those," Izzy whispered.

"Care to share with the class?" Maya asked, unable to keep the edge from her voice.

"No," Ronan said flatly, and for a moment the tension between them crackled like lightning. He turned to his computer guru. "Let's do it. Zara, can you—"

"Already coding. Give me a sec."

Maya moved closer to Ronan, lowering her voice. "You can't shut me out of parts of this investigation just because they're classified."

He turned, bringing them face to face. "Some secrets aren't mine to share."

"But they're Griffin's secrets too, aren't they?" She held his gaze. "The man we're trying to save?"

Something shifted in his expression—surprise, maybe even admiration. But before he could respond, Zara spoke up.

"What do you think?" She threw up an announcement on the big monitors mounted to the walls.

SECURITY CONSULTANT NEEDED

Boutique risk management firm seeks experienced security specialist

Location: Santa Monica, CA

Requirements:
- *8-10 years military/security experience*
- *Advanced training in Nordic emergency protocols*
- *Familiarity with Ghost surveillance systems*
- *Must be certified in Echo-Eight containment procedures*

Project involves assessment of library security systems.

Submit credentials to: Dr. Sarah Nightingale

Coastal Research Division

Reference ID: SEAL-1408-M3

Ronan clapped. "Outstanding, Major. Outstanding."

The Knight Tactical crew eyed the posting, looking as clueless as she felt.

"Care to fill us in?" Christian asked before she could.

Axel stepped up to the closest screen and went down the list. "Nordic equals Copenhagen. Obviously."

Christian rolled his eyes. "For sure. I think we're following. Go on."

"Right." Axel pointed to the next line. "Ghost is Griff's call sign. Echo-Eight, our team designation. Ocean Beach was Griff's preferred surf spot before he joined the Navy."

"The meeting will take place at 1408. That's an inside joke," Izzy added. "Old Ax-man here could never get anywhere on time, so we always started our workouts and meetings at eight after the hour. Only we never clued him in."

Christian grunted. "Then M3 is Muscle Beach on Third Street. I like it."

Ronan and Maya—everyone but his own people—stared at the man.

"What?" Christian attempted to look innocent. "I'm not all good looks."

"He's right," Ronan said. "It's perfect. Only the team would know about Axel's timing issue, and Griffin would recognize—"

Star interrupted, urgency sharpening her voice. "We've got another problem. Someone else is accessing Marcus's encrypted cloud files. Right now."

"Define 'someone else,'" Christian demanded, moving to Star's station.

"Multiple searches," she responded. "All VA facilities in Southern California. Patient records, staff schedules, security protocols—" She went still. "They're methodically accessing every clinic Marcus flagged. Like they're hunting."

"Hunting Griffin?" Maya asked.

"Or hunting anyone Marcus was trying to protect." Kenji's voice was grim. "Those disappearances and deaths your friends traced? They're accelerating. Three in the past week."

Star pulled up a timeline. "If this pattern holds—"

"We've got less than forty-eight hours before the next one," Ethan finished.

Maya felt Ronan tense beside her. "Griffin knew. That's why he's surfacing now."

"He's not just leaving us breadcrumbs," Axel said quietly. "He's running out of time."

24

PARENT TRAP

RONAN WATCHED his team demolish the impressive spread of sandwiches and snacks Christian and Ethan had assembled. Some things never changed—Deke still ate enough for three people, Izzy still stole pickles off everyone's plates, and Kenji still arranged his food in precise geometric patterns before eating.

The familiar scene twisted something in his chest. For a moment, it could have been any mission briefing from before. Before Copenhagen.

"Man, you guys eat like this every day?" Izzy asked around a mouthful of turkey club. "We were lucky to get MREs between ops."

"The perks of private sector work." Austin grinned.

"Got something." Zara's voice cut through the chatter. Kenji moved to peer over her shoulder. "We've been running current VA medical records in Southern California against Marcus's flagged cases ..."

"These test panels." Kenji leaned closer, sandwich forgotten. "They're ordering the same specialized bloodwork. Hormone levels, genetic markers—" He broke off, face darkening. "Every victim had these tests ordered within two weeks of their death or disappearance. And forty-eight hours after the tests, they were gone."

"Same labs?" Maya asked.

"Different facilities, same protocols." Zara pulled up more files. "And ... wow. Two new matches. Tests ordered yesterday."

Ronan felt his stomach drop. "Where?"

"Ventura VA clinic. A male." Her voice tightened. "And Long Beach. A female."

"Identical panels." Kenji's medical training showed in his precise terminology. "And none of the tests indicated by their presenting symptoms."

"Why?" Christian pressed.

"That's the ten-million-dollar question," Kenji finished quietly.

"Alright," Christian said, pulling up a map. "We've got three priorities and a ticking clock. Two potential victims and Griffin."

Zara bit her lip. "That's at least two hours between facilities."

"Which means we split up," Ronan said. "Two rescue teams, one contact team."

"I'll coordinate from here with Star and Ethan," Zara said. "We'll monitor all channels, keep everyone connected."

Jack studied the map, years of tactical planning evident in his quick assessment. "Kenji, you're with Austin in Ventura."

"Deke, Izzy," Jack continued. "You're with me in Long Beach. Place is way bigger, and way closer to lots of law enforcement. Better that we have a three-person team. The helo'll be fueled and ready in fifteen."

Izzy's eyes lit up. "That Agusta on the pad? Sweet."

"Try not to modify our helicopter mid-flight," Christian said dryly.

"And us?" Maya asked quietly.

Christian's jaw tightened. "You, me and Boy Wonder here are going ghost hunting." His tone suggested he wasn't thrilled about the arrangement.

Axel cleared his throat. "I should stay here too. Help coordinate." His meaningful look told Ronan he'd keep an eye on both teams, watch for patterns they might miss.

And avoid a dreaded helo flight.

Ronan felt Maya's presence beside him, that mixture of attraction and wariness that seemed to define their relationship. Now they'd be working together, no buffer, no distractions.

"If Griffin's watching the library," she said, "we need to move fast."

"Yeah." Ronan watched his teams gear up, falling into familiar patterns despite the years apart.

"Hey," Izzy called from the door. "Try not to disappear on us again, yeah?"

The words were light, but they hit like a punch to the gut. "Not this time," he managed.

"Three targets, three teams," Jack said, studying the map. "Two potential victims and Griffin's breadcrumb trail."

Maya's dad stepped forward, face set like a bulldog. "I'm going with my daughter to Santa Monica—"

"No." The response came from multiple voices.

"Dad," Maya said carefully, "every cop in LA County knows your face."

Lawrence's expression darkened. "I can be discreet."

Christian stifled a laugh.

Lawrence shot him a look.

Maya rubbed her temples.

Ronan leaned closer. "Parents, right? If my mother were here …"

"Woof," Axel added with a grin.

Jack pulled up the logistics screen. "Alright, we've got my Phenom, the Agusta, and it looks like my father-in-law's got one of his Pilatus PC-12 NGXs ready for action. My wife and her dad own a private air transportation company."

"Must be nice," Ronan muttered.

"Three birds, three pilots," Austin noted. "Jack and I can take two, but we need—"

"Ronan," Axel interrupted, eyes gleaming. "Though I have to ask ... can you even handle something built in this century, Ro?"

Jack raised an eyebrow at Ronan. "Want to try? The Pilatus has that new Pratt & Whitney PT6E-67XP engine ..."

Yeah. He did. In the worst possible way. He could already feel the controls beneath his hands. Smell that new-plane smell ...

"Touch screen avionics?" he asked, trying and failing to sound casual.

"Full Honeywell Epic 2.0 suite," Jack confirmed.

"You sure you're up for all that modern gadgetry?" Axel's grin widened. "No more analog gauges to tap when they stick ..."

"I piloted one last month, actually." Ronan paused. "In a simulator."

The room erupted in groans and laughter.

The teams were finalizing assignments when the command center door swung open.

A shockwave blew through the room. It was always like this. Every. Time.

His stomach dropped. *No. Please, no.*

Victoria Quinn swept in, all five-foot-nine of her wrapped in a designer suit that easily cost more than his monthly rent. Her signature red hair was shorter now, but she still moved like she owned whatever room she entered. His mother. The last person on earth he expected.

Or needed here.

Her gaze went straight to him, assessing. Concerned.

Apparently reassured he was still in one piece, she addressed the room like a monarch addressing an adoring crowd. "I heard you could use some help," she announced, then stopped short at the sight of Lawrence Chen.

Her green eyes widened. "Well. The legendary Detective Chen. That serial arsonist case in '98? Brilliant work with the paint analysis."

Lawrence, who'd been reaching for his badge, froze. "You ... you followed that case?"

"Darling, I tried to get an interview with you for months." Her smile was pure charm. "But you were so delightfully elusive."

Maya rolled her eyes as her father actually blushed.

"Mom," Ronan ground out. "How did you—"

"A source," she said primly. "A very reliable source who thought an investigative journalist might be useful." She fixed him with that familiar penetrating stare. "Did you really think I wouldn't find out?"

"Wait. No." Ronan waved his hands in the air. "This is not how we work. We don't bring in civilian—"

"Actually," Christian interrupted, surprising everyone. "We could use the help. Victoria has contacts we don't." He tipped his chin at Lawrence. "And Captain Chen's got decades of insight into law enforcement."

Ronan glared at his brother. Christian defending the woman who'd ruined his family?

"I knew you were a bright bunch," Victoria added, settling gracefully into a chair beside Lawrence, who looked like Christmas had come early.

Ronan watched in horror as his mother and Lawrence Chen fell into an animated discussion about cold cases and corruption patterns, his mother's hand occasionally touching

Lawrence's arm for emphasis. Maya caught his eye, her expression a perfect mirror of his own dismay.

"Wheels up in twenty," Jack announced, mercifully breaking the moment. "Ronan, you good with the Pilatus?"

"Yes," he said too quickly, grateful for the escape. "Very good. Extremely good."

Christian stood. "Suit up and meet me in the armory in five. Let's do this."

Great. Just great. Trapped in a small aircraft with his brother, the woman who tied his stomach in knots, and the knowledge that his mother would be waiting here when they returned.

"Moving out!" Ronan announced, perhaps a bit too loudly. He headed for his quarters, heard Maya's quiet laugh behind him.

"Your mom's not so bad," she murmured as they walked.

He shot her a look. "Wait until she starts planning our wedding."

They both froze, realizing what he'd said. Christian, passing by, muttered something that sounded suspiciously like "smooth."

When did this become my life? Ronan wondered again. But as they headed for their rooms, he had to admit—if only to himself—that it felt better than the silence of the past three years.

Even if his mother was going to drive him insane.

25

RING WORK

"I'M TELLING YOU, that guy's been doing the rings for like an hour. Has to be Cirque du Soleil."

"Everything's Cirque du Soleil to you. This is Venice Beach—could just be Tuesday."

Ronan bit back a grim smile, tasting salt on his lips. If they only knew he was hunting a ghost, not auditioning for the circus. Though maybe a career change wouldn't be the worst idea, given how this day was going. The metal rings had grown slick under his calloused palms, and his shirt clung to his skin like a second layer.

He pulled himself up on the traveling rings again, muscles burning under the merciless August sun. Sweat trickled down his back, and the metal rings were hot enough to sting his palms. His fifth set, and still no sign of Griffin. The salt-laden breeze carried the mingled scents of coconut sunscreen, marijuana smoke, and cooking meat from the nearby food trucks. The air was thick with Venice Beach's signature cocktail—sweat and sand, fresh-squeezed oranges from the juice cart, hemp oil from the massage tent, and that indefinable mix of sunscreen and desperation that seemed to hover over the performer's circle. He scanned the crowd between reps, searching for that familiar ghost-quick movement, that shadow-shift that meant his friend was near. But spotting Griffin was like trying to catch smoke. Always had been. The man could vanish in an empty room if he wanted to.

Where are you, brother?

The weight of the past three years hung heavier than his own body on the rings. He'd had chosen to take the fall for Copenhagen, had walked into that Board of Inquiry knowing exactly what he was doing. It had been the right call—he might not have taken the shot himself, but he'd been CO. He put Griff in that situation. Griff begged him to tell the truth, but it wouldn't have helped. Whether he pulled the trigger or not, he would have been punished. No reason for both of their careers to go down in flames.

But he knew Griffin's burden was far worse. Living with letting someone else pay for your choices ... that was a special kind of hell.

He dropped down onto the sunbaked sand, grabbed his water bottle, using the motion to check his peripherals. The bottle was warm, water tasting of plastic. Griff would be here somewhere. Average height, average build, dark hair high and tight—a thousand guys on this boardwalk fit that description. But none of them moved like Ghost. None of them had that coiled-spring energy that made Griffin the fastest operator Ronan had ever seen.

A burst of laughter from the basketball courts mixed with the endless rhythm of waves and the thrum of skateboard wheels on concrete. The cacophony of Venice Beach on a summer afternoon should have provided perfect cover, but instead, every noise set his combat instincts humming.

"LAPD, making another pass," Maya's voice came through his earpiece, disguised by her pretense of narrating a workout video. She stood a few yards away, phone up, looking California-casual in shorts and a tank top. But Ronan could see the tension in her shoulders, the way she shifted her weight every few seconds, combat-ready despite her relaxed pose.

"Copy," Christian replied from his food truck position. "That's four units in ten minutes."

Ronan forced himself back onto the rings, using the exercise to mask his own growing unease. Sweat stung his eyes. With BOLOs out for him and Maya, Southern California was the last place they should be right now. But Griffin had chosen this spot for a reason. The crowds pressed closer as the afternoon heat drove more tourists toward the relative cool of the ocean breeze. Each new face was a potential threat.

An LAPD-issue SUV rolled by again, its tinted windows reflecting the relentless sun. Ronan's scalp prickled with familiar combat instincts, the same sixth sense that had saved his life a dozen times downrange. They were exposed here, vulnerable. And Griffin still hadn't ...

Maya's voice cut through his thoughts, barely audible over a nearby busker's electric guitar. "Three o'clock. LA County bike patrol officer by the smoothie stand."

Ronan twisted, letting his momentum on the rings give him a natural-looking view of the target. The "officer" wore his watch high on his wrist—classic agency tell. The man's shirt was too crisp, too new. Real beach patrol wore uniform tees faded by sun and salt air.

The press of bodies around them grew thicker. Tourists seeking shade clustered under the palms, their chatter and children's squeals creating a wall of sound that made tracking movement even harder. The scent of grilled fish and hot pavement mixed with sunscreen and sweat.

Come on, Ghost. Where are you?

LOST HOPE

A street performer—one of those silver-painted living statues—broke his pose as Ronan completed another set. The man moved with mechanical jerks toward the rings, his tip bucket extended. Nothing unusual for Venice Beach, except ...

The performer's eyes met Ronan's for a fraction of a second beneath the metallic paint. In that instant, Ronan recognized the micro-expression code they'd used a hundred times in the field. *Ghost.* His heart slammed against his ribs, muscle memory recognizing his friend even as his brain caught up.

He dropped a dollar in the bucket, felt paper brush his palm. The statue moved on, working the crowd with robotic movements. Just another hustler on the boardwalk. But Ronan's fingers burned where they'd touched Griffin's for that split second.

Ronan palmed the note while reaching for his water bottle, the paper damp with sweat against his skin. "Package received," he murmured into comms, his voice nearly lost in the screech of a nearby seagull fighting over dropped french fries.

"What package?" Maya kept her phone up, still playing tourist. The late afternoon sun caught the tension in her jaw. "I don't—"

A bead of sweat tracked down his spine. The crowd seemed to press closer, bodies hemming them in on all sides. The sickly-sweet smell of cannabis drifted past, mixed with hot tar from the softening asphalt.

Ronan unfolded the note behind his bottle, the familiar block letters hitting him like a punch to the gut: FOLLOW PROTOCOL 7. EYES HIGH + LOW. MEET WHERE KINGS PLAYED. "That was Griff. We're blown."

Christian's voice tightened in their earpieces. "Drone, northwest approach."

Ronan crushed the note, letting his gaze drift up naturally, as if shading his eyes from the sun. The drone was there, a dark speck against the bleached-blue sky, moving with deliberate precision. Not the lazy wandering of a tourist's toy. The whine of its rotors carried on the breeze, a persistent whisper of surveillance.

"Moving to secondary," he said quietly, grabbing his gym bag. The canvas strap was gritty with sand, still hot from baking in the sun. But as he turned toward their exit route, Maya's sharp intake of breath stopped him.

"Two SUVs just blocked Ocean Front Walk," she reported. Through her camera's viewfinder, he watched her track the vehicles—black paint gleaming, windows tinted impenetrable. "And the police checkpoint at the pier ..."

"They're checking IDs." Christian's voice was grim. "Box formation. They're closing the net."

The temperature seemed to drop ten degrees despite the August heat. Ronan's mind raced. Protocol 7 was their old scattered-retreat strategy. But with watchers on the ground, eyes in the sky, and Griffin's warning about kings ...

Kings. *The chess players*.

The daily gathering of chess players at the beach tables. Where Griffin had taught him that knight's gambit, years ago. Where they'd waited out a surveillance team during that op in 19—

"They knew," he said softly, understanding hitting him like a physical blow. The crowd's chatter faded to white noise, replaced by the thundering of his pulse. "They knew we were coming before we did."

26

KNIGHT'S DEFENSE

Maya's lungs burned as she rounded the corner onto Speedway, Ronan and Christian hard on her heels, the taste of salt and adrenaline sharp on her tongue. The drone's whine sliced through the tourist chatter behind them, getting closer. When Ronan grabbed her arm and yanked her into the narrow gap between buildings, she didn't resist. The brick walls radiated August heat, making the already tight space feel like an oven.

"We could try the tunnels under the old canals," Ronan suggested, his voice low and urgent.

Christian shook his head. "They'll have those covered. Those tunnels are in every tourist guide now."

"Then we fight our way out." Ronan's jaw clenched. "Together."

The look he gave her made her stomach flip, despite the danger. Or maybe because of it.

"That's exactly what they want," Christian snapped. He moved closer to Ronan, dropping his voice. "Think. They're looking for a team. Three people moving together? Might as well paint targets on our backs."

"We're not splitting up." Ronan's voice held that familiar steel, the tone that had commanded SEAL teams through impossible situations.

"He's right." The words hurt coming out, but Maya forced herself to continue. "I can blend in with the shopping crowd on Abbot Kinney. You two—"

"No." Ronan stepped toward her, close enough that she could feel the heat coming off his body, smell the salt on his skin. "Maya—"

"You're painting a target on her if she stays with us," Christian growled, getting in Ronan's face. "But alone? She's just another tourist."

Maya touched Ronan's arm, felt the tension thrumming through his muscles. "He's right. I've got this."

The conflict in Ronan's eyes made her chest tighten. She wanted to say something more, something to ease that look. But another drone buzzed closer, and their time was up.

She watched her teammates disappear in opposite directions, Ronan's reluctance visible in every line of his body until he vanished into the crowd. *Focus. Move.* Eyes alert for the drone, she slipped out of the alley and joined a cluster of women leaving a wine bar, mimicking their loose-limbed strut and carefree laughter.

Her phone buzzed. An unfamiliar number: Chess masters moved inside. King's gambit in play.

Had to be Griffin Hawkins. She'd have to ask him later how he'd gotten this number—the phone was brand new, supplied by Knight Tactical less than forty-eight hours ago. Then again, this was Ghost. He probably had the number before she did.

The chess masters moving inside—that had to mean the players had left their usual outdoor tables. Thanks to her father's drill-sergeant training, she could hold her own at a chess board. A king's gambit was an aggressive opening move, sacrificing a pawn to gain position.

Message received. You want me to make an obvious move to draw attention.

She forced herself not to tense as two men in tactical pants and too-new tourist shirts passed by. Feds. FBI. NCIS. Did it really matter?

The women she'd joined turned into a boutique. Maya kept walking, every sense straining. Another buzz: Knight to queen's bishop 4. Clock running.

A knight's move—an indirect approach. Queen's bishop meant the left side of the playing field. Maya counted the cross streets. Four blocks left would put her behind the famous shopping street's main stores.

She slipped into the next alley, pressing her back against sun-warmed brick as an LAPD cruiser crawled past. The smell of coffee from the hipster café next door mingled with rotting sweetness from nearby dumpsters. Sweat trickled down her neck, but she didn't dare move to wipe it away.

Her gaze caught on a barista clearing tables outside the café. The servers wore shirts with chess pieces printed on them, part of some brand identity. *Of course. Chess masters moved inside—he's literally telling me which café.*

Her phone buzzed again: Rook takes pawn. Service entrance clear.

A direct assault on an exposed piece—Griffin was warning her the service entrance would only be clear momentarily.

The café's back door was still propped open from the barista's trash run. Maya counted to three, then moved. But as she reached for the handle, a new sound froze her in place —the distinctive scrape of uniform shoes on asphalt.

Christian's voice crackled in her earpiece. "Creating a distraction near Muscle Beach. Local talent's about to get rowdy." In the distance, she heard raised voices, the sound of an impromptu strength competition drawing crowds.

But her attention was locked on the shadow moving at the far end of the alley. The figure stepped forward—

"Hold up, ma'am." A female officer moved into view, hand on her holstered weapon. "I need to see some ID."

Her heart thundered, but Maya let her shoulders slump in fake relief. "Oh wonderful! An actual officer. Some creep's been following me since Pacific Avenue." She fumbled in her purse, hands shaking—not entirely an act. "I ducked back here to call my boyfriend ..."

Ronan's voice, tight with tension, came through her earpiece. "I've got two operatives in sight. One in a pink golf shirt. The other's wearing striped board shorts and a white tee. They haven't spotted me yet, but probably just a matter of time."

"I got you," Christian responded.

The officer studied Maya's offered ID—a quick Knight Tactical creation that would hold up to basic scrutiny. "There have been some incidents in the area. Maybe you should—"

A crash of weights hitting concrete echoed from Muscle Beach, followed by angry shouts. The officer's radio crackled to life. "All units, disturbance at Muscle Beach recreation area ..."

Maya watched indecision war on the woman's face.

Come on, Christian. Make it good.

"Dispatch, I've got a civilian complaint to check ..." The officer keyed her radio, then turned back to Maya. "Ma'am, I suggest you move to a more public—"

The radio erupted again. "Officers needed, situation escalating—"

Ronan's voice cut through her earpiece: "Golf Shirt is moving your way, Maya. Get clear."

The officer's radio crackled again with demands for

backup. She thrust Maya's ID back at her. "Stay in public areas," she ordered, already moving toward the growing chaos at Muscle Beach.

Maya waited three heartbeats before slipping through the café's service entrance. The blast of air conditioning raised goosebumps on her sun-heated skin. Through her earpiece, she heard Christian's satisfied grunt. "That's right, brother, show them how much you can lift. No, no—form's all wrong. Here, let me ..."

"Golf Shirt just badged the local cops on the corner." Ronan's voice was barely a whisper. "Looks like they're setting up a checkpoint on Rose Avenue."

Maya moved through the kitchen, nodding to a startled prep cook as she passed.

Her phone vibrated: Bishop to king's level. Time check.

Griffin was directing her upstairs, warning her to hurry.

"They're searching phones at the checkpoint," Christian reported between shouted encouragement to his impromptu weightlifting competition. "Looking for specific numbers."

Maya found the stairs, taking them two at a time. Below, she heard Ronan's sharp intake of breath. "Board Shorts just made me. Moving to secondary exit."

She paused to delete Griffin's texts. The upper floor was dim after the bright alley, scattered chess tables occupied by serious-faced players. No Griffin. But there, on a table near the fire escape: a knight piece lying on its side. Queen's bishop 4—fourth table from the left wall.

"Checkpoint's got dogs now," Christian's voice was tight. "Time to bail."

She heard boots on the stairs behind her. *Think.* The café's windows overlooked Abbot Kinney, police vehicles visible at both ends of the block. The fire escape would be watched. Which meant ...

Her phone buzzed one last time: Queen takes knight's pawn.

Maya deleted the final message just as heavy footsteps hit the top landing. She moved toward the chess table, blood rushing in her ears, mind racing through her options. The bailout point was eight blocks away, through a maze of police checkpoints and agency surveillance. She had no backup, no clear route, and—

A hand gripped her elbow. She nearly struck out before a familiar voice, barely a whisper, reached her. "Queen to king's side." Griffin Hawkins, dressed as a busboy, baseball cap pulled low. The slightest traces of silver paint rimmed his light blue eyes. Her relief lasted exactly one second before she registered the tension in his grip. Whatever was happening, this wasn't the clean extraction they'd planned.

"Golf Shirt is on the stairs," she murmured, tilting her head like she was checking her phone.

"Copy that. His partner has the alley covered." Griffin's casual pose belied the urgency in his voice. "We're about to make a very noisy exit. When I move, stay on my six."

"Wait." She fumbled in the pocket of her shorts, pulling out the extra set of earbuds they each carried in case they met up with Griffin.

He palmed the tiny devices before fitting them in his ears. "Nice. I'm a go on comms," he said.

Through her earpiece, she heard Ronan gulping for air, clearly running hard. "Welcome to the party, Ghost."

"Sitrep?" Griffin asked.

Christian answered. "Bailout position's blown. You got a plan B, Hawkins?"

"Copy that." Griffin's eyes scanned the rooftop. "How do you feel about Thai food, Agent Chen?"

Maya followed his gaze to the adjacent rooftop, where steam billowed from industrial exhaust fans. The smell of basil and ginger wafted up from below. "I hate Thai food," she muttered, but she was already moving. Behind them, the roof access door burst open.

Griffin shoved her hard toward the building's edge just as the first shots cracked against the concrete. "Move now, complain later!"

27

CONTACT BURNS

THE ANCIENT FIRE escape shed rust like dead skin, each step a metallic protest. Kitchen exhaust battled with the smell of corroded iron, masking their presence from the heavily armed men above. Three rooftops' worth of running had turned Maya's legs to rubber, but Griffin wasn't done leading them through this vertical maze.

Before she could get her bearings, Griffin shoved her toward a scratched and dented service door. He yanked it open and pulled her inside. The sudden transition from underground tunnel to fluorescent-lit kitchen making her head spin.

Boardwalk Bangkok, her mind registered automatically, catching glimpses of red and gold signage as they slipped past startled kitchen staff. Maya's tactical training kicked in, categorizing the space even as they moved through it. Two main exits. Three possible weapons within reach. Four workers who could either help or hinder. Usually, she analyzed scenes like this from a pursuer's perspective. Being on the other side of the hunt sent ice down her spine.

Steam billowed from industrial dishwashers, providing

momentary cover. The clatter of pots and shouts in Spanish covered their footsteps. But there was no hiding from the tactical teams that had to be converging on their position—teams that shouldn't have known where to look.

The smell of garlic and seared meat made her stomach clench, reminding her they'd been running this op for hours. Her muscles burned from the constant tension of staying alert while playing tourist.

Maya caught Griffin working his phone one-handed even as he guided her through the busy kitchen. When he noticed her watching, he gave a grim smile. "Insurance," he murmured. He tucked the phone away before she could see more.

Through her earpiece, Ronan's measured breathing told her he was still running. From the sound of it, taking evasive action.

Christian's voice cut through the kitchen noise. "Creating a diversion at the checkpoint. These bodybuilders are very interested in proper form."

Griffin guided them past a walk-in freezer, his hand signals indicating multiple hostiles converging. Maya caught a glimpse of their reflection in a steel cabinet—they looked exactly like what they were: fugitives.

"Ronan, south exit," Griffin commanded through his own comms, his voice barely a whisper. "Christian, create chaos at the checkpoint."

"Copy that, Ghost." Christian's reply was followed by the sound of weights crashing and men shouting.

They emerged into a wine cellar. Griffin pulled up a trapdoor Maya would have sworn was just part of the flooring. "Venice canal maintenance tunnels. Ladies first."

"Whole tactical team moving in," Ronan reported. "They're not even trying to be subtle now."

The tunnel was dank, the air thick with decades of moisture. Griffin produced a small flashlight, illuminating ancient brickwork. "This way. Ronan, Christian—mark your positions."

Maya heard their locations, realized Griffin was leading them in a converging pattern. Smart. The tunnels would conceal their meet up from their pursuers. And the drones.

But as they approached the junction point, Griffin stopped abruptly. "Company."

Flashlight beams bounced off the curved walls ahead. Behind them, more lights appeared. The tactical team had known about the tunnels.

"Ghost ..." Ronan's warning came just as multiple tactical teams converged from both directions.

Maya's pulse hammered in her throat as flashlight beams cut through the tunnel's darkness. The dank air felt suddenly thinner, harder to breathe. Her back pressed against slick brick, every nerve ending screaming for action. But years of training held her still, held her ready.

She cataloged their situation with brutal clarity: two exits blocked, unknown number of hostiles, limited cover, and the copper-penny taste of fear in her mouth. They were underground, in the dark, outnumbered.

And she and Ronan, at least, were suspects in at least two murders, and untold breaches of national security. Whether the tactical teams were good guys or enemies, they'd have no trouble explaining why they shot the four of them dead.

Her fingers found the grip of her weapon, the familiar texture steadying her. The tunnel's acoustics carried the soft clicks of multiple weapons being readied. The sound sent ice down her spine even as her muscles coiled for action.

A beam of light cut through the tunnel darkness, deliberately aimed to blind them. Maya caught glimpses as the light shifted: tactical gear, professional stance. The leader moved with the kind of effortless control she'd only seen in elite

SWAT operators, his weapon an extension of his body. This wasn't some rent-a-cop or weekend warrior. Every movement screamed federal training, but not the kind they advertised in recruitment videos.

When he spoke, his voice carried both authority and amusement, bouncing off the tunnel walls. "Last chance, Hawkins!" The accent was pure Midwest, heartland America. Not what she'd expected from their shadowy pursuers. "You've got nowhere left to run."

Griffin's thumb moved across his phone screen, the glow highlighting his razor-sharp focus. "You might want to reconsider," he called back. His voice held that dangerous edge Maya had learned to recognize. "I've got two years of Sullivan's intel. Every clinic. Every lab. Every victim. One click, and it all goes public."

"You're bluffing." But there was a new tension in that heartland voice, a flicker of uncertainty that hadn't been there before.

"Try me." Griffin's thumb hovered over the screen. "I've got enough to bury everyone involved. Your choice—back off, or watch your whole operation implode."

"Upload whatever you want. We own the channels." The team leader's voice echoed off the bricks.

Griffin's laugh was soft, deadly. "I'm not talking about news outlets." He thumbed something on his phone. "I'm talking FBI. CIA. NSA. All getting real-time data about American operatives disappearing American veterans. Think you can contain that?"

Flashlight beams caught the sweat on Griffin's face. This was no bluff—Maya could read the tension in every line of his body.

Shots exploded outside the tunnel. Griff shoved her behind a support column. The back of her head collided with the wall, making her see stars. Return fire lit up the darkness as bullets crossed the entrance. Through the muzzle flashes, she caught Griffin's subtle movements—the quick press of devices against the tunnel supports. Some kind of explosive charges, most likely.

"Run. Now. Back the way we came." Griffin's voice competed with the firefight. "Go!"

She understood instantly. While they'd been talking, he'd been positioning the charges between them and the enemy—and setting up their exit strategy.

She turned and ran back the way they'd come.

"Hold your fire!" The leader's voice cracked with authority. "Hawkins has a—" His words cut off as Griffin triggered the explosion.

The blast was controlled but devastating in the enclosed space. Shards of cement filled the air behind them as they ran, buying precious seconds. They emerged through a maintenance shaft two blocks from their extraction point, her ears still ringing from the detonations.

TWO FAMILIAR FIGURES rushed toward them. Blood trickled down the side of Christian's face. Ronan was cradling his left arm, his shirt torn and bloody. Griffin looked worst of all—pale, limping, but his eyes burned with a fierce intensity.

"Car. Now." He pushed them toward the waiting Knight Tactical SUV. "They'll have every asset in play within minutes."

Maya heard sirens converging as they peeled away from the curb. Griffin slumped against the seat, finally letting exhaustion show.

"They shouldn't have known," he said quietly, pressing a hand against his shoulder where blood was seeping through. "Someone leaked the meet. And they were willing to kill us all to contain this."

Griff and Christian exchanged grim looks. "We need to get back to headquarters," Christian said, applying pressure to his own wound. "Figure out if they tracked you, or us."

"Or if we've got another problem entirely," Ronan added, his voice tight with pain and concern.

Maya caught Ronan's eye. After years in Homicide, she knew that look—the one suspects got when they realized they weren't the predator anymore. They were the prey.

28

OLD WOUNDS

Once safe in the Pilatus, Ronan studied his friend. Beneath the edgy energy, the man looked exhausted. Ronan figured he probably looked the same. Only with a bullet hole in his bicep.

He inclined his head at his long-lost teammate. "Good to see you."

Griff looked up from the med kit Christian had produced. "Right back atcha." He frowned over the neat assortment of implements and bandages, ducking his head away.

The pain in Ronan's arm was overshadowed by the twinge of guilt that twisted his guts. The secret he and Griff shared bonded them more tightly than any of the others on their team. Not in a good way.

Kit in hand, Griff ordered Ronan to sit back. "This is gonna hurt," he warned before digging in.

No joke.

Ronan gritted his teeth as Griffin cleaned the wound. The plane's cabin lights were harsh, revealing every scrape and blood stain they'd collected during their escape. Outside the

Pilatus's windows, the Van Nuys tarmac shimmered in the late afternoon heat.

"Stop being such a baby," Griffin muttered, probing the wound with experienced hands. "It's just a through-and-through. No nerve or bone involvement. I'll get you patched up until Kenji can do his doctor thing."

"Just a—" Ronan broke off with a hiss as Griffin applied antiseptic. "Easy for you to say. You're not the one who has to fly this thing with a hole in his arm."

"Just don't scratch the aircraft," Christian spoke up from where he was bandaging his own arm. "It's ridiculously expensive to have these things worked on."

Ronan couldn't help smirking. "Put it on my tab."

"Body's writing checks your bank account can't back, dude."

For sure. Nice of Bio Bro to remind him he was the poor relation. Nothing like kicking a guy when he was down. He glared at Christian, but the man was too busy checking the sight lines from the plane's windows to pay him any attention.

Griff packed up the med kit. "Maybe I should take the controls. You're looking a little pasty."

"You couldn't fly a paper airplane," Ronan shot back, but the familiar banter helped distract from the pain. "That last landing in Kandahar was especially bad."

"That was one time—"

"That was three times," Ronan corrected. "Okay. No. Two. The third time doesn't count. The plane was already on fire when you took control. I'll give you that one."

"'Cause you're so generous." Griffin jabbed the needle into Ronan's arm.

Ronan tried to laugh, but it turned into a grunt of pain. His eyes found Maya, sitting quietly in one of the leather seats. She hadn't said much since they'd made it to the plane, her face drawn and pale. It wasn't like her—in the few days he'd known her, she'd been all sharp wit and sharper insights. Reminded him of her father, a little, though he'd never tell her that.

Griff set aside the kit and checked the dressing one last time. "You'll live. Probably."

"Your bedside manner hasn't improved," Ronan muttered, testing his range of motion.

"Neither has your ability to dodge bullets." Griffin eyed Christian. "We need to move. Once our tail strikes out searching traffic cams, they'll start checking airfields."

"Copy that." Christian nodded toward Maya. "You okay over there?"

She looked up, seemed to shake herself out of whatever thoughts had held her. "Just wondering how they knew where to find us."

Ronan caught the way Griffin's hands stilled for just a moment. There was more here—much more—than their friend had revealed.

"First," Ronan said, pushing himself up with only a small wince, "we get airborne. Then you're going to tell us exactly what kind of hornet's nest we just kicked."

The secure radio crackled as he headed into the cockpit, stopping him. "Knight One, this is Base. Sitrep."

Christian moved to the comm panel in the passenger area. "Base, Knight One. Package retrieved. Minimal casualties." He glanced at Ronan's shoulder. "Couple of scratches. Nothing serious."

"What about my plane?" Jack's voice rose.

"All good, my man. Just shot up the ancillary equipment. Ronan took a round through the shoulder, but it's all good."

"Opposition?" Jack's voice was tight.

"Heavy. Local law enforcement plus private contractors.

Someone had advance intel on our location." Christian paused. "High-level coordination. They knew exactly where to look."

A long silence filled the channel. Then, "Get in the air as quick as you can. Both retrieval teams are airborne. Austin's group and mine. Both packages secured."

Something in Jack's tone made Ronan look up from his pre-flight checks. There was more there—something unsaid.

"The packages?" Christian asked carefully.

"Let's just say ... they're not exactly what we expected. You'll understand when you see them. Base out."

Maya stirred from her seat. "I don't know Jack very well, but cryptic is never good."

"Neither is the FAA notification I'm seeing," Christian said, checking his tablet. "They're implementing special screening protocols at all airfields within three hundred miles."

"Sounds like we've overstayed our welcome," Griffin said, sliding into the co-pilot's seat with the ease of someone who'd done it many times before. He started the second set of pre-flight checks without being asked. "Transponder off?"

"Roger that." Ronan was just thinking the same thing. With the transponder off, they'd be invisible to flight tracking radar.

Ronan caught Maya and Christian exchanging looks as they moved toward the back lounge. The pain in his shoulder was becoming a dull throb, manageable now that the adrenaline was wearing off.

He pushed the throttles forward, feeling the familiar surge of the engines. Whatever they'd stumbled into, it was bigger than a simple extraction.

They maintained radio silence until reaching cruising altitude, the San Fernando Valley falling away beneath them. Ronan adjusted their heading, his jaw tight against the burning in his shoulder. The local anesthetic was already wearing thin, each small movement a reminder of torn muscle and tissue.

"So this is what a SEAL looks like when he's pretending not to be in pain." Maya's voice came from just behind the cockpit door.

"I don't pretend anything, Special Agent." He kept his eyes forward, fighting a smile despite the throbbing in his arm.

"Right. And that wasn't you telling Christian 'it's just a scratch' while bleeding all over the tarmac?" She moved into his peripheral vision, holding out water and pills. "Take these."

"Worried about me?"

"You mean am I concerned about the several million dollars' worth of aircraft you're currently piloting? Yes." But her voice held something that belied the snark.

"Admit it, Chen. You care."

"I care about not dying in a fiery crash because our pilot is too macho to take pain meds."

"Your concern is touching."

Without a word, she set the water and pills on his console and headed back into the lounge.

Griffin let the cockpit fall silent for the better part of an hour, watching the last rays of sunlight paint the clouds. "You know, for a guy who can engineer a hot extract under the worst possible conditions, you're remarkably blind at close range."

"If this is about leaving you hanging during that paintball rematch with the Marines ... though I have to admit, seeing a SEAL get lit up in rainbow colors made my whole month."

"This is about you still carrying my shot from Copenhagen." Griffin's voice dropped. "Three years of letting people think you took down that doctor. And for what? To protect me? I made my choice."

Ronan adjusted their heading, hiding a wince. The pain meds weren't doing nearly enough. "And I made mine."

"But you never let me have a say. I'm good with the truth coming out. Always have been." Griffin's voice roughened, sanded with anger. "You've got the team back. Good people. They deserve the whole truth, not some sanitized report where you took responsibility for my call."

"What I've got," Ronan cut him off, "is a bullet hole in my arm and two hours of flying ahead. So unless you want me to pass out somewhere over the Sierra Nevada, we're done talking."

A wave of dizziness hit Ronan hard enough that he had to focus on his breathing. Griffin noticed, his hand moving to the co-pilot controls without comment.

"I've got it," Ronan ground out.

"Sure you do. Just like you 'had it' when—"

The cockpit door opened. Maya eyed him with laser focus. Her lips flattened into a sharp line. "Griffin, he's grey. Why is he grey?"

"Because he's a stubborn—"

"I'm right here," Ronan muttered.

She snorted. "Yes, you are. Barely. We're still an hour out. Can you make it, or should we set down?"

The genuine concern in her voice made him turn his head, meeting her eyes. Bad idea. This close, he could see flecks of gold in the brown. Could see worry warring with something else entirely.

"I can make it."

"You sure about that?" But her hand had settled on his uninjured shoulder, steady and warm.

"I've flown with worse."

"That's not actually reassuring." But she squeezed his

shoulder gently before stepping back. "Just ... call if you need anything?"

After she left, Griffin shook his head. "You're both ridiculous."

"Shut up and help me fly this plane."

But for the first time since they'd taken off, Griffin was smiling. "Whatever you say, brother. Whatever you say."

29

FUZZY LANDING

Ronan brought the plane down on a decent line, compensating for the tremor in his hands. Not his best landing, but nobody died, and he didn't scratch the plane, so he'd count that as a win.

"Show-off," Griffin muttered from the co-pilot seat.

"Says the man who once landed a chopper in a sandstorm." Ronan started shutdown procedures, each movement sending fresh fire through his arm from shoulder to fingers.

The Knight Tactical hangar was organized chaos. Axel stood at the front of the welcoming committee, his usual stoic expression cracking into relief when Griffin emerged. The two men embraced briefly, Axel clapping Griffin on the back.

"Good to have you back, brother."

"Good to be—" Griffin's response cut off as Kenji practically tackled him.

"You absolute jerk," Kenji said, grinning. "Do you know how much paperwork you caused when you walked out of that last debrief without the CO's permission?"

Ronan watched Griffin's smile tighten, not quite reaching

his eyes. Before he could analyze that, his mother rushed him.

"Mom, I'm fine—"

"You were shot. Again." She eyed his bandages while simultaneously pulling out her recorder. "Now, about these clinic infiltrations—"

"Not now, Mom."

Izzy appeared at Ronan's side. "You look bad."

"Thanks."

"Med bay's waiting. And those two"—Ethan nodded toward a corner where two people were examining Knight Tactical's security setup with enthusiasm—"are making us very nervous."

The two rescued veterans, both middle-aged, one male, the other female, were roaming away from Jack and Austin. Mike Rutherford, former Army Ranger, was pointing out what he considered to be potential blind spots in their security system. Katherine Genovese, the retired Marine, had somehow acquired a tablet and appeared to be taking notes.

"This is outstanding! What a set up you people have," Kate announced. "Hey, Rutherford, they've got thermal imaging!"

"That's proprietary info," Austin protested.

"Son, I had better tech in Fallujah," Mike replied. "Now, about these camera angles ..."

Maya materialized next to Ronan, steadying him when he swayed slightly. "Medical. Now. You need to let Kenji take a look."

"I need to debrief—"

"You need stitches." Her hand brushed his good arm. "The conspiracy will wait ten minutes."

"Five."

"Ten." Her tone brooked no argument. "Axel's got this."

Indeed, Axel had moved to intercept Lawrence Chen, who

was trailing Ronan's mom with his own tablet, adding commentary to her interviews. Axel's expression suggested he was reconsidering several life choices.

"Fine. Ten minutes." Ronan caught Griffin watching him and Maya, something unreadable in his expression. Before he could ask, Griffin turned away, focusing intently on whatever Kenji was saying.

"Make it fifteen," Star called from nearby. "Your landing was crooked."

"My landing was perfect."

"Your landing," Maya said softly, steering him toward medical, "was stubborn. Like the pilot."

Her hand was still on his arm. He told himself the warmth spreading through his chest was just blood loss.

Behind them, Kate's voice rose: "Hey, is that a weapons testing range? Mike, they've got a weapons testing range!"

"Ma'am, that's restrict—" Austin's protest faded into resignation.

Ronan caught Axel's eye. His second-in-command shook his head slightly—Griffin was different. They both saw it. The question was why.

"Stop thinking so loud," Maya murmured. "Medical first. Mysteries second."

He let her guide him toward the Knight Tactical medical bay tucked in next to the workout area, very aware of her fingers still resting just above his elbow. He'd give it ten minutes, then they needed answers.

In the end, he endured twenty minutes of Maya hovering while Kenji cleaned and re-stitched his arm. Not that he minded having Maya around. She reminded him of the ocean—calm on the surface but with currents that could pull you under if you weren't careful. And he was definitely in danger of drowning, especially when she looked at him with that mix of concern and exasperation.

The painkillers they gave him were barely enough to take the edge off—his insistence on staying clear-headed meant settling for something just above aspirin. Maya's eyeroll suggested exactly what she thought of that decision.

Finally, Kenji snapped off his latex gloves. "He'll do."

While Kenji cleaned up, Maya helped Ronan shrug back into his shirt. "Be careful. If you pull those stitches playing hero again, I'm letting your mom interview you while you're on the good drugs."

"That's just cruel."

Her smile didn't quite hide her concern. "Then don't pull your stitches."

They could hear the two vets' enthusiastic voices carrying from the command center, punctuated by what sounded like Ethan and Zara giving them a technical rundown of the surveillance systems. His mother's rapid-fire questions provided a steady backbeat to the chaos.

Through the windows of the medical bay, he saw Griffin standing slightly apart from the others, posture rigid as Axel and Deke tried to draw him into conversation.

"Something's wrong," Maya said quietly.

Ronan finished buttoning his shirt one-handed. "Let's go find out what."

30

TRIP WIRES

The command center had reached a new level of controlled chaos by the time Ronan and Maya arrived. Lawrence had apparently bonded with Kate over surveillance tech, the two of them hunched over his tablet while he demonstrated something involving thermal imaging. Mike Rutherford was regaling Victoria with a story about his Ranger days that had Christian pinching the bridge of his nose.

Jack and Austin were in their customary positions at the head of the conference table next to a stone-faced Deke, all of them looking slightly stunned. Ronan could see where the two energetic retirees, combined with the forces of nature that were his mother, and Lawrence Chen, might set anyone back on their heels. The top-tier security company had morphed into a mash-up of Golden Girls meets Die Hard.

Ronan tried to steer his mother away from the gray-haired Ranger. "Mom, that's not actually relevant to—"

"Everything's relevant," she countered, recording device at the ready. "Now, Mr. Rutherford, you were saying about the blood tests?"

The word 'blood tests' caught Kenji's attention. He looked up from his borrowed station, where he and Star had been combing through data. "What blood tests?"

"The ones that made no sense," Kate said, finally looking up from Lawrence's tablet. "I went in for a cortisone shot for my sciatica. Somehow ended up giving enough blood for a platelet drive."

Mike nodded. "Same here. Physical therapy for my knee turned into a vampire convention."

"Standard protocol includes basic panels," Kenji explained, but Mike was already shaking his head.

"Not like this. They took multiple vials, different colored tops. Said something about a new veteran wellness program."

Griffin's head snapped up. He'd been studying a terminal in the corner, deliberately distant from the group. "When exactly?"

"Three weeks ago," Kate said. "Right after they changed my regular doctor."

"Four weeks for me," Mike added. "Different clinic, same deal. New doc, lots of tests."

Maya's father tapped his glasses against his chin. "Something about that library's been bugging me. Star, honey, could you access the usage logs for the Santa Monica library for the past month?"

She laughed. "In a heartbeat."

He nodded slowly. "Not hard to do, huh?"

Zara snorted this time. "A seventh grader could do it. Maybe a really talented fourth grader."

He zoned in on Griff. "So really, anybody could."

Griffin went still.

"Back in '89, we had this case—a serial burglar who specialized in home break-ins," Lawrence explained. "He was smart. Only hit high-end homes in isolated areas. Places with expensive security systems that were somehow on the fritz. We interrogated every employee at every alarm company, right down to the janitors. Nothing. Took us a year to catch him. Turns out, his accomplice was at the Building Department. Any permits issued for home security systems got passed along to him. I think the minute you searched for those VA files, you lit up their radar somehow." He turned to Star and Ethan and Zara. "That's doable, right?"

The three computer whizzes murmured their assent.

"But I used a secure terminal protocol," Griffin protested quietly.

"Doesn't matter." Lawrence clapped him on the shoulder. "They weren't tracking you, son. They were tracking what you were looking for. Anyone digging into those specific medical records would trigger their system."

"Then they'd follow the tracks," Zara added, locking eyes with Star. "Eventually, they'd get past your protocol."

Star nodded. "And they'd locate the exact terminals."

Ronan watched understanding dawn on Axel's face. "They set up a digital tripwire."

Lawrence tapped the end of his nose. "Bingo. Just like my thief used permit requests. Only now it's all algorithms and cloud computing whatchamacallits. Same detective work, different century."

The room went quiet. Even Victoria's pen stopped moving.

"The research you were doing," Lawrence said carefully. "It wasn't just about current VA patients, was it?"

Griffin stared at his hands, fingers working against each other. "You guys already know Tank was working at the VA outreach center in San Diego. A couple of months ago, a woman came in. Her uncle, a Gulf War vet, vanished. Police said he probably just took off—guy had some minor mental health issues, history of disappearing for a few days. But she knew something was wrong. Tank told the woman he'd check into it."

"Why Marcus?" Victoria asked, pen poised.

Ronan's arm throbbed as he shifted position, something about Griffin's tension setting off warning bells.

"He worked the outreach desk twice a week. Veterans trusted him." Griffin's jaw tightened, and he pushed himself up to pace the small space. "Turns out, the uncle had gone to the local VA clinic for some kind of minor health thing. High blood pressure or something."

The familiar cold settled in Ronan's gut—the same feeling he got before missions went sideways.

Griffin stopped at the window, his reflection stark against the darkness outside. "Anyway, three days later, the guy disappears. Tank messed around in the clinic files. Saw a whole handful of similar cases. Mostly nobody reported them because the vets either lived alone, or died. Suicides or accidents."

Kate made a small sound, and Mike's hand found hers.

Ronan's hands clenched involuntarily. He could see where this was going.

"The deeper he dug, the more suspect cases he found. And he'd barely touched the clinics in Southern California." Griffin turned back, meeting Ronan's eyes. "So he called me."

The pain meds were wearing off, but Ronan barely noticed now. His whole focus was on Griffin, who seemed to be carrying the weight of what came next.

"Marcus called me because ..." Griffin's voice roughened. He dropped into his chair like his legs wouldn't hold him. "Because he knew I'd believe him. That I'd understand why a bunch of vulnerable vets suddenly deciding to vanish wasn't right."

"How many?" Ronan forced the words past the tightness in his throat.

Griffin's hands trembled slightly as he reached for his water. "Fifteen vets so far that we confirmed. All in the last eight months. They'd get called in for new evaluations, medical tests, biometric scans—way more extensive than usual VA protocols. Then they'd vanish."

Mike's hand went to the bandage at the crook of his arm where they'd taken blood samples.

The silence that followed felt like a physical presence until Christian leaned forward, breaking it. "They're harvesting their data before killing them." He clasped his hands behind his neck, squeezing hard. "The why we can work out later. I say we start with the who and the what."

"Copy that," Austin answered before Ronan could.

Murmurs of assent filled the space.

Hands on his hips, Axel paced the outer edges of the room. "Then we need to look at the footage. Security cameras, waiting room videos, anything from the VA facilities where these tests happened."

Star squinted at her monitor. "The Santa Monica clinic keeps their security feeds for ninety days. Policy after an incident with the pharmacy break-in last year."

Zara nodded, her gaze on her own bank of monitors. "Same with the West LA facility. Plus they upgraded their system recently. Better resolution."

"We'll need all of it." Ronan eyed the group. "Every frame from both Mike and Kate's visits, plus any footage we can find from the other clinics Marcus investigated."

Star was already typing. "Pulling emergency backup servers now. They know we're closing in. If they're altering records—"

"They might have missed the security footage," Lawrence finished, nodding. "Basic detective work. People always forget about the cameras."

"We'll work in shifts," Jack decided. "Cross-reference

everything. Medical staff, orderlies, anyone who had contact with the victims on Marcus's list."

Griffin stood abruptly. "I'll take first shift."

Maya caught the look Ronan and Axel exchanged. None of them liked the edge in Griffin's voice, but they needed answers.

Maya touched Ronan's arm lightly. "Take a break. I'll start the first review."

He studied her face—the concern there wasn't just professional anymore. "You picking up profiling habits from your dad?"

"No." A ghost of a smile touched her lips. "Just getting better at reading you."

The moment stretched between them until Deke cleared his throat. "Before we dive in, might be good to take five. Say a prayer for Marcus. For all of them."

Griffin's shoulders tensed. "Prayer didn't save those vets."

"No," Deke agreed quietly. "But it gave Marcus the courage to act when he saw something wrong. Sometimes that's all we can do—recognize evil and stand against it."

Ronan felt the weight of those words. He'd spent years putting barriers between himself and faith, between himself and connection. In hindsight, that might have been the wrong choice.

31

MIDNIGHT INTEL

THE COFFEE BURNED HER THROAT, but at least it gave her hands something to do besides shake. Maya was five cups deep into the night, riding the edge between caffeine jitters and post-firefight adrenaline crash. Eight hours since the warehouse. Since the gunfire and the running and watching Ronan take that hit. The memory made her chest tight all over again.

The massive command center felt oddly intimate with just the core team remaining. Ethan and Christian maintained their silent vigil at the bank of monitors while Griffin wore a path in the carpet behind them. Ronan hadn't moved from the satellite feed station in over an hour, though Maya caught him watching Griffin's pacing in the screen's reflection. Her father and Victoria had taken up positions at the conference table, presumably to review evidence, though they seemed more interested in trading meaningful glances when they thought no one was looking. The others had been ordered to rest, leaving the night shift to those too wired or worried to sleep.

Her dad's soft snoring broke the silence. He'd dozed off

watching Victoria work, his face softer than Maya had seen it in years. Even in sleep, he angled toward the journalist like a flower tracking the sun. Ronan's mom, with her sharp wit and flowing scarves, somehow managed to look elegant even after hours of crisis. Maya ran a hand through her own practical bob, feeling the sweat-stiff strands. She'd never been that kind of woman. Never sparked that kind of fascination in men. She was all clean lines and quiet competence, like the moths that visited her apartment's porch light—drawn to brightness but forever in the shadows of more brilliant creatures.

She shifted in her chair, every muscle screaming. She'd never run like that before, never felt such pure animal terror mixed with fierce determination. Her palms still stung from catching herself on concrete, and her shoulder ached where she'd slammed into a wall during their escape. But they'd made it. They were alive.

The command center's blue-tinged quiet felt surreal after the chaos. Maya watched faces flicker past on her monitor, fighting exhaustion. She was starting to understand what had drawn her father to this life—the razor's edge of purpose and danger, the rush of facing impossible odds. The way it forged bonds nothing else could touch.

Maybe that's what he saw in Ronan's driven mom. That spark of shared danger and purpose that Maya had always been too careful, too controlled to chase. She'd built her life around being reliable. Dependable. The steady one who kept the wheels turning while others chased excitement.

But today had changed something. Running for their lives, heart pounding, every sense razor-sharp—she'd felt more alive than in all her years of careful planning.

Her gaze drifted to Ronan across the room. Even injured, he radiated that quiet authority she'd noticed from minute one. But now she understood it better. She'd seen him in action, maintaining control even while bleeding, getting his team out safely. The kind of leadership her father used to talk about, back when she was young enough to still hero-worship his war stories.

A movement caught her attention—Ronan shifting in his chair, trying to hide a wince. Her chest tightened again. The image of blood spreading across his sleeve was still too fresh. For the first time in her life, she understood the kind of fear that could make someone reckless. The kind that made you forget about being careful and controlled.

"You should rest," she said quietly.

"I'm fine." But he met her eyes, and something passed between them in that look. Understanding. Concern. Maybe something more.

A sharp chime cut through the quiet.

"Got something," Ethan called from his station.

Maya moved to look, very aware of Ronan doing the same. Their shoulders brushed as they leaned in. On the screen, a grainy image showed a man in blue scrubs loading samples into a van.

"Facial recognition got a hit," Ethan said. "Guy's name is Trevor Abramian. Works for Pacific Coast Medical Labs as a courier."

"And?" Austin prompted.

"And he moonlights as a security guard. For Sentinel Security, among others."

The room went quiet. Maya felt Ronan tense beside her.

"Could be nothing," Christian said slowly. "Lots of guys work multiple jobs these days. Especially in San Diego."

"Run his financials," Ronan ordered.

Ethan typed. "Three part-time security gigs. Rent's eating half his income. Looks like he spends the other half on bodybuilding supplements and video games. Nothing suspicious in his bank records."

Lawrence stirred in his chair. "Why is a private lab picking up VA samples anyway? Don't they have their own facilities?"

"They do," Griffin confirmed. "Full labs at every major center."

"Track the van," Ronan said. "Where did those samples go?"

Ethan pulled up traffic cam footage, following the white van's progress through San Diego streets. "Looks normal. Straight to Pacific Coast Labs, right on schedule."

Maya felt the team's energy deflating. Another dead end.

"Wait." Ronan leaned closer. "Can you access the lab's delivery logs? See what happened to those samples?"

"Give me a minute." Ethan's typing intensified. "Okay, got it. Samples logged in at 2:47 p.m. by ... huh."

"What?"

"Different name. Dr. James McClelland signed for them."

Griffin went very still. "McClelland? I know that name. Marcus had it in his notes."

"Running facial recognition now," Ethan said. "Tapping into the lab's security footage from—" He stopped abruptly.

An overweight Caucasian man in a lab coat was handing a box to a tall, stubbled forty-something man with stiff, military bearing. Handsome, but stark. Cruel, even.

"That's impossible," Christian said sharply.

"No. Way." Austin blinked hard. "No. Way."

Ronan jabbed a finger at the screen. "And he is?"

"Reynaldo Pantone." Christian's voice rose in disbelief. "Chief Operations Officer of Sentinel Security."

Ethan's hands were already moving. "Cross-referencing Abramian's delivery schedule with Marcus's list of missing vets."

Screens flickered as data populated. Maya watched the

dates flash by, her throat tight. Three months ago. Two months. Six weeks ...

"There." Griffin's voice was like gravel. "Every time a vet disappeared, Abramian had picked up samples from their VA clinic somewhere between three and ten days beforehand."

"And every batch went to McClelland personally," Ethan added. "He's not showing his face at the VA clinics. He's got Abramian doing the legwork, then handles the samples himself at the lab."

Ronan grunted. "And we've got proof of the connection between Pantone and McClelland. On the day, a set of samples was delivered to a Pacific lab no less."

"Perfect deniability," Lawrence said, fully awake now. "Private security company with military contracts. A legitimate medical lab as cover ..."

"Whatever they're doing with those biological samples, it ain't good," Griffin muttered.

"It's on now." Frowning hard, Christian pulled out his cell. "Time to get Jack."

32

NIGHT KITCHEN

RONAN LEANED against the conference room wall, using the pressure to brace his injured arm. The pain meds were wearing off again, but he kept his expression neutral. Three a.m., and the room hummed with barely contained energy despite the hour.

The scent of Christian's stress-baking filled the air—fresh croissants, cinnamon rolls, something with chocolate. The pastries covered one end of the long table, alongside a professional-grade espresso machine. Steam hissed as he pulled another shot.

Jack stood at the head of the table, sleeves pushed up, hair standing on end. He studied the screens where Star had arranged their evidence in neat columns: Abramian's delivery routes, McClelland's lab records, Pantone's connection to Sentinel Security.

"Walk me through it again," Jack said. "From the beginning."

Dale Bosch, a Knight Tactical member and former NCIS director, tapped his tablet. Despite being called in at 0300, the man looked pressed and polished. "Sentinel Security has government contracts, more of them than we do, so they have easy access to military installations, VA facilities, and for sure sensitive operations."

Austin reached for his third espresso. "And their COO is paying visits to the doctor in charge of processing stolen biometric data from veterans."

"Who end up dead," Axel added quietly.

Kenji cleared his throat. "The VA contracts out some lab work, but nothing this specialized. And definitely not identity verification protocols."

Ronan watched Maya's father study the evidence. The retired investigator's rumpled appearance couldn't hide his sharp focus. Like father, like daughter.

Griff paced near the windows, while Zara and Star huddled over laptops. Izzy cleaned her sidearm, the repetitive motion betraying her tension. Deke and Maya sat silent, but Ronan could practically see them gaming out tactical scenarios in their heads.

"We can't just walk into Sentinel Security and start asking questions," Christian said, sliding fresh espressos in front of Jack and Bosch. "They've got too much legitimate cover."

"And political protection," Bosch added. "Their CEO plays golf with three senators."

Jack bit his lip. "I'll run this new intel by the admiral, but I can tell you, he'll want us to dig deeper before he runs any of this past Buck Richardson."

"The lab, then," Ronan said, pushing off the wall and ignoring the flare of pain. "Pacific Coast Medical. That's where the evidence is."

Jack's eyes narrowed, studying him. "You're thinking infiltration?"

"For sure. We need proof of what they're doing with those samples. How they're building the identity packages if that's really what they're doing."

"And fast," Griffin added. "They'll notice Kate and Mike's disappearances pretty quick. They'll be cleaning house."

The room went quiet except for the soft whir of laptops and the espresso machine's hum. Ronan felt the weight of Jack's assessment. He kept his posture carefully neutral, refusing to show weakness.

"Thoughts?" Jack asked the room.

"Maybe it's time to shine a spotlight on this," Ronan's mom suggested. "I know the news directors at every major station. We could—"

Ronan bit back a groan. "Mom, stop. We're messing with classified intel. You'd just get shut down. Or arrested."

Whether because of the pain radiating from his wound, or the lack of sleep, or just the constant pressure of being around his mother and his silent bio bro, irritation flashed through him. But it quickly dissipated. Victoria might have been a mostly absentee mom, but the woman loved him. Almost as much as she loved being in the center of the action.

"McClelland's the weak link." Jack redirected the conversation.

Exactly what he'd been thinking. "So we grab him, make him talk. He'll crack."

"Kidnapping?" Maya's voice cut through the tension. "That's a federal offense."

"Yeah? And? So is murder. They killed Tank. And your partner. We don't even know how many others. I'll risk a little kidnapping."

Axel crossed his arms over his massive chest. "Copy that, bro."

"He's right," Griffin said, knuckles white around his coffee cup. "I'm all for it."

Christian shook his head. "Think this through, guys. If we grab McClelland, Pantone knows instantly. Best case, they scatter. Worst case, they eliminate loose ends and take their operation underground."

"More bodies," Austin agreed. "We need something concrete linking the VA samples to Pantone without tipping our hand."

Griffin slammed his cup down, coffee sloshing. "How?"

The raw pain in the man's voice filled the room. Ronan pushed off the wall, ignoring his shoulder's protest, and crossed to his friend. He placed a hand on Griffin's shoulder, steady pressure grounding him. "We'll get them. The right way. So it sticks. So they can't wiggle out on technicalities." He held Griffin's gaze until some of the fury ebbed. "Tank and Tom Benson deserve a conviction that holds up in court. So do all those vets who 'disappeared.'"

The room went quiet, watching the exchange. Even his mom's perfect composure softened slightly.

He felt Maya's gaze on him as he steadied Griffin, and when he looked up, their eyes met. Something in her expression had changed—less wariness, more ... what? Understanding? Respect? The intensity of her dark eyes made him want to look away and hold her gaze at the same time. He was used to people seeing the soldier, the commander, the man of action. But Maya saw deeper, and that unsettled him in ways he wasn't ready to examine.

He forced his attention back to Griff, to the mission, to anything but the way Maya's presence filled his awareness even from across the room.

Jack's expression tightened. "We need to be careful here. Pantone could be operating independently. One corrupt executive doesn't necessarily implicate all of Sentinel Security."

"Agreed." Ronan straightened, shoulder protesting. "Which means we need to tackle this from two angles. First, is Pantone a lone operator, or is Sentinel involved? Second ..." He met Griffin's haunted eyes. "What's worth killing for?

What are they doing with those samples that requires eliminating witnesses?"

The questions landed heavy in the pre-dawn quiet.

Zara's hands stilled above her keyboard. "I think I know," she breathed. "Biological passports. They've got everything they need—DNA, fingerprints, complete medical histories, military credentials ..."

"Z's right. Perfect foundation for foolproof forgeries," Kenji added. "The kind that would pass any biometric verification system."

Lawrence frowned. "But fake IDs are a dime a dozen. Even good ones. Give me an hour and I could get you ten of them. Why go to these lengths?"

The answer punched Ronan in the gut. "Because they're not building street-level forgeries. They're creating military credentials. The kind that get you past nuclear facility checkpoints. Biological screening. Classified installations."

The room went dead silent.

"Two teams," Jack said finally. "We split this. One group investigates Pantone, the other gets proof of what that lab is really producing."

Ronan nodded. "Zara, Star, Ethan—you're our best bet for tracing Pantone's digital footprint."

"But you'll need a techie to run the VA op," Star pointed out. "I say Ethan and Zara work the Pantone angle here. I'll go with the team."

"Belay that," Ethan spoke up. "I'll go. You and Zara have a better handle on the new AI protocols. I got this."

Star kissed her husband on the cheek before addressing the group. "See? He's learning. Instead of an order, he makes it a compliment. Smooth move, Mr. Hernandez. Very smooth."

The cyber-security operative grinned hard. "Sometimes you can teach an old dog new tricks."

It was a good move. Ronan had to admit, he would have flat ordered his wife to stay back. He could learn a thing or two from these domesticated warriors.

"Good plan," Jack agreed. "The rest of us hit the lab."

"Not you." Jack's voice was firm. "That arm needs time."

"I'm going." Ronan kept his voice level, but his hands clenched. They weren't sidelining him. Not for this.

To his surprise, Maya spoke up. "He goes." Her tone brooked no argument. "But you stay in the van," she added, fixing Ronan with a look that somehow managed to be both commanding and concerned. "That's non-negotiable."

Ronan held her gaze, fighting a smile. "Deal." Behind his back, his fingers crossed—an automatic gesture he hadn't used since childhood. But something in Maya's eyes said she knew exactly what he was thinking.

He'd worry about that later. Right now, they had work to do. And less than five hours to plan for it.

33

HIGH WIRE

MAYA'S HANDS shook as she adjusted her scratchy polyester scrubs, already damp with sweat in the August heat. The badge hanging from her neck felt like a noose—"Angela Sanders, Lab Assistant"—complete with her photo altered just enough to match her current appearance.

"Run it one more time," Jack said, studying the clinic's layout on his tablet. "Everyone clear on why Maya's going in?"

"Because I'm the least valuable in a tactical situation," Maya said dryly.

"No." Ronan's voice was sharp. "Because we need our combat-trained operators positioned for rapid response if this goes sideways. You've got the investigative experience to know what we're looking for, but Christian and Kenji need to be free to move if you need extraction."

"And I've got their surveillance feeds on a continuous loop," Ethan added from behind one of his multiple laptops. "No one's going to see any faces we don't want them to see."

Christian nodded. "Maya finds what we need. We stay ready to get her out. Clean and simple."

Simple. Right. Maya pushed her fake glasses higher, the unfamiliar weight strange on her nose. The thick headband pulled her hair back severely, making her face look smaller, more uncertain. Perfect for the role of nervous junior lab tech. Her heart hammered against her ribs—method acting at its finest.

"Run the entry sequence again," Ronan said beside her, his voice low and steady. Even confined to the van, he radiated contained energy. Maya caught the slight wince as he shifted, though he tried to hide it.

"Enter through the staff entrance," she recited, fingering the lanyard. "Badge in, check my phone like I'm confirming directions."

"Good. Then?"

"Follow the route Star mapped out. Second floor, east wing. Records room." Her voice caught. "Pretty different from serving warrants with LAPD."

"That's why you've got us." Jack's voice was reassuring. "You find the evidence, we handle the rest."

"And that's why I'm stuck in this stupid van," Ronan muttered.

"Team Two in position," Christian's voice crackled through their earpieces. "Security's light—one guard at reception, one patrolling. Kenji and I are ready at the north entrance to create a distraction, if needed."

"Cameras looped," Ethan confirmed. "You're clear, Maya."

"Remember," Kenji added, "if anyone questions you, you're covering Jessica's shift. She's out with food poisoning. All the details are in your phone if they ask."

Maya nodded, throat tight. Ronan's hand found hers, warm and calloused. The simple touch steadied her more than she wanted to admit.

"Jack, we're ready," he said.

"Green light," Jack's voice came through. "Maya, you're up."

She reached for the door handle, but Ronan kept hold of her hand. "Hey." His voice was soft, just for her. "I've got your back. We all do."

"Thought you were staying in the van," she managed a weak smile.

"Close enough to get to you if needed."

"But not as close as he'd like to be." From the back of the van, Izzy muttered to Axel, "They're not fooling anyone."

Maya felt heat creep into her cheeks, but Ronan just smiled—that rare, genuine smile that transformed his whole face. "Go show these Special Forces boys how LAPD gets it done."

She stepped into the suffocating heat, letting her shoulders curl inward, making herself smaller. Less confident. Her sensible shoes scuffed against sunbaked concrete as she approached the staff entrance, while behind her, the weight of her team's presence felt like armor.

Maya swiped her badge with deliberate hesitation, letting out a small breath when the light turned green. The blast of AC hit her as she entered, raising goosebumps on her sweaty skin. Inside, the clinic had that universal medical facility feel—linoleum floors, fluorescent lights, the sharp bite of disinfectant.

She fumbled with her phone, the way Star had coached her. New employees always checked directions, double-checked room numbers. She'd seen it countless times during investigations—the way uncertainty made people smaller, less noticeable.

"Guard at the desk is streaming the Dodgers game," Christian murmured in her ear. "You're clear."

The elevator doors opened with a tired ding. Maya stepped inside, pressed two, and used the moment alone to steady her breathing. Not so different from undercover work with LAPD. Except for the team of Special Forces operators backing her up.

"Doing great," Ronan's voice was warm in her earpiece. "Maintenance cart heading this way—hold the elevator on two until it passes."

She jabbed the 'door closed' button as the elevator settled. The squeak of wheels passed, then faded.

"Clear," Austin confirmed. "Kenji, Christian—you've got eyes on both stairwells?"

"Locked down," Christian replied. "We've got your exit routes covered, Maya."

She stepped out, hearing the soft buzz of voices from the labs down the hall. Real techs, doing real work. Her pulse quickened.

"Left at the water fountain," Kenji directed. "Records room is third door."

She rounded the corner and nearly collided with a man in a lab coat. Her heart stopped.

"Oh! Sorry!" She fumbled her phone, letting it clatter to the floor. "I'm so sorry. I'm new, covering for Jessica, and I'm completely turned around …"

The man barely glanced at her, stepping around with a distracted, "No problem."

"Nice recovery," Ronan said softly in her ear. "You're doing fine."

She retrieved her phone with shaking hands, the badge swinging against her chest. Twenty more feet to the records room. Nineteen. Eighteen …

Maya swiped her badge at the records room door, her heart stuttering until the lock clicked open. She slipped inside, into cool darkness broken only by the glow of computer monitors.

"I'm in," she whispered. "Now what?"

The room smelled of paper and electronics. Rows of filing cabinets stretched into shadows. A desk near the door offered a clear view of the entrance. Maya slid into the chair, trying not to think about whose workspace she was invading.

"Plug in the USB," Ethan directed. "It'll auto-launch and copy their database structure. Look for anything dated in the last three months."

Maya's fingers trembled as she inserted the drive. The screen flickered, lines of code scrolling past.

"Lab tech heading your way." Christian warned in her ear.

"Hide the USB," Ronan ordered. "Look busy."

Maya minimized the window of the copying program and pulled up a random file just as footsteps approached. They continued on down the hallway. She let out a shaky breath.

"Transfer at twenty percent," Ethan reported. "Keep an eye on that door."

"Guys," Austin cut in, "McClelland just pulled into the parking lot."

Maya's stomach dropped. In her ear, she heard Ronan curse softly.

"McClelland's taking the east elevator," Austin reported.

"Time for plan B." Christian's voice was steady. "Kenji?"

"On it. Maya, you'll hear a code blue announcement. That's your cue to get out."

"Transfer at sixty percent," Star said. "We need three more minutes."

A minute later, the man himself strode into view, white coat billowing around his thighs as he strode down the hallway. Head down, he eyed the tablet in his hand, frowning.

Maya's mouth went dry as she watched him approach. No reason he'd head into the room. She had to stay calm. She forced herself to breathe normally, to look busy but not suspicious. After all, she was supposed to be in the building

—just another lab tech covering a shift. If he entered, she'd plead ignorance. Wasn't this Jessica's station?

He had no way of knowing what was on her screen, no reason to question her presence. Still, her pulse thundered in her ears as his footsteps drew closer. Suddenly, alarms blared. "Code Blue, Lab Three! Code Blue, Lab Three!"

McClelland's head snapped up. He hesitated, then hurried onward, toward the labs on the far side of the floor. Maya watched him disappear around the corner.

"Transfer at eighty-five percent," Ethan said.

Through her earpiece, Maya heard the controlled chaos Kenji and Christian were creating. Something about contaminated samples and exposure risks. They had the entire floor's attention.

"Ninety-five percent. And transfer complete," Ethan announced. "Get out. Now."

Maya yanked the USB free and stood—then froze. Footsteps and voices were approaching from both directions—McClelland returning from the false alarm, and what sounded like security responding to his call about unauthorized access to the records system.

She was boxed in. The elevator would be watched, the stairs monitored. McClelland, or the security team that would follow, would be well within his rights to have the new temporary employee—who wasn't even supposed to be in the computer area—searched.

Which left only one option.

"Window," Ronan's voice was tight. "The maintenance ledge."

Her hands shook as she eased the window open. Four stories up, the late afternoon sun threw harsh shadows across the narrow, concrete ledge. It had looked manageable during planning. Now, with her sweaty hands and trembling legs, it looked impossible.

Maya hesitated.

"You've got this," Ronan's voice steadied her. "Just like we practiced."

She swung one leg out, then the other, pressing her back against the rough brick. The polyester scrubs caught against the wall as she inched sideways.

She tried not to look down. She tried not to think about the wind that lifted her loose scrub top, or the way her sensible shoes offered zero grip on the ledge.

Three shuffling steps. Her thigh muscles burned. A bird swooped past, startling her, and her fingers scraped against the brick as she caught herself. Four more steps.

"Almost there," Ronan murmured in her ear. The tension in his voice told her he was watching through the surveillance feed. "Fire escape is just past the drainpipe."

The metal platform seemed miles away. Her glasses slipped down her nose, and she didn't dare adjust them. Inside, she heard voices growing closer to the records room. Any second now, they'd discover the transfer.

Maya's law enforcement training screamed at her with every unauthorized step. Breaking and entering. Corporate espionage. If she was caught, her career wouldn't just be over—she'd be facing federal charges. Everything she'd worked for, destroyed in one afternoon.

But then she thought of Marcus and Tom. Of Kate and Mike, who'd barely escaped. Of all those veterans who hadn't. Sometimes justice needed a push. Sometimes the system that was supposed to protect people became the very thing enabling their destruction.

Her foot slipped, heart lurching as pebbles skittered down the building's face. The by-the-book FBI agent in her head was still listing federal statutes she was violating, but another voice was stronger now—the voice that had first drawn her to law enforcement. The one that said protecting people mattered more than protecting protocols.

"Maya." Ronan's voice again, somehow knowing she needed the anchor. "You're doing great. Just keep moving."

That voice. The one that had been systematically dismantling her careful professional boundaries since day one. The one that made her question everything she thought she knew about right and wrong, about duty and justice. About herself.

She reached the fire escape with trembling arms, metal ringing dully under her feet as she practically fell onto the platform. No time to recover. Voices erupted from the records room behind her as she flew down the stairs, each clang of her footsteps echoing off the building's face. The last flight swayed under her descent.

Heart pounding, she flew down the stairs, jumped the last few feet to the pavement, and ran. She burst out of the alley into blazing sunlight. Ronan stood in the middle of the parking lot, tension radiating from every line of his body. Their eyes met.

Maya's face split into a fierce grin as she jogged toward him, USB drive clutched tight in her hand. She'd done it.

"I told you to stay in the van," she said as she reached him, breathless and triumphant.

His answering smile was equal parts relief and pride. "And I told you I had your back."

For a split second, time stopped. The sun caught his features exactly right, softening the usual hard edges, and Maya felt that familiar flutter in her chest. He looked at her like she'd just conquered the world, not just stolen some files. Like she was someone worth breaking protocol for, worth leaving the safety of the van for. It was the kind of look that made her wonder what else he might break the rules for.

And how much she wanted to find out.

"If you two are done making eyes at each other," Jack's voice cut in, "let's move. McClelland's calling security."

They ran for the van together, Maya's victory thrumming through her veins. Behind them, alarms wailed.

34

FREEFALL

The van's door slid shut with a bang that matched Ronan's thundering pulse. His hands wouldn't stop shaking—leftover adrenaline from watching Maya traverse that ledge, four stories up. He'd made the call. He'd told her to do it. And now the image of her balanced on that narrow strip of concrete was burned into his brain.

He'd done hundreds of ops, lost good operators, buried friends. But watching her out there, knowing he couldn't reach her ... The fear had been different. Visceral. Personal in a way that terrified him more than any firefight.

Maya sprawled in the seat beside him, face flushed, eyes bright with triumph, clutching that stupid USB drive like a trophy. "Mission accomplished," she said, her grin infectious, reckless. Beautiful.

He tried to return her smile, to share in her victory, but his chest was too tight. She'd done exactly what they'd trained for, executed it perfectly. So why couldn't he shake this bone-deep dread?

Jack took a corner too fast, tires squealing. Ronan's shoulder slammed into the van's wall, sending pain shooting down his arm. The physical pain was almost welcome—easier to handle than the emotional chaos threatening to overwhelm him.

"You okay?" Maya's hand was on his arm, her victory-high instantly replaced with concern.

"Fine." He wasn't. Not even close. The image of her on that ledge was on repeat in his head. One slip. One wrong move. His good hand clenched into a fist. Years leading Special Forces ops, and he'd never felt this off-balance. This exposed. This vulnerable.

They'd practiced the maneuver at Knight Tactical Headquarters, but that had been different. Controlled. With safety gear and spotters. He'd never actually expected her to have to actually do it. Had never anticipated how it would feel to watch her take that risk, knowing all he could do was talk her through it.

"That," Christian called from the back, peeling off his lab coat, "was some seriously impressive improvisation, Maya."

"It was seriously something," he muttered, before he could stop himself.

"The ledge was your idea, remember?" Kenji added, grinning.

"That was theoretical." He clenched his jaw. "Not a fourth-story reality." Not watching someone he was falling for risk her life while he sat helpless in a van. The thought hit him like a physical blow. *Falling for her*. When had that happened?

Maya's triumphant smile faltered. "You're the one who told me to use the window exit."

"Because we were out of options." His voice came out clipped, tight. Clinical. "Not because it was a good plan."

"It worked." But the victory had drained from her voice, replaced by something harder. More defensive.

"Children," Jack's voice carried from the driver's seat, "save the lovers' quarrel for later. Ethan, what did we get?"

Ronan's gaze slid away from her face, down to her trembling hands. She'd been scared too, he realized. She'd just handled it better than he did. That knowledge should have made him feel better. Instead, it twisted something in his gut. She'd do it again. Without hesitation. It was who she was.

"Downloading now," Ethan announced. "Wow. Maya, this is ... this is everything. Collection protocols, processing procedures, even a client wish list of orders ..."

"See?" Maya's smile was softer now, just for him. "Worth a little ledge-walking."

The intimacy in her expression punched him straight in the solar plexus. He couldn't do this. Couldn't watch her take these risks, knowing how he felt. Couldn't let his feelings compromise either of their safety. Some ugly tangle there.

"Next time, we find a different exit strategy." His voice was flat, professional. Distant.

"Next time?" Her eyebrows arched. "Planning to get me into more trouble, Commander Quinn?"

"Planning to keep you out of it," he muttered. The high of completing a successful op was wearing off way faster than usual, replaced by cold certainty. He had to shut this down. Now. Before it went any further.

"These two are worse than a Hallmark movie," Christian stage-whispered to Kenji.

"Shut up," Ronan barked, his sharp tone making Maya flinch. She studied his face, confusion replacing her earlier warmth. He forced himself to look away, to focus on the mission. It was better this way. Had to be.

35

CRUISING ALTITUDE

Half an hour later, the sleek jet had left the LA Basin far behind.

Maya leaned her head against the aircraft's small window, watching the sun-bleached sky cruise past. The vibration of the plane's engine thrummed through her body, matching the lingering buzz of adrenaline in her veins. She'd never felt anything like it—the crystalline clarity of action, the pure focus of mission parameters, the rush of split-second decisions that worked.

Now she understood why people got addicted to this life.

Across the aisle, Ronan sat rigid, staring straight ahead, jaw clenched. He hadn't said two words to her since they'd boarded. The warmth from their earlier moments in the van had vanished, replaced by this ... wall. She'd seen him shift moods before, but this was different. Colder. Almost angry.

She closed her eyes, forcing herself to breathe deeply. It wasn't her job to figure him out. She'd learned that lesson the hard way with her father—some people just ran hot and cold. Trying to navigate their emotional weather patterns only left you exhausted and confused.

The mission was successful. They had the data. No one got hurt. That's what mattered.

Still ... she couldn't help remembering how his hand had felt on hers in the van, the way his eyes had softened when she'd made it back safely. For a moment there, she'd thought ...

Stop it, she told herself firmly. Focus on the win. On how good it felt to contribute, to use her skills in a whole new way. To prove she belonged on this team, whether Ronan Quinn approved or not.

Rays of sunlight caught the wing, flashing golden. She bowed her head, letting the familiar words of gratitude flow through her mind. *Thank You for watching over us. For keeping us safe. For giving me the strength and clarity to do what needed to be done.*

The plane banked slightly, beginning its descent to Hope Landing. She straightened, squaring her shoulders. She was an NCIS agent who'd just completed her first successful covert operation. She'd scaled a building, outsmarted security, and retrieved crucial evidence.

If Ronan Quinn wanted to sulk about it, that was his problem.

But even as she thought it, she caught him watching her reflection in his window. For just a second, his expression was unguarded—something raw and afraid in his eyes that made her breath catch. Then he noticed her looking and the wall slammed back into place.

She turned back to her own window, puzzled and slightly unsettled. There was more going on here than just his usual mercurial moods. But that was a mystery for another day. She had a mission debrief to focus on, and the lingering sweet taste of victory to savor.

Star's voice crackled over the plane's comm system, startling her. "Hope Landing One, this is Base. Got something you need to hear."

Ronan straightened in his seat, all business now. "Go ahead, Base."

"I played a hunch, and it worked." Star sounded smug. "We've got McClelland on tape admitting to the connection with Pantone."

"She's brilliant," Zara said. "I don't think it took her five minutes to digitize an AI Pantone voice that would fool any voice-activated security. Not that McClelland even questioned who he was actually talking to."

Austin grinned at them from the co-pilot seat. "This, I gotta hear."

"Coming right up," Star announced.

The recording filled the cabin, crisp and clear. "The collection rate isn't fast enough." The fake Pantone's voice was sharp. "We were supposed to deliver way more IDs by now. The buyer is getting impatient. You know that's not good."

"You try running a medical facility and keeping this quiet," McClellan snapped. "These protocols take time."

"Time we don't have. Double the intake. I don't care how you do it."

"And risk exposure? Your employer—"

"Sentinel isn't involved in this conversation. Just do your job, Doctor."

Maya watched Ronan's expression tighten at the mention of Sentinel.

Ethan clapped loudly. "Rock, on woman! Outstanding work."

"What do you think? Pretty good, huh?" Star prompted. "We used AI voice synthesis based on his press conferences and public appearances. McClellan bought it completely. His responses confirm Pantone's running this operation."

"But not whether he's acting alone or on Sentinel's orders," Jack added from the cockpit.

Maya watched the team process this. Christian and Kenji exchanged looks. Even Ethan stopped typing.

"We need to take this to the admiral," Christian said finally, breaking the silence. "He'll want to be read in before we make another move. Let him decide how to proceed."

"Agreed," Jack called back. "We're wheels down in ten. Maya, great work today."

Maya nodded, but her attention was on Ronan. The setting sun caught his profile, highlighting the tension in his jaw. Whatever was eating at him went deeper than just her ledge-walking stunt. She'd bet her badge on it.

But right now, they had bigger problems. An admiral to brief. A conspiracy to unravel. And somewhere in the gathering darkness, a former military official named Pantone who was selling out his own country, one stolen identity at a time.

The plane banked, giving Maya her first real overview of Hope Landing in the daylight. The valley spread out below them like something from a postcard—dense pine forests parting to reveal a small town nestled between two gleaming lakes. Lake Bigler's vast expanse stretched to the north, while tiny Reed Lake sparkled to the south.

"Density altitude's a beast in this heat," Jack announced from the cockpit. "Going to need every foot of runway."

Maya watched as they descended, the details of the town emerging from the landscape. So different from San Diego's sprawling concrete and endless coastline, boxed in by desert on three sides. Here, everything was green and wild and alive, the mountains rising protective walls around the valley.

She hadn't even had time to explore since arriving. Hadn't walked the neat downtown streets or hiked the trails she could see threading through the forest. Hadn't done anything but chase leads and dodge bullets.

The thought sobered her. Once this was over—assuming they survived it—there'd be no going back. Even if they cleared her name, she knew how federal agencies worked. They didn't forgive trouble-makers, didn't forget agents who made waves. Her career with NCIS was effectively over before it had really begun.

The plane touched down with a gentle bump, Jack compensating for the tricky altitude with practiced ease. Maya stared out at the forested valley, surprised by how little the thought of leaving NCIS bothered her. She could talk it through with Dale Bosch, get his perspective, but she already knew. Sometimes doors closed so others could open.

Unbidden, her mind painted a picture: a life here, in this mountain sanctuary. Morning runs around the lake, evenings watching sunset paint the peaks. A small house in the woods. A certain former Special Forces commander with storm-gray eyes and a rare, transformative smile ...

She shut that thought down hard. Whatever spark had been growing between them was dead. Ronan had made his feelings clear with his cold shoulder act. No point dreaming about impossible things.

"Maya?" Christian's voice broke through her reverie. "We're here."

She unbuckled, gathering her gear with deliberate focus. Dreams of what might have been would have to wait.

Still, as they deplaned under the late afternoon light, the air heavy with pine and summer heat, Maya couldn't quite shake the feeling that she'd found something here. Not just a case to solve or a wrong to right, but a place that called to her soul.

Whether it called to anyone else's remained to be seen.

36

FAMILIAR GROUND

Ronan strode into Knight Tactical's ops center, deliberately taking a position at the far end of the conference table. Through the floor-to-ceiling windows, late afternoon sun painted the valley in gold, a breathtaking view. He barely noticed.

His team filtered in behind him—Axel claiming the chair to his right, Kenji and Deke settling in across from them. The easy familiarity they'd developed over years of missions felt like a lifeline now. How many more times would they gather like this?

Once this op was over, they'd scatter. Back to their lives. Their homes. Their families. All the things he'd never managed to build.

Christian was already there with Ethan and Star, the three of them hunched over multiple screens. Jack and Austin disappeared to take a few hours with their families—something about their kids' soccer tournament. Must be nice, having somewhere to go, someone waiting. Someone who mattered more than the next mission.

Zara and Izzy occupied their usual corner, heads bent over

laptops. Griff lounged against the wall, his usual sardonic expression in place. "Nice of you to join us, boss."

The nickname hit harder than usual. Once this was over ... what? Back to ferrying questionable cargo in a beaten-up plane? Starting over somewhere new? Alone?

Christian glanced up, his expression unreadable. Whatever tentative understanding they'd reached as brothers felt fragile in the fluorescent lights of the ops center. Another relationship he'd probably manage to screw up, given time.

Maya entered last, taking a seat near the door. The physical distance between them felt like miles. Good. That's what he wanted.

Maybe if he reminded himself enough, he'd come to believe it.

A massive screen flickered to life, revealing Admiral Knight on what appeared to be his yacht's bridge. Even at zero one hundred Mediterranean time, the man radiated energy that put Ronan's exhausted team to shame. Behind him, moonlight silvered the calm waters, the night sky perfectly clear in that way unique to the Italian coast.

Ronan fought back another yawn. After thirty-six hours with no real sleep, the admiral's alertness felt like a personal attack. Around the table, his team wasn't faring much better. Even Christian had given up pretense, his third coffee of the hour going cold beside his laptop. But the admiral looked ready to take on the world, his intense focus a reminder of how he'd earned that fourth star.

"I've been trying to contact Buck Richardson since Jack clued me in on your latest intel. He's gone dark," Knight began without preamble, the time difference clearly irrelevant to his concerns. The tension in his face stood out sharply in the bridge's low lighting. "I can't find anyone that's heard from him since yesterday morning ..."

"That tracks with the timeline we're seeing, sir." Zara

studied her monitor. "All Sentinel's secure channels went quiet after Maya's infiltration."

Star leaned forward, her usual energy subdued. "We're seeing systematic shutdowns across their network, Admiral. Like they're—"

"They're purging systems," Maya added. "Standard procedure after—"

"After a breach," Ronan finished, then immediately regretted it. Their tactical synchronization was still perfect.

But instead of the smile that would have earned him a day ago, this time, hurt flashed across her face before she masked it.

Keep things professional, he reminded himself silently. *Mission focus only.*

Across the table, Christian's eyebrows lifted slightly. Axel shot him a look that said he wasn't fooling anyone. Ronan ignored them both, just like he ignored the hollow ache in his chest every time Maya spoke. Just like he ignored the way everyone in the room was pretending not to notice the growing tension between them.

Professional. Distant. Safe.

"What about the medical records?" Kenji asked, his usual calm voice carrying an edge. The team medic had taken the VA deaths personally—they all had, but for him it was different. These were people he might have treated, might have saved.

"Working on decryption," Zara replied, sharing a screen with Ethan. The two tech experts had been trading coding duties for hours, their usual competitive banter replaced by grim focus. "But the preliminary analysis shows they're running a network."

Deke leaned forward, his quiet presence drawing attention. "The question is why. What's the endgame?" The former chaplain's eyes held that penetrating look Ronan had learned to respect—and sometimes fear. Like he could see straight through people's defenses to their core.

"Whatever it is," Griff said from his position by the wall, "it's big enough to spook Richardson into hiding."

Christian straightened, his tactical mind visibly engaging. "That man doesn't spook easily. I've known him for years through the admiral. This isn't like him."

"Unless he knew we were coming," Star added. "The timing of the systems shutdown—"

"They knew exactly what we'd found," Maya finished.

He'd been about to make the same observation. Again, with the perfect tactical synchronization. Ronan forced himself not to look at her, but he could feel her presence across the room like a physical thing.

The admiral's voice cut through their speculation. "Which is why I'm heading back. Minerva's meeting the kids in Capri—that'll keep her occupied while I help you all handle this mess."

"Sir," Christian started, leaning forward, "given the security implications—"

"This isn't up for debate, Murphy." The admiral's tone brooked no argument, but there was something else in his expression. Pain, maybe. Betrayal. "Buck Richardson's been my friend for thirty years. No way I'm accusing a good man of treason. Not until we've got ironclad evidence. If he's involved in this, I want to look him in the eye when we take him down."

Ronan understood that kind of loyalty. That need to face betrayal head-on. It was part of what made walking away from Maya so hard ...

The admiral eyed an expensive dive watch. "Minerva's going to have a fit, but I can make it back to port in under three hours. That puts me in the air by zero five hundred local time at the worst. Then fifteen hours flight time, give or take. I'll be wheels down around twelve hundred local time." He eyed his drooping crew. "Let's call a meeting for thirteen hundred. In the meantime, get me as much intel as you can. And people? Go get some sleep. That's an order."

He ended the call, leaving them with action items and a growing sense of urgency.

Christian rose, clapping his hands together. "You heard the man. R and R, including serious rack time, is officially mandatory."

Before the group could disperse, the hangar door below burst open, admitting his mother in full force. Lawrence Chen trailed her up the stairs with an apologetic expression. "There you all are! I brought sustenance. Nobody thinks clearly on an empty stomach."

She brandished several bags from the DreamBurger outlet in the tiny airport terminal. Ronan's stomach betrayed him with a growl, even as his mother's presence made him tense further.

"Victoria," Christian started, "we're kind of in the middle of—"

"Of starving yourselves while overthinking everything?" She began distributing containers with military precision.

Axel pressed a hand to his flat belly. "Mrs. Quinn, you are the best."

Her smile dazzled. "Of course, I am. But I'm pleased to no end that you know it, dear."

Maya's dad caught Ronan's eye and shrugged helplessly. Clearly, he'd tried and failed to prevent this invasion.

Before Ronan could process the complicated emotions of his mother feeding his brother's team—his team—like they were all one big happy family, Maya approached his end of the table. "We should discuss the entry protocols."

"Send them to Kenji," Ronan cut her off, standing abruptly. "He'll coordinate with tactical."

He saw the flash of anger in her eyes, the slight straightening of her spine. "Right. Keep it professional. Got it."

She turned on her heel and walked out. The room fell awkwardly silent.

"Real smooth, boss," Griff commented dryly.

Victoria paused in her dumpling distribution, eyes sharp. "That young lady—"

"Mom." Ronan's voice held a warning even he rarely used. "Don't."

She pressed her lips together, clearly holding back whatever maternal wisdom she'd been about to dispense. Lawrence placed a gentle hand on her arm, and she subsided, but her eyes spoke volumes.

Axel paused, fries halfway to his mouth. "You're being an idiot," he muttered, too low for anyone else to hear.

"Whatever. Just stay focused," Ronan growled back.

"Oh, I am. Are you?"

Ronan ignored them all, gathering his papers with sharp movements. He needed air. Space. Distance. His future stretched out before him like a blank page—tattered, torn, and utterly empty. Just the way it had to be.

Just the way he'd chosen to make it.

"The burgers will get cold," his mother called after him as he headed for the door.

He kept walking. Behind him, he heard Axel accept a container with excessive enthusiasm, heard Christian thank their mother with careful politeness, heard the normal sounds of people connecting, belonging, building something he couldn't let himself have.

The door closed behind him with a final click.

Perfect. Now he had two women in his life he needed to avoid. At least his mother would keep trying. Maya was smart enough to know better.

37

RAW EDGES

THE NEXT MORNING, Ronan stared at his reflection in the bedroom window, hardly recognizing the man looking back at him. Dark circles shadowed his eyes, testament to another night of broken sleep. The nightmares had been worse than usual—Maya on that ledge, but this time she fell. Maya in that alley where her partner died, but this time he couldn't reach her in time. Maya bleeding out while he watched, helpless, useless ...

He scrubbed a hand over his face. Even awake, he couldn't escape her. Everything circled back to those moments of connection, that easy synchronization, the way she fit into his life like she'd always been there. And that was exactly the problem.

He couldn't do it. Couldn't watch her walk into danger day after day, knowing each mission could be her last. Her partner's execution had only confirmed what he already knew—law enforcement, intelligence work, it was all a game of Russian roulette. Eventually, the chamber wouldn't be empty.

A knock at his door interrupted his brooding. "Go away."

Axel pushed in anyway, bearing coffee and what smelled like Victoria's cinnamon rolls. "Thought you might need breakfast."

"What I need is to be left alone."

"Yeah, because that's working out so well for you." Axel set the offerings down with exaggerated care. "You look like hell, by the way."

"Thanks." Ronan's tone could have frozen lava. "Anything else?"

"Just trying to help, man."

"I don't need—"

Another knock cut him off. Christian this time, already dressed for working out. "Gym. Ten minutes."

"Pass. Got a headache."

Christian's expression hardened into what Ronan privately thought of as his commander face. "That wasn't a request, little brother. Team's waiting. And check the attitude, dude." He paused in the doorway, eyes glinting. "Make that five minutes, or I'm coming back to drag you down by that pretty hair of yours."

Axel snorted into his coffee. "You heard him, dude. I'm gonna guess he's not kidding."

Ronan didn't care. "Get out. Both of you."

Christian just smiled. "Four minutes now."

Axel followed his bio bro out. The door closed behind them with quiet finality. He gripped the windowsill, a wave of dizziness making the room tilt slightly. The pain meds were wearing off, but he couldn't take more on an empty stomach.

He slumped back onto the bed. Maya loved her work—it was obvious in every move she made, every insight she offered. He couldn't ask her to give that up. Wouldn't want her to be anything less than what she was. But he couldn't be the one waiting, wondering, watching the clock until she came home.

If she came home.

Better to end it now. Better to be the jerk who pushed her away than the man who held her back. Or worse, the man who had to bury her.

His phone buzzed—a text from Christian: *Three minutes.*

Ronan growled and pushed himself up. Fine. He'd go work out. Maybe physical exhaustion would quiet the voice in his head that kept whispering he was making the biggest mistake of his life.

He threw on some borrowed workout clothes and skulked downstairs to the gym like a man heading to his execution. If this was some kind of intervention, with Maya waiting ... but the scene that greeted him stopped him cold.

Eight teenagers occupied various stations around the gym, most of them built like brick walls, one wiry girl outlifting several of the boys. Hockey players, he realized, recognizing the Tahoe Grizzlies logo on their workout gear.

"Team," Christian's voice carried across the gym with practiced authority. "Special treat today. This is Commander Quinn, former Navy SEAL." There was unmistakable pride in his voice that made Ronan's head snap around. "He's going to show you what a real workout looks like. Or at least as much as he can with that gimpy arm of his."

The teenagers straightened immediately, athletic competitiveness sparking in their eyes. Ronan was still processing Christian's introduction when his brother clapped him on the shoulder. "Show them what you've got, Commander."

Oh it was on. He might not be able to participate much with a bum arm, but he could run them through the workout of their lives. He demonstrated what he could one-handed, his injured arm held carefully against his body. Even that small movement sent a warning pulse of pain through his body.

An hour later, even the cockiest player was dripping sweat, but their grins were infectious. Sophie, the wiry girl, had particularly impressive form on her burpees. Ronan found himself fully engaged, demonstrating techniques, getting pulled into their casual banter.

"Dude," one of the boys nudged another, "they do the same thing!"

"What thing?" Sophie asked, between sets.

"That weird neck crack before they demonstrate something. Look—Coach Murphy just did it, and Commander Quinn did it like three times during warm-up."

Both brothers froze, then turned to look at each other. Ronan hadn't even noticed the habit, but now that it was pointed out ...

Christian laughed, surprising Ronan again. "Well, might as well tell you—Commander Quinn here is actually my baby brother."

"Baby brother?" Sophie's eyes went wide. "No way!"

"Way," Christian grinned. "Though he hates when I call him that."

The easy way Christian owned their relationship, the obvious pride in his voice—threw Ronan off balance.

He leaned against the wall, trying to make it look casual rather than necessary. The room had taken on a subtle spinning quality that he didn't like at all. He should probably consult Kenji.

As they wrapped up, Sophie approached him. "Thanks, Commander Quinn. Think you could show me that modified pull-up sequence again next time? I mean, once your arm heals and everything."

Next time. The words hit him unexpectedly hard. "I, uh ..."

"He'll be here Thursday," Christian answered for him. "Can't let my little brother show me up with just one session, right?"

The last teenager waved goodbye, leaving the brothers alone in the suddenly quiet gym. Christian started racking weights, his movements automatic.

The room seemed to swim slightly. He'd been so focused on the kids, he hadn't noticed how the dull throb in his arm had escalated to a steady burn. Maybe he should have eaten those cinnamon rolls after all.

"Sophie's mom works three jobs," Christian said casually. "Dad's not in the picture. Kid taught herself to skate on borrowed gear at public sessions. Now she's looking at D1 scholarships."

Using his good arm, Ronan helped rerack a set of dumbbells. "Yeah?"

"Blue? Living with his grandma after both parents got locked up. Jamal's family lost everything in the Paradise fire, moved here for a fresh start. Every one of these kids has a story." Christian paused, something fierce in his expression. "But they show up. Every practice, every workout. Keep their grades up, stay clean. That's all I ask. Foundation covers the rest—gear, ice time, tournament fees."

"You're changing lives," Ronan said quietly, meaning it.

Christian shrugged, but Ronan caught the pleased look that crossed his face. "You should think about coaching. You're good with them."

Ronan barked out a laugh. "Right. The Hollywood kid who's never been on skates. That'll work great."

"You could learn—"

"Like you did? Growing up in Colorado with skiing trips and hunting weekends and perfect nuclear family ice skating sessions?" The bitterness in his voice surprised even him. "Besides, I'll be gone as soon as this mess is cleared up."

Christian stopped moving, turned to face him fully. "Gone where?"

"Somewhere." Ronan kept his eyes on the weight rack. "Haven't figured that out yet."

"Right. Because running away is definitely the answer." Christian's voice held an edge. "You know what these kids have taught me? Sometimes the hardest thing isn't surviving the bad stuff. It's learning to accept the good stuff when it comes along."

"Deep thoughts from Coach Murphy?" Ronan tried for sarcasm, but it fell flat.

"Just something to think about, little brother." Christian grabbed his water bottle, but before he could say more, the gym door opened.

Maya stood in the doorway, gym bag slung over one shoulder, early morning light casting her silhouette. For a moment, no one moved. The air hardened with unspoken words.

Her eyes met his for a fraction of a second before sliding away.

He managed a curt nod, focusing intently on rewrapping a loose jump rope, his movements precise. Professional. Distant.

She crossed to the far side of the gym, her steps measured, spine straight enough to make a drill sergeant proud. The soft thud of her bag hitting the floor echoed in the loaded silence.

Christian let out a low whistle. "You know, I wondered if you inherited your mom's emotional intelligence or Dad's complete lack of the same." He shouldered his bag. "Question answered."

"Shut up."

"Hey, just observing." Christian paused at the door.

"Though I gotta say, for a tactical genius, you're being impressively stupid right now."

The door closed behind him, leaving Ronan alone with the neatly racked weights, the perfectly coiled jump rope, and the growing certainty that he was systematically destroying every good thing in his life.

Nothing new there.

38

FIGHTING FORM

Maya waited until Ronan's footsteps faded before she unleashed her first punch at the heavy bag. The impact jarred through her wrapped knuckles, satisfaction mixing with fury. Another punch. And another. Each one harder than the last.

Wounded warrior act. Right.

She'd fallen for it like some rookie. Let herself believe there was something real beneath those walls he built. That all those moments of connection—finishing each other's tactical thoughts, moving in perfect sync during the op, the way he'd looked at her when he thought no one was watching—meant something.

The bag swung wildly as she landed a particularly vicious combination. Her father's voice cut through the rhythm of her strikes.

"Your elbow is dropping."

"Not now, Dad." She caught the bag, steadying it, refusing to turn around.

"Want to talk about it?"

Seriously? Hard no.

As if she needed to walk her father through the way she'd

let herself get played by another emotionally unavailable man with a hero complex. "Nope."

She heard him inhale sharply and immediately regretted the harsh response. It wasn't his fault her mother had left them both. Just like it wasn't his fault Maya had apparently inherited his terrible taste in partners.

"Maya—"

"I'm sorry." She finally turned to face him, saw the hurt in his eyes that he tried to hide. "That wasn't fair. I'm just ..."

"Angry?" His smile was gentle. "I remember that feeling."

"I thought ..." She slammed another punch into the bag, her voice tight. "I thought we were building something. Something real. I'm such an idiot."

"You're many things, sweetheart. An idiot isn't one of them."

She wanted to believe him. Wanted to believe she hadn't completely misread everything. But the memory of Ronan's cold dismissal, the way he wouldn't even look at her anymore, made her jaw clench.

"I need to shower." She unwrapped her hands with sharp, angry movements. "Got a briefing to prep for."

Her father stepped aside, letting her pass, but his quiet words followed her: "Sometimes people push away what they want most because they're afraid of losing it."

"Yeah?" She paused at the door. "Well, mission accomplished there."

The hallway offered no escape from her thoughts. Every corner held some memory—Ronan's laughter during their late-night strategy session, the brush of his shoulder against hers as they reviewed intel, that moment in the van when she'd thought ...

"Maya!"

She turned to find Zara hurrying toward her, tablet in hand, excitement radiating from every movement.

Zara grabbed her arm. "We cracked it. The medical records, the money trail, everything. Conference room, now. Everyone's assembling."

Maya glanced down at her workout clothes, then at her new friend's urgent expression. "Five minutes?"

As she hurried toward her room, she pushed everything else aside. She was good at that—compartmentalizing, focusing on the mission. It's what made her excellent at her job.

It's also what made her terrible at relationships.

39

DEEPER PATTERNS

THE CONFERENCE ROOM hummed with tension as Maya slipped into one of the few remaining seats—unfortunately, right next to Ronan. She forced herself to focus on Zara and Ethan, who were practically vibrating with nervous energy as they pulled up multiple screens of data.

"We found it," Zara announced. "The biological passports aren't just being collected—they're being sold. And we can prove who's buying."

Star nodded, highlighting a series of transactions. "These transfers all route through Cyprus shell companies, but look at the encryption signature."

"Krechet Strategic," Ronan said, leaning forward. Maya caught his slight wince—his shoulder was bothering him again, not that he'd admit it. "They're not even trying to hide it."

Maya shifted in her seat, hyperaware of his proximity. "For those of us who don't speak alphabet soup?"

"Russian military intelligence front," Ronan explained, his voice sliding into that focused tactical tone she'd grown to ... appreciate professionally. "They pose as independent contractors, but they're Kremlin muscle. Run by Mikhail Yastrebov—ex-FSB colonel with ties to Putin's inner circle."

"The biomarkers, the genetic profiles, the medical histories," Ethan added, pulling up more data. "They're not just stealing identities—they're buying complete biological passports."

The implications hit Maya like a physical blow. Her years with the LAPD had taught her to follow evidence trails, but this ... this was bigger than anything she'd imagined. She felt Ronan tense beside her, knew he'd reached the same conclusion.

"So we've got proof," she said, the words tasting like ash. "The Russians are—"

"Buying murdered veterans' identities to insert deep cover operatives," Ronan finished, their old synchronization betraying them both.

Across the table, Christian and Jack exchanged grim looks. Austin muttered something that sounded like a prayer. Deke's usually calm expression had hardened into something dangerous.

"Well," Griff drawled from his corner, breaking the heavy silence, "guess that explains why Pantone's nowhere to be found. Man's probably halfway to Moscow by now."

"If he's lucky," Axel added darkly.

Kenji leaned forward, medical training evident in his precise questioning. "The biomarkers in those samples—they weren't just for identification, were they?"

Star picked up the thread. "With this kind of data, they could create covers that would pass any DNA screening. Medical records, genetic histories, everything."

Maya felt sick. All those veterans ... all those families thinking their loved ones had died of natural causes ... Or disappeared. She clenched her jaw, trying to maintain professional distance. But when Ronan shifted slightly, his arm barely brushing hers, she couldn't help but react. The tiny contact sent electricity through her system, and she hated herself for it.

Maya could practically feel the tension radiating off him. Which she totally shouldn't even notice. What was she, thirteen?

Still, it was hard not to notice how ragged he looked. Worse than the rest of them, for sure. Of course, he was the only one who'd been shot. Christian's little scratch hardly seemed to count. Yeah, Ronan was awfully pale. Beneath the table, she clenched her hands. The guy was an adult. If he needed medical attention, he could ask for it. Not. Her. Problem.

She forced herself to focus on the screens, on the data, on anything but the man beside her who could finish her sentences but couldn't seem to look her in the eye anymore.

They had bigger problems than her broken heart.

Admiral Knight strode into the conference room, his presence immediately commanding attention despite his rumpled appearance. With his sharp, blue eyes and that distinctive weathered face, he looked exactly like his photos—a naval legend somehow crossed with a lived-in William Macy. The room stood.

"Commander Quinn." The admiral extended his hand to Ronan. "Good to finally meet you in person. Your reputation precedes you." His gaze swept the room, taking in the team. "All of you. Impressive work so far."

Jack took point on the briefing, with Austin adding tactical details. Maya forced herself to focus on their voices, not on the way Ronan's fingers drummed against his thigh when he was processing intel. A tell she definitely hadn't catalogued. Because that would be ridiculous.

"So that's where we are, sir," Jack concluded. "The question is how to proceed with Sentinel. And Buck Richardson."

The admiral's face tightened at his friend's name. He stood at the head of the table, hands clasped behind his back, silent for a long moment. Maya recognized the pose from a thousand military briefings—a commander weighing options, calculating risks.

"Pantone's our key," he said finally. "We find him, we get our answers about Richardson and everything else." The admiral's jaw clenched. "Where is he?"

"Give us an hour." Zara's fingers were already flying across her keyboard. "We've got partial traces on his digital signature, and I've got contacts in Cyprus who—"

"Thirty minutes," Star cut in, shooting Zara a competitive look. "Those routing nodes you found? They're active. He's moving money right now."

"Twenty," Ethan countered, already heading for the door. "The encryption's good, but it's not that good."

Admiral Knight's weathered face cracked into a slight smile. "I like your team, Quinn."

"Sir." Christian stood. "Permission to prep for immediate deployment? Austin and Izzy can help me get the aircraft ready while the cyber team does their thing."

"Granted." The admiral's gaze swept the room one final time. "The rest of you gear up. The second we have coordinates, we move."

Maya felt Ronan tense beside her again, knew he was about to speak before he even opened his mouth.

"Rules of engagement, sir?" Ronan asked, and Maya definitely didn't notice how his voice got slightly deeper when he was in tactical mode.

"Bring him in. Alive." The admiral's smile held no humor. "I've got some questions for Mr. Pantone about my old friend Buck."

The meeting broke up, people filing out with purpose. Maya gathered her tablet, hyperaware of Ronan still at the table, presumably waiting for her to leave first. The awkward dance of avoidance was getting old.

She turned toward the door just as he stood. They both stopped, caught in that weird space between leaving and staying, between speaking and silence.

"We should ..." she started.

"Maybe we need to ..." he said at the same time.

They both fell silent.

"Talk?" she finished, hating how hopeful she sounded. Professional. She was supposed to be keeping this professional.

Something flickered in his eyes—pain? regret?—before that wall came down again. "About the mission parameters," he said stiffly. "We should coordinate our approach to Pantone."

Of course. The mission. Because that's all this was now.

"Right." She squared her shoulders. "The mission. Send me your tactical outline when it's ready, Commander."

She walked out before he could respond, her steps measured, her spine straight. Behind her, she heard him exhale sharply, heard the soft thud of his fist hitting the conference table.

Good. Let him hurt too.

40

CHAIN OF COMMAND

RONAN KNEW it was an ambush the moment he walked into the kitchen. The admiral leaned against the counter, Christian lounged by the coffeemaker, and Jack blocked the doorway. Three military men, all wearing identical expressions that spoke of news—and something else.

"We found Pantone," the admiral said without preamble. "He's holed up in a converted Nike missile site in the Marin Headlands."

Ronan paused halfway to the coffee pot. "A missile site."

"Some tech billionaire turned it into a safe house," Christian explained. "Underground bunkers, secret passageways, the whole nine yards."

"You're kidding." Ronan reached for a mug. "What's next—sharks with laser beams?"

Knight's mouth twitched. "According to our intel, the renovation kept most of the original Cold War infrastructure. Multiple levels, blast doors, emergency power systems. Added some modern amenities—luxury living quarters, state-of-the-art security."

"And a secret tunnel to the bay," Christian added. "Because apparently that's a thing now."

"Wheels up in thirty," Jack said. "Ethan's getting us detailed schematics, Austin and Izzy are prepping the Pilatus and the Eurocopter."

Ronan sipped his coffee, waiting.

The three men exchanged looks.

"About the team composition," the admiral began carefully. "Given the nature of the operation—"

"Maya needs to be there." The words were out before Ronan could second-guess them. His grip tightened on the mug as three sets of eyebrows rose in perfect synchronization.

Yeah, he was surprised, too. He might hate the idea of her being in danger. Might not even be able to live with the consequences, but thinking about her being sidelined to make him feel better flat broke him.

The three men exchanged looks.

"She's not going." Knight didn't waste time with preliminaries.

"This isn't an NCIS operation," Jack added. "We're going in hot against mercenaries in an underground fortress."

"She's a qualified federal agent—"

"Who's never done a black ops insertion," Christian cut in. "This isn't a criticism, little brother. It's operational reality."

Ronan set his mug down carefully. "With all due respect, she's proven herself more than capable—"

"In controlled situations," the admiral said. "With backup. With clear rules of engagement."

"She handled herself fine at the clinic."

"That was different," Jack said. "This is a whole other level of—"

"Of what?" Ronan challenged. "Risk? Complexity?

Because I've seen her tactical assessments. She thinks faster on her feet than half our team."

Christian straightened, his expression hardening. "We were hoping you'd tell her."

"I'm not ..." Ronan ran a hand through his hair. "Look, she's not exactly interested in my opinions right now."

"Wonder why." Christian folded his arms across his chest. "You're the one who brought her to the party. It's your job to handle this."

"She's not a situation to be handled. She's a highly qualified agent who—"

"Who you're not thinking clearly about," the admiral interrupted quietly.

Ronan fell silent. Three sets of knowing eyes watched him, waiting. "We need her on this. And she's earned it."

"You sure about that?" Jack's tone was careful. "This isn't exactly standard law enforcement."

"She's NCIS." Ronan fought to keep his voice steady. He couldn't believe he was about to say this. "We could use federal oversight, chain of custody for evidence collection. She knows the case inside out." And she deserved this. She'd more than earned her place on the team, whether he liked it or not.

"It's going to be a hot insertion," Christian said quietly. "Underground fortress, armed hostiles—"

"You think I don't know that?" The edge in his voice surprised even him. He drew a deep breath. "Look, she's qualified. More than qualified. And this isn't about ..." He trailed off.

"About what?" His mother's voice from the doorway made him close his eyes briefly. Of course she'd show up now. "About you trying to protect a woman you have feelings for? Or about you finally figuring out you can't?"

He turned to find her watching him with knowing eyes.

"Actually," Ronan met his mother's gaze, "I was about to say it isn't about what makes me comfortable. It's about doing the job right. And loyalty to a team member who's proven themselves."

Something shifted in his mother's expression—pride, maybe, or recognition.

"You were twelve," she said softly, "when that editor told me the Middle East was 'no place for a woman reporter.' Remember what you said?"

He did. The memory hit him like a physical thing—his mother's determined face, so like Maya's when she took on a challenge. His own righteous fury at anyone trying to limit her.

"I said it was stupid," he answered. "That you were smarter than him anyway."

"And now?"

Ronan looked at the mission plans spread across the counter, thought about Maya's quick tactical mind, her steady hands, her unwavering courage. Everything in him screamed to keep her safe, protected, away from danger.

But that wasn't who she was. And it wasn't who he was, either.

"Now I'm saying she's part of this operation." His voice strengthened with conviction. "Not because we need federal oversight, though we do. Not because she's qualified, though she is." He met each pair of eyes in turn. "Because she's earned it. Because it's right."

"Even though it scares you to death?" his mom asked quietly.

"Especially because of that." Ronan's laugh held no humor. "Trying to protect people by controlling their choices—that's not protection. That's fear winning."

"Well," his mother's smile was approving, "look who finally grew up."

"Does this mean," Maya's voice from the doorway made them all turn, "you're done being an overprotective jerk?"

She stood there in tactical gear, chin lifted in that familiar challenging angle. His heart contracted painfully, but he forced himself to really look at her—not as someone to protect, but as the capable agent she was.

"Probably not," he admitted. "But I'm working on it."

Something softened in her expression. "Good enough." She moved to study the schematics. "What's our infiltration route?"

Then he stepped up beside her, pointing to the water access tunnel. "Here's what we know …"

Ronan watched her examine the schematics, memorizing the tilt of her head, the way her finger traced possible entry points, how she finished his tactical thoughts before he voiced them. One more op. He could do this one last time—be professional, keep his distance, get the job done. Then he'd head off into the sunset. Find a job overseas. Something, anything, to put enough distance between them that he wouldn't have to face this gut-wrenching fear every time she walked into danger.

He ignored the voice in his head that sounded suspiciously like his mother, asking if he really thought running would make it hurt any less.

41

SUNSET WATCH

The command vehicle's air conditioning struggled against the late afternoon heat. Ronan swiped a hand over his sweaty forehead and shifted in the passenger seat, trying to find a position that didn't aggravate his wound. Two days wasn't nearly enough healing time, but no way he'd sit this out. Not with Maya there.

Through the windshield, he watched Ethan setting up the drone equipment, muttering about sight lines and thermal imaging. The van was parked in what looked like an ordinary scenic overlook, offering a clear view of both the Golden Gate Bridge and the converted Nike missile site. Tourists came and went, snapping photos, completely unaware of the fortress beneath their feet.

"I mean, seriously?" Ethan's voice crackled through the comms. "Underground lair. Secret passages. Probably has a white cat somewhere in there."

The driver's side door opened and Maya slid in, bringing a wave of fresh air and tension with her. "Deke's team is in position," she reported, all business. "They've found the maintenance tunnel entrance."

Ronan nodded, pulling up the thermal imaging on his tablet. His arm protested the movement, and he couldn't quite hide the wince.

Maya noticed—of course she did. "Should you be—"

"I'm fine." The words came out sharper than intended. He softened his tone. "Christian's team?"

"Moving into tourist cover now." She pulled up her own tablet, careful to maintain the professional distance between them in the confined space. "Axel's complaining about the hiking boots."

"Of course he is."

They settled into an awkward silence, watching the feeds as their teams took position. The sun was starting to set, painting the bay in colors too beautiful for a mission like this. Tourist traffic was thinning out.

Ronan knew he should focus entirely on the operation, on monitoring their teams, on watching for threats. Instead, he found himself asking, "What's next for you? After this is over?"

He felt rather than saw her surprise at the question. "Assuming we survive your tech billionaire's Bond villain basement?"

"Assuming."

Maya was quiet for a moment, studying the feeds. "There's work to be done at Hope Landing. Real work, not just cleaning up Richardson's mess." She paused. "The whole team could do good there. You all could."

The suggestion caught him off guard. "My team's not a thing. Not anymore."

"You should be. You're good for each other."

Before he could process that—or his unexpected reaction to it—Christian's voice cut through on comms.

The sun had nearly set now, painting the command vehicle's interior in deepening shadows. In the dim light, it was harder to maintain the careful distance between them. Harder to ignore the familiar way she analyzed data, the quick insights he'd come to rely on these past few days.

"Maya ..." he started, not sure what he was going to say.

Her tablet chirped. "Movement in the tunnel," she reported, instantly professional. "Deke's team has contact."

The mission was starting. Whatever he'd been about to say would have to wait.

It always did.

They watched Deke's body cam footage as his team moved through the maintenance tunnel. The infrastructure was pure Cold War—thick concrete walls, heavy blast doors, emergency lighting that cast everything in sickly green.

"Point team reaching first junction," Deke whispered. "No contact."

Ronan frowned at the thermal imaging. "Too quiet. We should be seeing patrols."

"Underground's clear," Christian reported from his position. "Moving to phase two."

Maya suddenly sat forward. "Wait. Pull up the power grid readings."

Ronan did, his shoulder protesting. The numbers scrolled across his screen.

"Look at the usage patterns," she said. "For a facility this size, running this much security ..." She pointed to specific sections. "These sectors are drawing almost no power."

"Because they're empty," Ronan realized. He studied the tactical overlay with fresh eyes. "They're not defending the facility. They're ..." His military training kicked in. " All teams, hold position. This isn't a defense pattern—it's an evacuation."

"What?" Jack's voice crackled through comms.

"They're pulling out," Ronan explained. "Leaving just

enough security to make it look normal from the outside. The real action's somewhere else."

Maya was already pulling up the building schematics. "There has to be another exit. Something not on the plans ..."

"All that matters is Pantone's still here," Christian cut in. "Thermal's showing a cluster of heat signatures in the main command center. Has to be him."

Ronan's instincts screamed trap, but they couldn't risk losing their only lead to Richardson. His shoulder throbbed, reminding him he was stuck here while the teams went in.

"Proceed with infiltration," he ordered. "But watch your backs. Something's not right."

Maya looked at him, and he saw his own concern mirrored in her eyes. They both knew what happened when things seemed too easy.

His arm burned. He shifted again, catching Maya's quick glance.

"You should take something for that," she said quietly.

"I'm fine." But he couldn't quite hide his wince as he reached for the comm controls. "Deke, status?"

"Approaching command center from the west. Still no resistance."

"Christian?"

"East corridor secured. Something's hinky here. These security measures look active, but ..."

"But they're not actually protecting anything," Ronan finished. He'd seen enough military operations to recognize the signs. "They're for show."

On the thermal imaging, the heat signatures in the command center remained stationary. Too stationary.

"Contact, east wing!" Christian's voice cut through comms. "Ethan, I need eyes on that corner!"

"On it." Through the drone feed, they watched Ethan

smoothly redirect his surveillance. "Two tangos, moving tactical. Wait—confirmed Sentinel gear."

"Taking them," Jack reported. "Austin, cover that exit."

Multiple shots fired, precise and controlled.

"Tangos down," Christian said. "But these guys are definitely Sentinel. Professional training, top-tier gear."

"More movement," Deke reported. "They're falling back to the command center."

"Ethan," Jack cut in, "get me thermal on the north corridor."

"Already scanning. Got multiple signatures converging on your position."

Maya grabbed Ronan's good arm. "Look at the power signatures in the sub-basement."

He saw it immediately. While everyone was focused on the command center, something was drawing power three levels down. "It's a diversion," he said. "Deke, hold position. Christian, get eyes on that sub-basement. Jack—"

"Taking fire!" Austin's voice. "Heavy resistance from the west."

"Moving to support," Ethan reported. "Christian, watch your six."

"I see Pantone," Jack called out. "He's running. Ethan, can you track him?"

"Negative, too much interference. Christian?"

"I've got him," Christian confirmed. "Moving to intercept."

Then a single shot. Different from the others. Deeper. Then silence.

"Report," Ronan demanded. "Someone report."

"Pantone's down," Christian's voice was tight. "Sniper round. Professional."

"What?" Maya leaned forward. "From where?"

"Unknown shooter," Jack said. "But that wasn't us."

"Whoever took that shot knew exactly what they were doing," Austin added.

Ronan stared at the feeds, at Pantone's crumpled form, at their only link to Richardson lying dead on cold concrete. Around him, his team's voices continued reporting positions, movements, threats—the smooth coordination of highly trained operators.

But none of it mattered now. "Who just shot our only lead?"

Kenji was examining something—a uniform patch. "I grabbed this off one of the guys in the group that shot Pantone."

"What is that?" Maya asked.

Austin glanced over, his expression hardening. "That's a Sentinel Security identifier. Executive protection division."

"His own security detail killed him?" Christian's voice was sharp with disbelief. "Why would they take out their boss?"

"Richardson's dirty," Ethan finally said, looking up from his tablet. "Has to be. No other reason for this level of cleanup."

That felt right. Of course. Pantone was the number two guy at Sentinel. No way his own people took him out without orders from higher up. And they all knew there was only one guy above him …

The van's interior lights cast harsh shadows as Jack pulled out his secured sat phone.

"Sir," Jack said into the phone. "Mission completed, but with complications." He paused, listening. "Yes sir. Pantone's dead. But there's more—it was his own security detail that took the shot."

"Tell him about the patch," Christian suggested, but Jack was already shaking his head at something the admiral was saying.

"Sir?" Jack's voice changed subtly. Everyone in the van noticed. "Sir, what's wrong?"

"When?" Jack demanded. "How many—" He broke off, listening. "Yes, sir. We'll head back immediately."

Jack's haunted expression made Ronan's chest tighten. "What is it?"

Jaw hard, Jack swallowed. "The admiral's wife is missing."

42

CODE BLACK

Dawn painted the windows of Knight Tactical's top floor orange-gold as Ronan surveyed the crowded briefing room. Ten hours since Minerva Knight disappeared somewhere between the harbor in Napoli and the restaurant in Capri where she planned to meet her daughters. His entire arm, hot and inflamed, pulsed with each heartbeat, sending fresh waves of heat through his system, but he forced himself to focus on the assembled team.

The admiral stood at the head of the conference table, outwardly composed but Ronan could read the devastation in the slight slump of his shoulders, the shadows under his eyes. Watching his mentor maintain his professional demeanor while his wife was missing hit Ronan harder than he'd expected. This was exactly why he'd kept relationships at arm's length all these years—the terrifying vulnerability of having someone to lose.

Jack stood with his core unit—Austin, Christian, and Dale—near the main display screen. Dale's wife, FBI Special Agent Tamra, was already coordinating with European authorities. Even Jack's brother Chase was there, still in his

Hope Landing FD uniform. Their grim expressions matched the gravity of the situation. Ronan caught Maya watching him with careful concern and forced himself straighter. He couldn't afford to let fever or emotion compromise him now, not when the admiral needed them operating at peak efficiency.

"Seely and Patrick are standing by," Jack reported. "Can be in the air from their locations in thirty if we need them."

The admiral managed a slight smile. "Let's hope we don't need to interrupt their vacations just yet."

Ronan's own team filled the other side of the room. Deke had just finished leading a quiet prayer, his steady presence a counterpoint to the tension. Not how Ronan would have spent the time, but who was he to comment? Deke's words certainly calmed Griff, at least. Handguns lined up on the table in front of her, Izzy methodically worked her way down the row, inspecting and cleaning. Zara hunched over laptops with Star and Ethan, while Kenji divided his attention between monitoring Ronan's condition and conferring with Jack. Axel paced near the window, radiating contained fury.

His mom's hand rested on the admiral's shoulder, her usual elegant poise masking her worry for him and his wife. Beside her, Maya's dad studied the timeline they'd constructed on the wall, his detective's mind clearly working the puzzle from every angle.

Even Mike and Kate, the retired vets they'd recently rescued, had insisted on joining in. "I know Russian operations," Mike had said simply. "If that's where this leads …"

Maya stood close enough that Ronan caught her quick, assessing glance. Close enough to catch him if his strength failed—which it wouldn't. Couldn't. Not with this much at stake.

"Last contact was zero nine hundred local," Christian reported. "The charter office confirmed Mrs. Knight's departure from the Port of Naples, heading for Capri. Scheduled to meet her daughters for lunch at La Fontelina."

"Never made it to the restaurant," Jack added, his usual easy manner stripped away. "Girls waited two hours before raising the alarm."

"And no sign of the boat? Why is there no sign of that boat?" The admiral's voice remained controlled, professional, but Victoria's hand tightened on his shoulder.

Still typing, Zara shook her head. "Harbor cameras show departure, heading southeast toward Capri. After that, nothing. Like the boat just ... vanished. The skipper, too."

"If they find the boat at all, it'll be floating face down in the Med," Christian muttered.

The secure line's harsh buzz cut through the room.

Everyone stilled.

Zara nodded at the admiral. "Ready to trace. Go ahead, sir."

The admiral grabbed his phone. "Speak."

A digitally altered voice filled the room. "Your wife is quite comfortable, John. For now."

Ronan watched the man's face freeze, decades of military control masking everything except a slight whitening around his mouth.

"Prove it," the admiral said flatly.

"Arrangements can be made. But first—Knight Tactical stands down. All operations cease immediately." A pause. "Especially concerning recent events regarding the Veteran's Administration."

Jack's team exchanged sharp looks with Ronan's people.

"You're asking me to trust my wife's safety to an anonymous voice," Knight said.

"Trust isn't required. Compliance is. We want three of your companions." The voice sharpened. "Ronan Quinn. Maya Chen. Axel Reinhardt. Surrender them so we can remit them to federal authorities, and we'll release Mrs. Knight."

The room went deadly quiet. Ronan fought a wave of dizziness, felt Maya's steadying hand brush his back. Across the room, Axel had gone completely still.

"Video proof," Knight demanded. "Now."

The main screen flickered. The man's wife appeared, gray hair in disarray, swaying slightly in a straight-backed chair, but otherwise not in obvious distress. Standard waterfront backdrop behind her, could be anywhere. Her eyes were slightly unfocused, narcotics, probably, but there was still calculation in them.

"Tell the girls I love them," she managed, voice steady despite the slur. "And John—about that Annapolis toast … it was the right—"

The feed cut abruptly.

"Two hours," the voice returned, "to begin arrangements for their surrender."

The line went dead. Zara shook her head—no trace. Izzy swore softly.

"Wait." Knight's voice cut through the stunned silence. "Play it back. That last thing she said."

Zara reversed the feed. Minerva's face filled the screen again, managing to look composed despite her situation.

The admiral went absolutely still. Something flashed across his face—recognition, then rage, instantly controlled.

"Sir?" Jack asked quietly.

"Thirty years ago. Only four of us in the room." Knight's voice was carefully neutral. "A specific speech about power and shadows. About never needing to hide your strength."

Victoria touched his arm. "John?"

The admiral blinked hard, his face going slack with shock. "Richardson. She's telling us Buck Richardson is behind this."

"Hope Landing ground, this is Mooney Three One One Echo. Requesting clearance to land on runway zero niner. Anybody home?" The bland announcement came over the speaker connected to Hope Landing's tiny control tower. Unmanned, at this hour.

Ethan's voice was clipped: "Incoming aircraft requesting clearance to land. Private Cirrus Vision Jet." He turned away from his keyboard, blinking in surprise. "It's Buck Richardson's plane, sir."

"Right on cue," the admiral said softly. Ronan heard decades of friendship turned to ash in those three words.

Jack growled. "No way that's a coincidence."

Fury flashed through Knight's eyes. "Roger that, son. The man always did try way too hard. It'll be the death of him."

Clearly, he meant that literally.

The room swayed dangerously, but Ronan locked his knees, gripping the edge of the table. Maya's hand settled firmly against his back, steadying him while appearing to simply stand close. He caught Kenji's sharp look and forced himself straighter, knowing the medic would bench him in a heartbeat if he showed weakness now.

Knight strode to the console next to Ethan and punched the send button. "Hello, Buck. Your timing is impeccable, as always. Come on in." He stepped away from the transmitter. "All right, people. Game on." He paused, giving each of them a piercing look. "Whatever the man has planned, we play along."

Jack shot to attention. "Yes, sir."

"Tactical thoughts, sir?" Christian asked.

"We'll wing this one. One thing you can count on with Buck Richardson. He never fails to telegraph his punches. If you see a verbal opening, go for it. The rest of us will follow. And under no circumstances do we clue him in that we know. Everyone copy?"

"Sir. Yes, sir," they answered in near-unison.

"Meeting adjourned," Knight ordered. "Jack and Austin, escort Richardson up. The rest of you have one hour to give me options."

Maya kept her hand against Ronan's back as the room cleared, her touch light enough to seem casual but firm enough to help him stay upright. In the hallway, he leaned briefly against the wall, letting the cool surface draw some heat from his fevered skin.

"You're burning up," she whispered, and he heard the familiar edge of exasperation in her voice. The one that said she thought he was being an idiot but would back his play anyway. "But if you pass out during the op ..."

"I won't." He pushed off the wall, fighting to keep his stride steady as they headed for the tactical room. They both knew what was coming next—Richardson would arrive playing concerned friend, and they'd need every operator in place for what would follow.

Maya's muttered "stubborn idiot" told him exactly what she thought of his assurances, but she'd play along. For now. It would have to be enough.

43

FAULT LINES

Maya was already reading Richardson's body language as he swept into the tactical room. Seven years in Homicide had taught her to catalog the subtle tells—the too-precise timing of his concerned expression, the calculated urgency in his stride, the way his eyes flickered over tactical displays before settling on the admiral.

"John." He gripped the admiral's shoulder. "What do you need? Sentinel resources are at your disposal. Sky's the limit."

Through the surveillance feeds, Maya watched Jack's team silently securing positions around the building's perimeter. On her tactical display, Star's fingers flew across keys, manufacturing the appearance of desperate search patterns.

"First," the admiral gestured to the screens, "I need to understand what happened with Pantone."

Richardson's pause was microscopic. "Awful business. Internal investigation is ongoing, but I haven't had direct contact with him in weeks. Man went completely dark on us."

Maya caught her father's subtle head tilt—he'd spotted

something too. Richardson's right hand tapped twice against his leg as he spoke. Classic tell.

"The biological passport situation," the admiral said. "We traced it back to him."

Richardson's mask slipped for just a fraction of a second. "I ... what situation?"

As the admiral outlined their findings, Maya noticed Axel go rigid by the window. His face had drained of color, eyes fixed on Richardson with shocked recognition. Before she could move, Austin had positioned himself nearby, ready to intervene.

Then Maya saw it—a pattern in the data scrolling across her screen. Encrypted transmissions piggy-backing on Richardson's arrival signal. She glanced at Ronan, saw him tracking the same anomaly.

"The important thing now," Richardson pivoted smoothly, "is finding Minerva. Have the kidnappers made any demands?"

"They have," the admiral said heavily. "Very specific ones."

Richardson leaned forward, concern perfect except for the predatory gleam in his eyes. "Tell me everything. Maybe I can help negotiate ..."

Knight looked like he'd just aged decades. "They want Quinn, Reinhardt, and Detective Chen. That's not going to happen."

"John." Richardson's voice carried careful concern. "That's poor tactical thinking, my friend. Think about what you're saying. Your wife's life—"

"I won't hand innocent people over to kidnappers." The admiral's tone was steel.

Despite Knight's refusal, Jack's team shift subtly closer to their positions. Christian blocked the exit while Jack, Austin and Ethan separated her and Ronan from Axel and the rest of Ronan's team.

She went cold.

An act, right?

Richardson crossed to the tactical display, his concern sharpening to something harder. "Who says they're innocent? Have you seen the evidence against them? Because I have. Even if they're innocent of the charges, which I highly doubt, they're only going to compromise this rescue. Look at them, John. Really look. Quinn's running a fever that should have him hospitalized. Detective Chen's emotional involvement has compromised her judgment. And Reinhardt ..." He gestured at Axel's rigid stance by the window. "I read the man's file. He's clearly unstable."

Knight looked like he'd swallowed dirt. "You're out of line, Buck."

"Am I?" Richardson's mask slipped, showing something cold beneath. "Or am I the only one willing to state the obvious? You have three compromised operatives making increasingly dangerous decisions in a hostage situation. Operatives who could be used to save your wife's life. You need to be clear here, John."

Maya saw Jack's team continuing their careful repositioning—subtle movements that looked random but were cutting her, Ronan, and Axel off from the rest of the room. Professional. Practiced.

"Secure them." Richardson's authority filled the room. "Now. Before their instability gets someone killed."

"How dare you—" Victoria started forward, but Austin smoothly intercepted her, gripping her upper arms.

Richardson's hand moved to his jacket pocket. "Think about your position, John. We'll do our best to rescue Minerva without having to negotiate, but what if we fail? Can you really tell me you're not willing to trade these … folks … for your innocent wife?"

Maya watched the trap closing. Saw the team's growing tension as they recognized what was coming.

"But I'm jumping the gun here. All I'm saying is they need to be contained until we see where this goes," Richardson continued, voice hardening. His eyes locked with Knight's. "Make the hard call, John. Before someone else makes it for you. Your wife is counting on you. So is your team."

Christian clapped his hands together, shooting Richardson a heartfelt look. "Copy that, sir. If these three are dirty, we're gonna look like fools."

"Or co-conspirators," Richardson added ruefully. "You're better than that. All of you."

The Knight Tactical operatives in the room jumped on that, each playing to Richardson's point, showing shock. Anger. And in a brilliant touch, disappointment in their leader.

And concern. The kind you showed for a doddering uncle long past his prime.

The silence stretched razor-thin. Then the admiral broke … or pretended to break.

Her heart leapt into her throat. She lifted a prayer for their safety. And for Mrs. Knight. Because if Admiral Knight wasn't the best actor she'd ever seen … she and Ronan and Axel might well not survive this.

Shrinking before her eyes, Knight gestured weakly. "Jack."

"Sir?"

"Secure Quinn, Reinhardt, and Agent Chen."

Maya's father stepped forward, face thunderous.

"John, no—" Victoria's protest cut through the room.

"Either shut up," the admiral's voice could have frozen

flame, "or you can join them. In fact, you need to be secured. Maya's father, too."

"I'm on it," Ethan announced, shoving back from the table. "Ma'am?" He gestured toward the exit. Ronan's mom shot him a deadly look before flouncing out ahead of him.

"Put those two vets with them," the admiral called out after him.

Jack and Christian stepped forward to secure the three of them while the others watched Ronan's friends for any signs of heroics, but none of his people moved. They managed to look both concerned, and relieved.

At least she hoped their expressions were acting.

Christian whispered, "Be ready for anything," as he secured her wrists.

Richardson swept the three of them with a critical eye before clapping his old friend on the shoulder. "That's the right move, John. Trust me."

Gaze haunted, the admiral pressed a hand to his belly, as if trying to tamp down a wave of nausea. Which, given the circumstances, could be all too real. "It doesn't feel that way."

Richardson's satisfaction was palpable now. But he missed what Maya saw—the team's silent communication, their practiced movements, their absolute trust in each other and their leader.

"Look," Richardson continued. "We don't necessarily have to turn these three over. Between your operatives and mine, it's likely we'll be able to rescue Minerva without making the exchange. Or my people could locate her first. Don't give up hope."

Knight managed a sickly smile. "Thanks for that."

"My pleasure." He spun on his heel, heading for the door. "I'm going to need a secure line. I want to bring my people up to speed."

The air instantly returned to the room. The man sure did love the sound of his own voice. If things went to plan, he'd have decades to hear himself talk. Alone in a Supermax cell.

She and Ronan and Axel might be zip-tied, but they weren't alone. Whatever game Richardson was playing, he'd just made his first serious mistake: underestimating the loyalty of a tactical team. Even a frayed one.

Hands behind his back, Ronan swayed slightly. His skin had gone even grayer. He looked long past done.

Maya sent up a silent prayer wishing, not for the first time, that he could feel its comfort—that sometimes the strongest thing you could do was admit you couldn't do it alone. But Ronan Quinn had spent his life relying on nothing but himself and his training. She just hoped that would be enough. Because the way Richardson was watching them, like a cat with cornered mice, told her the real fight was just beginning.

44

DEAD DROP

The August heat hammered down as Christian roughly guided Ronan up the Pilatus's stairs, his grip unnecessarily tight. "Move it, scum," he snarled, loud enough for Richardson to hear. The tarmac shimmered in the late morning sun, making the private airfield's isolation feel even more pronounced.

Sweat darkened Ronan's shirt where Christian's fingers dug into his injured arm. To anyone watching, it looked like deliberate cruelty. Only Ronan felt the gentle squeeze that followed. "Sorry," Christian whispered without moving his lips.

Behind them, Jack shoved Maya and Axel forward, his face twisted in disgust. "Can't believe we worked with these pieces of filth." He steered them none-too-gently toward their seats.

Richardson had stuck close over the past two hours as he negotiated with the kidnappers and he and the admiral planned the rescue flight to Italy. Not much opportunity for anyone to confer with Ronan or Maya or Axel. Exactly what Richardson wanted, for sure. Ronan's team feigned disinterest and stayed away completely. The admiral's wife wasn't their concern. Nor were Ronan and Axel. Traitors to be handed over.

That left Christian, Jack and Austin to rotate as their guards. The one unguarded moment he got, Austin assured them that they'd be sending reinforcements. "We've got an Embraer jet on standby. It's a hundred knots per hour faster than your ride. And our ceiling's ten thousand feet higher. Richardson will never see us. We'll be on the ground long before you hit the Med. We're hoping we can extract Mrs. K before you land, but stay on your toes. No idea how this is going to go down."

The rushed communication had buoyed Ronan's spirits. Weak as he felt, he wasn't sure how much help he'd be when the time came. But knowing they'd have friendlies on the ground helped.

"Buck, we're going to need someone to watch over the prisoners." The admiral's voice carried from the co-pilot's seat. "We should bring Murphy. Extra security—"

"Your boy's brother?" Richardson's laugh was sharp. "No offense, Christian, but blood tells."

Christian leapt forward, face red, fist cocked, Jack barely catching him before he reached Richardson. "I'll take you down."

"Stand down," Jack barked, though his own face had hardened at Richardson's jab.

"My father's choices aren't mine," Christian spat, shrugging off Jack's restraining grip. The fury in his voice wasn't entirely feigned.

"Exactly my point," Richardson said smoothly. "Family loyalty can be ... unpredictable."

"Then Jack," the admiral pressed. "These prisoners need watching—"

Richardson continued with his preflight. "The kidnappers were clear, John. No extra personnel. It was hard enough convincing them to let me fly you over." He checked his watch. "Speaking of which, we're burning daylight. My team from Greece will be in position in six hours. They'll stay out of sight, until I can persuade the kidnappers they mean no harm. But we need to get going if we're going to meet the deadline." He twisted himself around in the captain's seat until he could lock eyes with Jack and Christian, blocking the aisle between the three of them and the cockpit. "Check their restraints one more time."

"Sir." Jack sounded way too much the eager flunky. But as he bent over Maya, he winked.

Christian hovered over Ronan. "Hold still," he barked, though Ronan hadn't moved.

His brother tugged at the restraints, and then, suddenly they fell away only to be instantly replaced.

"Izzy and Star came up with these," Christian whispered, voice barely audible. "Three taps on the fastener and they pop off."

He gripped Ronan's good shoulder. "Wish I was going with you, bro."

Radiating pretend rage, Ronan refused to meet his brother's eyes. "You should come. I'd love to make it a one-way trip, dude."

Christian laughed harshly. "I bet. Sorry, this is a private vacay. Just for you and your two buddies here. It ends with identical prison cells." Christian clapped him hard on his injured shoulder, drawing a sharp groan, and backed away to tend to Axel's restraints.

He was telling Ronan that they all three had new bindings. Nice.

When the time came, that would help. A lot.

Christian saw to Axel's bindings, his movements sharp

with apparent anger. "All secured, sir," he reported to Jack. "Though why we're bothering with procedure for traitors ..."

"Because we're professionals," Jack cut him off. "Unlike some people." His glare at the prisoners crackled with convincing hatred.

As they descended the stairs, Christian turned back. "Rot in hell, baby bro," he snarled at Ronan. "I'm only thankful our father never gave you his name."

Jack paused in the doorway, saluting the older men. "Good hunting, sirs."

As the jet's door closed with a final, heavy thunk, Ronan's gaze fell on Maya's cross necklace, glinting in the pre-dawn light. He'd always respected her faith, even if he couldn't share it. Had admired how she found strength in something he couldn't see or touch or quantify. But now ...

For the first time in his life, he found himself reaching for that same invisible lifeline. The words felt clumsy, foreign in his mind. He didn't know the proper way to do this, didn't know if there were rules or protocols. But he figured if there was a God up there, He'd understand raw honesty.

Not for him. He chose this life. Chose the risks, the battles, the scars. But Maya, fierce, smart, beautiful Maya, wasn't a warrior. Hadn't signed up for this. Neither had Minerva Knight.

The prayer rose from somewhere deeper than thought: *Keep them safe. Please. I'll pay whatever price You want, take whatever hits are coming, just ... let them walk away from this.*

No. Matter. What.

It felt like making a contract with the universe itself. Like the words carried a weight that changed something fundamental in the air around them. He didn't know if anyone was listening, but he meant every syllable with an intensity that surprised him.

He slumped tiredly in his seat, his brain buzzing. The

antibiotics Kenji had managed to slip him were finally kicking in. His head felt clearer than it had in hours, though fire still crawled beneath the bandages on his shoulder. Through the Pilatus's windows, darkness had given way to dawn over the Atlantic. Six hours into a nine-hour flight to Italy.

Richardson's voice drifted back from the cockpit as he adjusted their heading. Former Air Force pilot, current traitor, apparently. The admiral sat beside him as co-pilot—Richardson's idea, keeping the man who'd "orchestrated" their transfer close. Making him complicit.

To allegedly face kidnappers. To save Minerva.

Right.

"This makes zero sense," Maya muttered, quiet enough that the cockpit crew couldn't hear. "Why drag us to Italy just to bring us back to face charges in the States?"

Axel's first words in hours were barely a whisper: "Because we're not supposed to come back. Easier to disappear us on foreign soil."

"Richardson and his goons are planning to make it look like we were in on the kidnapping," Ronan added.

Maya flinched.

"Sorry," he muttered.

She straightened her narrow shoulders as much as she could with her hands tied behind her back. "Don't be. It's the truth."

We got this. He willed her to understand the unspoken reassurance he didn't dare say aloud.

Turbulence rattled the Pilatus. Across the aisle, Axel went rigid. The former SEAL's breathing had shifted—short, sharp inhales that had nothing to do with the plane's movement. His eyes had that thousand-yard stare Ronan recognized from the last couple of years of their deployment. Ever since the disaster in Damascus.

"Hey." Ronan kept his voice low, steady. "Stay with me,

bro. You're on a stupid-swanky private jet." He watched Axel's hands clench. "Maya's on your left. I'm on your right. Buck Richardson's flying, which is actually pretty funny if you think about it."

Maya noticed it immediately, shifted to press her shoulder against Axel's. "Ground yourself, big guy. Feel the seat. Smell the leather. Listen to Richardson being an arrogant ass up there, telling the admiral about his flight hours."

Axel's breath hitched. His whisper was raw: "Last time I was zip-tied on a plane—"

"Was then. This is now." Ronan kept his tone matter-of-fact. "And these aren't real zip-ties. They're our ticket out. Remember the plan. Stay with us."

Slowly, deliberately, Axel flexed his hands. Inhaled. Exhaled. "The plan," he repeated. "Right." His voice steadied. "Sorry."

"Don't be," Maya murmured. "Just means you're human."

Ronan caught the admiral watching them, concern evident despite his careful mask of indifference. He gave the man a slight nod. All good.

The plane hit another patch of turbulence. This time, Axel didn't flinch.

Ronan fully expected Jack and Christian and Griff and the rest of their team to beat them to Italy, once they rescued the admiral's wife, or if they failed to locate and extract her before the planned exchange, it would be down to Ronan and Maya and Axel to handle Richardson and his crew.

Either way, the man had earned himself a fist to the face. Ronan was looking forward to it. A lot.

45

BATTLE PRAYER

THE HOURS CRAWLED by in a haze of carefully orchestrated movements. Every few hours, the admiral would unclip their restraints for bathroom breaks and to let them eat—always when Richardson was focused on navigation or radio checks. During one of these moments, Maya flexed her wrists, and Ronan caught himself wanting to reach for her hands, to massage away the marks from the restraints. The way she would've let him, before he'd pushed her away. Before he'd convinced himself that distance meant safety.

"Procedure," the admiral would say loudly if Richardson glanced back, his tone carrying just the right note of authoritative boredom. "Can't have them getting blood clots before they face charges." He'd replace the restraints with efficient movements that looked strict but never hurt, somehow always managing to position himself between them and Richardson's line of sight as they flexed their cramping muscles.

"Watch for my signals," the admiral whispered to him while Richardson was busy with the nav system. "Three taps means wait. Two is go, whatever that means. We'll be making this up on the fly."

Ronan had blinked his assent. He'd fill in Maya and Axel when he was certain Richardson wouldn't notice.

They choked down protein bars and water, Richardson watching them like a hawk, the admiral maintaining his act of cool disdain. The sun tracked across the sky outside their window, shadows lengthening as they crossed time zones.

Now, as morning approached over the Mediterranean, the cabin had settled into a tense quiet broken only by the drone of engines and Richardson's occasional radio checks with his teams. "Approaching Italian airspace," Richardson announced from the cockpit, his smugness carrying through the cabin. "John, would you check those coordinates again? The latest communication specified—"

"Upper Tyrrhenian, grid sector four," the admiral responded woodenly. "Isola del Giglio."

Ronan's head felt fuzzy again, his body hot, but he forced himself to focus. Knight's shoulders were rigid as he stared straight ahead through the cockpit window. To anyone else, he probably looked like a frightened husband hoping to get his wife back. But Ronan caught the subtle tap of his finger against the armrest. Three taps. *Wait*.

"Coming up on the western cliffs," Richardson announced.

Maya shifted beside Ronan. Playing her part perfectly—the angry detective, caught and helpless. "This is insane," she muttered, voice pitched to carry. "You can't seriously be trusting kidnappers—"

"Special Agent." Richardson's voice held exactly the right amount of stern compassion. "I understand your position, but right now, a woman's life is at stake. Sometimes we have to work outside normal channels. If it's possible to rescue my friend's wife without handing you over, we'll do it. You have my word."

Sure. Ronan just bet. Thankfully, their waiting reinforcements would make sure it didn't come to that.

The plane banked, and through the window, Ronan caught his first glimpse of the Italian coast. Somewhere down there, Minerva Knight was being held, Richardson's Sentinel Security operatives waiting to take them all out. Richardson probably planned to frame him and the others for the murders, too. What a shame the three of them would die trying to escape.

But Ronan's bet was on Knight Tactical, and the rest of his own crew. Priority one would be scouring the coast for Mrs. Knight, but a close second would be helping the four of them take Richardson down. Which they couldn't do until the woman was safe.

Richardson's voice carried back again, all professional concern: "Five minutes to the exchange point. John, I suggest you prepare yourself. This could get ... complicated."

With any luck, way more than Richardson knew.

The setting sun over the Tyrrhenian Sea painted the water blood red. The plane descended in a smooth arc toward a small private airstrip carved into the cliffs.

Richardson was still talking, his words meant for multiple audiences now. "Standard procedure would be to notify Italian authorities," he said, voice carrying clearly through the cabin. "But as the kidnappers pointed out, Mrs. Knight's safety has to be our priority. Sometimes ..." He paused for effect. "Sometimes we have to trust each other."

The admiral's hand moved to adjust a dial. Three taps again.

Yeah. He figured. They'd know when things got rolling.

Through the deepening twilight, Ronan caught movement

on the ground. Vehicles. People. Richardson's team getting into position, no doubt.

Maya's shoulder pressed against his. Offering support, and seeking it, even after everything. Even after he'd hurt her with his walls and his fear and his stubborn insistence that he knew best. He pressed back, throat tight. The best he could do under the circumstances. Besides, it would be better if she was edgy, as a real hostage would be. Though the tremor in her breathing wasn't entirely an act, and that was on him too.

Her cross caught the last rays of sunlight through the window, and he found himself reaching again for that tenuous connection he'd formed with her God. Not with words this time, just raw need and promise: *Let me make this right. Let me be brave enough to tear down these walls I built. Let me deserve her faith in me.*

"Final approach," Richardson announced. "John, keep an eye on those three. Let me handle the landing." His tone was perfect—professional concern masking steel. "Wouldn't want anything to go wrong at this stage."

Despite Richardson's ham hands with the controls, the plane touched down with barely a bump.

The plane taxied to a stop. Through the window, Ronan caught his first glimpse of their destination. His fever-muddled brain took a moment to process what he was seeing.

"You've got to be kidding me," Axel muttered.

Rising above the private airstrip, terraced into the cliffs like a wedding cake made of marble and glass, sprawled the Costa Bella Resort. Even in the gathering dusk, Ronan could make out the crowds of tourists on multiple levels of infinity pools and outdoor restaurants. Hundreds of civilians, all potential collateral damage.

"This complicates things." Maya's whisper carried carefully controlled tension.

Richardson's voice drifted back from the cockpit, smooth as aged whiskey: "You're going to stand out like sore thumbs in that tactical gear, but that can't be helped. My people have a plan." He glared at them. "And you'll follow it. To the letter, if you want Minerva Knight to survive the hour."

Ronan caught the admiral's subtle signal—three taps against the controls. *Wait*.

But watching the swarms of tourists moving through the resort's outdoor spaces, he wondered if they'd waited too long. One wrong move here, and innocent people would pay the price.

"Actually," Axel's voice was pitched for their ears only, "this might work in our favor. Hard to make people disappear with this many witnesses."

"Only if he cares about collateral damage." Maya's shoulder pressed against Ronan's, steadying him as another wave of fever hit. "Which, given what we know about his operations, I can't imagine he does."

The resort glittered against the darkening sky like a false promise. Beautiful. Exposed. Dangerous. They had one shot at this. One chance to play it exactly right. And now they had to do it in front of an audience.

46

EXCHANGE RATE

Maya had participated in her share of undercover operations, but this was pushing it. The gleaming marble lobby of the Costa Bella Resort echoed with tourists' excited whispers as Richardson led their strange procession past reception. Their tactical blacks stood out like ink stains against the resort's cream and gold palette. Maya's boots left faint scuffs on the polished floor, each step echoing under the murmur of fountains and soft classical music.

Richardson walked point in his carefully casual golf attire, while the admiral brought up the rear in full tactical gear. Between them, Maya, Ronan, and Axel shuffled along, hands bound.

After far too long in the same clothes, they looked exactly like captured operatives being moved under duress. Which they were, just not in the way Richardson thought.

The young woman at the reception desk kept her professional smile, but her fingers stilled over her keyboard. A bellhop nearly crashed his luggage cart. The security guard by the elevator touched his earpiece, clearly debating whether to intervene.

"Just ignore them, people," Richardson announced loudly, playing his producer role to the hilt. "The paparazzi always find us." He shot the guard a piercing look. "We're working a scene here. Didn't publicity call you?"

The man's mouth dropped open, but his hand remained poised over the mic on his shoulder.

Richardson waved his hands impatiently. "Il film, il film. Una produzione Americana!"

The staff exchanged glances, a few of them finally smiling weakly. The security guard stood down, shoulders softening. "Ah, sì, sì. Prego, continuate."

Richardson nodded shortly. "Grazie." He infused the politeness with irritation.

Maya forced herself to smile, channeling every actress she'd ever interviewed during her time in LA Homicide. The metallic taste of adrenaline coated her tongue. Somewhere in this resort, Knight Tactical operatives, and Ronan's friends, were searching for Minerva. Until they found her, everyone had to play their parts perfectly.

Beside her, Ronan stumbled slightly, his fever making him look exactly like a brooding action star who'd partied too hard.

A teenage girl darted forward with her phone raised. "Oh wow. Are you that guy from—"

"No autographs during filming, please!" Richardson intercepted her smoothly. But Maya caught the way his hand tightened on his phone, the subtle check for messages.

If she were planning this op, she'd be waiting to hear where they wanted the captives secured. Most likely, he planned to execute the three of them, and the admiral and his wife.

Though pretending to go through the exchange and let the Knights leave, thinking they'd dodged a bullet would be the more prudent thing to do. She didn't know the man well enough to guess.

"Method actors," the admiral explained to the growing crowd. His voice carried the tense tones of a harried production assistant. "They insist on absolute authenticity. Real restraints, real tension ..."

Real danger, Maya thought, catching another micro-expression flash across Richardson's face as he checked his phone again. The man was unraveling, but only someone trained to read killers would notice. The scent of his expensive cologne couldn't quite mask the sour edge of his sweat.

Whatever he had planned, it wasn't going well. She bit down hard on a smile. Score one for the good guys.

"Mr. Producer!" A woman in designer resort wear waved her phone. "Just one photo with your stars?"

"Oh, let them have their moment," the admiral said before Richardson could refuse. He gestured expansively at the soaring lobby ceiling. "The lighting in this space is perfect."

Maya stepped into another posed photo, maintaining her camera-ready smile while cataloging exits, threats, positions. Ronan jutted his chin at the east doors. Yup. She saw it. Two operatives posing as hotel staff. Another watching from the mezzanine. All looking increasingly tense. The click of tourist photos mixed with the splash of fountains, creating a surreal soundtrack to their dangerous charade.

"You're squinting," Richardson critiqued, his producer's mask slipping just slightly as his phone remained silent. "Let's move this somewhere more ... private."

"Actually," Ronan drawled, playing the difficult star perfectly despite his fever, "I'm feeling inspired by this space." Hands still pinned behind his back, he turned awkwardly toward the admiral. "Didn't you say something about the emotional resonance of public versus private personas?"

Knight launched into a long discourse on artistic authenticity that had the tourists enthralled and Richardson practically vibrating with contained tension. Maya could hear the strain in Richardson's breathing now, the slight catch each time he checked his silent phone.

She shifted closer to Ronan, feeling the heat radiating from him. Too hot. The infection was getting worse.

"You good?" she whispered through her publicity smile.

"Just ... enjoying my acting debut." His attempt at humor couldn't quite hide the fever strain, but his eyes were sharp as he tracked Richardson's increasing agitation.

Another tourist approached for photos. Richardson's smile turned brittle as he checked his phone yet again. Nothing.

Maybe because Minerva Knight wasn't where he thought she was.

Maya tasted copper and realized she'd bitten the inside of her cheek. Time to push.

"You know," she announced to their audience, pitching her voice to carry. "I'm really feeling this scene. The tension, the uncertainty ..." She met Richardson's eyes. "That growing realization when everything starts falling apart ..."

If looks could kill, Richardson would have just ended her. "Perhaps," he said, his cultured voice carrying just a hint of strain, "we should move this somewhere more private. The lighting in the garden would be perfect for—"

She shifted her weight, noting how Richardson's security team had subtly tightened their formation. The man on the mezzanine had disappeared—not a good sign. Through the crowd's excited chatter, she caught the admiral's barely audible inhale. He'd noticed too.

Any second now.

"Actually," she projected her voice to carry across the lobby, playing up her role as the difficult starlet, "I think we should do the confrontation scene right here." She stepped closer to Richardson, watching his pupils dilate. "You know, the one about betrayal?"

Richardson's phone finally lit up with a message. Maya watched the blood drain from his face as he read it.

"No," he said softly, all pretense of the charming producer vanishing. "No, that's not possible."

The tourists, sensing something had shifted but not understanding what, began to back away. The security guard by the door touched his earpiece, frowning.

Through the thinning crowd, Maya caught a glimpse of Griff at the bar, casually wiping a glass like he'd worked there all his life. He met her eyes for a fraction of a second, and his characteristic half-smile appeared. Behind him, Jack materialized from the service corridor, still in maintenance coveralls, flashing the OK sign while pretending to check his phone.

If Griff and Jack were here, looking this pleased with themselves, it could only mean one thing: they'd found Minerva. She was safe.

Mission accomplished. The most important part, anyway.

The admiral's transformation was subtle. The tension in his shoulders, coiled tight for days, eased by mere millimeters. But it was his eyes that gave him away to Maya. Behind that stern professional mask, they sparked with a fierce joy that made him look twenty years younger. For just a heartbeat, she glimpsed the young officer who'd first fallen in love decades ago.

Holding her gaze, he tapped his wrist twice. Ronan and Axel tensed imperceptibly on either side of her. They'd been waiting hours for this signal. Maya pressed the hidden catch in her restraints. Next to her, she heard the faint clicks as

Ronan and Axel did the same, their restraints dropping to the tile.

Fully in control now, the admiral straightened, his voice carrying the weight of absolute certainty: "Minerva's safe, Richardson. It's over."

The sound Richardson made was barely human—a strangled mix of rage and despair that made the nearest tourists flinch back in alarm. His carefully manicured hands curled into claws, and she saw the moment his control shattered completely.

47

CHECKMATE

Ronan felt the first explosion before he heard it—a deep vibration that rippled through his bones. The fever that had been simmering all day peaked suddenly, making the room tilt. He locked his knees, refusing to go down.

No way. Not now.

Another explosion above. Then another. The sprinkler system activated. The sudden cold water made him shiver. Emergency lights began to strobe, transforming the lobby into a fractured nightmare of red and white pulses. Each flash sent daggers through his skull.

Through fevered eyes, he saw Richardson's face twist into something triumphant and horrible. Maya moved—a blur of purpose through his wavering vision—but Richardson was faster than any of them expected. In one fluid motion, he grabbed Maya, spinning her around and pressing a gun to her temple.

"Nobody moves!" Richardson's voice carried over the chaos of the panicking crowd. "I'll kill her. You know I will."

Ronan's muscles screamed to launch forward, to do something, anything—but the fever had other plans. The room spun. He caught himself against a marble column. Water ran into his eyes, and he couldn't tell if it was sweat or from the sprinklers.

"Let her go, Buck." The admiral's voice cut through the chaos, steady and commanding despite everything. "There's nowhere left to run."

Richardson's laugh was hollow. "There's always a way out, John. You taught me that." He started backing toward the service corridor, dragging Maya with him. "Anyone follows, she dies."

Maya's eyes met Ronan's across the lobby. There was no fear in them—only calculation. He recognized that look. She was planning something.

Don't, he wanted to shout. Too dangerous. But the fever had stolen his voice.

Richardson reached the corridor entrance. In that moment, Maya moved—dropping her weight suddenly, twisting inside Richardson's grip. Her elbow shot up, catching him under the chin. The gun flew from his grip.

She rolled clear as Richardson stumbled backward.

"No!" Richardson's hand went to his jacket pocket, emerging with something small and metallic. A pill case.

The admiral was moving before anyone else could react. His shoulder caught Richardson in the midsection, driving him back into the wall. The pill case skittered across the floor, out of reach. Before Richardson could recover, the admiral's fist connected with his jaw in a punch that seemed to carry thirty years of betrayal behind it.

Richardson went down hard.

"I taught you a lot of things," the admiral said quietly, standing over his former friend. "But you never did learn not to underestimate the people around you."

The world spun again, and this time Ronan couldn't fight

it. As his knees buckled, all he could think was: I failed. Should have been me saving her. Should have ...

The last thing he heard before consciousness fled was Maya's voice: "Ronan! Stay with us!"

Yeah. About that.

He had so much to say to her. So much.

Don't leave. It was all he could do to lift the words up to the Almighty. *Please. Lord, don't let her leave.*

48

FIGHTING CHANCE

THE PLANES TOUCHED down at Hope Landing just before dawn, the sky turning pearl-gray over the mountains. Maya closed her eyes briefly, lifting a quiet prayer of thanks. For survival. For success. For the unconscious man being tended by Kenji two rows ahead.

"He'll be okay," Kenji said, catching her worried look. His usually stoic expression softened. "Trust me, I've patched this idiot up more times than I can count. The fever's already responding to treatment."

"You sure?" Izzy called from behind them. "Because I still owe him for that prank in Buenos Aires, and if he thinks dying will get him out of it—"

"Nobody's dying," Deke cut in, but his attempt at sternness was undermined by his grin. "Though I'd pay good money to see that prank revenge."

"Focus, children," Zara drawled, but Maya caught her checking Ronan's vitals for the hundredth time.

The moment the cargo ramp lowered, their little convoy was swarmed. Maya's father broke through first, but instead of the lecture she'd braced for, he just pulled her into a fierce hug.

"You're okay," he whispered.

"Told you I'd be careful," she mumbled into his shoulder.

"Careful?" came Mike's voice as he and Kate pushed through. "Is that what we're calling black market identity sales and explosions these days?"

"Don't forget kidnapping," Axel added helpfully.

Maya groaned. "Not helping."

Ronan's mother pushed past them in a cloud of lavender perfume. "My boy," she whispered, reaching for her son's hand as Kenji wheeled his stretcher past. Her eyes were wet, but her voice was steady. "Always fighting everyone's battles."

"We've got him, Mrs. Q," Griff assured her, appearing at her side like a protective shadow. "Kenji's the best. Even if he is way too smug about it."

"I heard that," Kenji called over his shoulder.

"You were meant to!"

"Children," the admiral's voice cut through the banter, warm with amusement. He approached with his wife on his arm, both of them looking tired but radiant. The newly-reunited couple couldn't seem to stop stealing glances at each other. "Let's get our patient inside before you start the comedy routine."

"John," Minerva chided gently, "let them have their moment." Her eyes softened as she looked at Ronan. "Though perhaps we should move this inside. I believe I owe this young man and his friends a considerable debt."

"We all do," the admiral said quietly.

Maya watched as Ronan's team fell into formation around his stretcher—Griff, Kenji, Izzy, Deke, Axel, and Zara—moving with the unconscious synchronization of people who'd trusted each other with their lives for years.

"They're something else, aren't they?" Kate said, coming to stand beside Maya. "Even after everything that happened with the discharge ... they never wavered. Not once."

"Family," Mike agreed, his arm around his wife. "The real kind."

"Speaking of family," Minerva said, her eyes twinkling as she looked between Maya and Ronan, "I do hope you'll all be staying close. We're planning a little get together as soon as Ronan's up for it."

"Minnie," the admiral warned, but he was smiling. "Let them breathe."

"I'm just saying—"

"We know exactly what you're saying, Love."

Later, after they'd gotten Ronan settled in Knight Tactical's medical bay, Maya found herself watching through the observation window as his team settled in for their vigil. Izzy had already claimed the best chair, her feet propped on Deke's lap as she worked on her laptop. Zara was arguing with Kenji about treatment protocols while Axel played referee. Griff stood slightly apart, that haunted look more pronounced now that the adrenaline had faded. He caught her eye and headed out into the hallway.

Maya approached him carefully. "Want to talk about it?"

He managed a small smile that didn't quite reach his eyes. "Thanks, but ... it's between me and Ronan. Something we need to work through together." His eyes went distant. "When he's better."

"Well, if you ever need an outside perspective ..."

"I'll know who to call." This smile was warmer. "You're good people, Maya. I see why he ..." He trailed off, shrugging.

Inside the room, Izzy was now threatening to draw mustaches on Ronan while he slept. Deke had produced a pack of cards from somewhere and was attempting to teach Zara some complicated variant of poker, while Kenji periodically reminded them to keep their voices down in the medical bay.

Maya watched them, something aching in her chest. This was what she wanted. Not just the missions or the adrenaline or even the chance to stop terrible things before they happened. She wanted this—the way they moved around each other like planets in a perfect orbit, the shorthand of inside jokes, the absolute certainty that any one of them would die for the others without hesitation. At LAPD and NCIS, she had colleagues.

Here, she could have family.

The realization settled over her like sunrise. She'd spent so long trying to follow her father's path, to be the daughter he wanted. But watching Ronan's team—his family—she finally understood. Sometimes the right path was the one that scared you most.

Ronan's team had only joined forces to help Marcus. Nothing said they'd turn into the next Knight Tactical. But even if it wasn't with Ronan, she wanted this. Maybe the admiral would see her potential?

If not, she'd keep looking until she discovered her own found family. Having seen genuine teamwork in action, she knew she couldn't live the rest of her life without it.

She needed air. She slipped out of the medical wing and into the morning sunshine, letting the crisp mountain breeze clear her head. Her father would be waiting—she'd seen him heading toward the main headquarters. The workout room, probably. Might as well get this over with. She'd made up her mind, after all. The past few days had shown her exactly where she belonged, even if it meant disappointing him. Taking a deep breath, she rounded the corner.

The familiar smell of leather and sweat hit her as she pushed open the gym door. Her father was already there, working the heavy bag with the focused intensity she remembered from childhood. Without turning, he caught a set of sparring gloves and tossed them her way.

"Your cross still dropping?" he asked, steadying the bag.

Maya smiled, wrapping her hands. Some things never changed. "Only when I'm tired."

"Which you must be." He moved to the mat, raising his guards. "Long few days."

She squared up across from him, feeling the familiar rhythm settle over them. Jab, cross, slip. Block, counter, move. They'd done this dance a thousand times.

"Dad, I—"

"You're leaving NCIS." He caught her hook, nodded approval at the follow-up she threw. "Not a question."

"Yes." She ducked under his combination. "What they do here, what Knight Tactical does ... it's not just about solving crimes or getting justice after the fact. They prevent the worst from happening in the first place. That's what I want to do."

She waited for the argument, the disappointment. Instead, he dropped his hands, his expression thoughtful.

"You know, when you were little, all I wanted was for you to follow in my footsteps." He smiled, touching his glove to her chin like he used to when she was small. "Took me too long to realize you needed to make your own path. And this" —he gestured toward the medical wing—"this looks like a pretty good path."

Maya blinked hard against sudden tears. "Really?"

"Really." He pulled her into a sweaty hug. "Just promise me one thing?"

"What's that?"

"When you and Ronan figure out whatever this is between you—and don't try to tell me there isn't something —you'll let your old man walk you down the aisle?"

"Dad!" But she was laughing, ducking away from his teasing jab.

"Just saying." He kissed her forehead. "I'm proud of you, baby girl. Always have been."

She stared him full in the face, chest tight. "Thank you."

He looked away. "Should have said those words way more often. I'm sorry about that."

"You're saying them now. That means everything."

Hands on his lean hips, he shuffled his feet, nodding in acknowledgement.

Needing to steer the conversation away from Ronan, away from her hopes that were nothing more than far off possibilities, she took charge.

"So let's talk about your love life," she said, mostly to lighten the moment, but also because she was intrigued. "You're pretty taken with Victoria Quinn."

His mouth dropped open. "Taken? I don't know about that."

"Dad. Don't even bother. You like her. A lot."

He squeezed the back of his neck, wincing. "That obvious?"

"Afraid so."

He got a dreamy look in his eyes. "She's a magnificent woman."

"Ask her out."

"What? No. The woman's got a demanding schedule. And my shifts are way too unpredictable."

She pulled off her gloves and made a face. "Wow. Is that an excuse I'm hearing? From the legendary Lawrence Chen? Really?"

He threw up his hands. "You're right. That's fair." He grinned at her. "How about this? I'll ask Victoria on a date if you talk to your guy. Neither one of us has anything to lose. What do you say?"

He was wrong. She had a lot to lose.

But she couldn't admit that aloud. Not to her father. Or herself. So she responded the only way she could. "Deal."

"Deal." Her father pulled her in for a bone-cracking hug, and then stowed his sparring equipment.

Maya watched him leave the gym, her smile fading. If only things were as clear-cut as her father saw them. A neat Hollywood ending where the guy gets the girl, the team welcomes her with open arms, and everyone lives happily ever after.

She unwrapped her hands slowly, studying her knuckles. The mission's success didn't change the fundamentals. Ronan was still Ronan—damaged, distant, wrapped in layers of armor she wasn't sure anyone could breach.

And Knight Tactical ... she'd helped with one mission, sure. But that didn't automatically translate to a job offer. These people had years of history, trust built in blood and fire. They'd worked together seamlessly while she'd just tried to keep up.

The bitter taste of reality settled on her tongue. She'd meant what she'd told her father about wanting this life, this mission. But wanting something and getting it were vastly different things.

Maya tossed the gloves in the bin and headed for the showers. Time to face the day—and whatever complications it brought—with clear eyes.

49

DAWN'S DUE

Ronan surfaced from the fever three days later in a private medical suite, an IV in his arm and the steady beep of monitors marking time. Something pressed against his chest, unfamiliar. His hand drifted up, fingers finding a metal chain and cross. He frowned, trying to remember where it had come from.

His first clear vision was Maya asleep in a chair beside his bed, her hand curled around his. When he shifted, her eyes opened instantly.

"Hey," she said, voice rough with exhaustion. "Welcome back."

He tried to speak, but his throat felt like sandpaper. She helped him with ice chips, her hands gentle.

While the blessed moisture melted in his mouth, his fingers drifted to his chest again, exploring the foreign object that had been nagging at his fuzzy consciousness. A chain, and a cross, substantial but not heavy. His thumb traced the contours, finding smooth edges worn by years of handling. The base was wider than the arms, tapering to clean lines that spoke of both strength and grace. Not ornate, but solid. The kind of cross a warrior would wear.

"What's this?" he managed finally, fingers still wrapped around it. The metal was warm from his skin.

Maya's expression softened. "It's Christian's. He wanted you to be safe." She hesitated. "He's been here every day, you know. Usually around dawn. Won't leave until someone else shows up."

The implications of that filtered slowly through Ronan's drug-hazed mind. Christian Murphy—his half-brother who'd barely acknowledged his existence for nearly three decades—had not only given him his cross but had been standing watch over him. Like family. Real family. The kind that showed up when it mattered.

Something tight unknotted in his chest. They needed to clear the air between them before he left Hope Landing. Twenty-eight years of silence was enough.

"Richardson?" he managed finally. "Where do we stand?"

"Can't shut the guy up." Axel's voice came from the doorway. He looked tired but steady, the haunted look from the explosions gone from his eyes. "The actual interviews are deeply classified. Not that that means a thing to Zara or Star or Ethan. Apparently, the man's given up everyone involved down to the building janitors. Turns out survival instinct trumps everything when you're facing multiple life sentences."

He moved farther into the room. "Oh, and we're all clear. BOLOs lifted. No more manhunts."

Christian appeared behind him, tablet in hand. "The network's falling apart. Richardson's people are scrambling to make deals. The admiral's been running operations nonstop, coordinating with agencies in three countries." He grinned. "Got some interesting intel about your fever, too."

LOST HOPE

Ronan tried to sit up, but Maya's hand on his chest kept him down. "What?" he asked.

"It wasn't the result of your wound. Kenji was on top of that from the minute you got shot. They dosed you," she said, and there was steel under the exhaustion in her voice. "At the reception. Low-grade bioweapon. Richardson's insurance policy. If things went south, he wanted to make sure at least one of us went down."

Christian looked like he wanted to murder someone. "Man figured he'd bargain for his freedom. The antidote for his escape." He scraped a hank of hair back off his face. "Idiot."

"The man always did like to hedge his bets," came a familiar voice. The admiral stepped into the increasingly crowded room, looking like he hadn't slept in days but somehow more alive than Ronan had seen him since they'd met. "Of course, he didn't count on your doc, Kenji, having experience with this particular compound."

Ronan's head was swimming again, but for different reasons. "So it's really over?"

The admiral opened his mouth to respond, but Ronan barely heard him. Maya's hand was still in his, and suddenly that was all he could focus on. Three days of fever dreams had clarified some things. Important things. Things he needed to tell her before—

His vision wavered slightly. Still not at full strength.

Griff filled the doorway. Something in his expression made Ronan's stomach tighten. He knew that look.

Maya must have sensed it too. She squeezed his hand once and stood. "We should let you rest."

"Wait." His voice was still rough. "Don't—I mean, we need to talk. Before you go. Promise?"

Her eyes softened. "Promise. I'll be back."

The others filed out, leaving him alone with Griff, who

settled into the chair Maya had vacated. For a long moment, neither spoke.

"Copenhagen," Griff said finally.

Just the word made Ronan's chest tighten. "We don't need to—"

"Yeah, we do." Griff leaned forward, elbows on his knees. "I can't keep hiding behind you on this. I took the shot. Whatever comes from that, I'll face it."

"I was trying to protect you. As commander, I would have gone down anyway. No reason for two of us to suffer."

"I know. But carrying this lie ..." Griff shook his head. "It's time to set it straight. Not officially, if you insist, but the team deserves to know."

It would change how they looked at Griff. The man had to know that. And yeah, judging from the pain creasing his face, he did. But okay. Really, it was Griff's right to insist.

Ronan closed his eyes. When he'd claimed responsibility for the shot, he'd thought he was doing the right thing. He never imagined the weight he'd place on his friend's shoulders. "You're right. But I want you with me when we tell them." He gestured at his hospital gown. "We'll do it first thing, once Kenji lets me wear grown up clothes again."

"Thank you." Griff's voice was quiet. After a pause, he added, "So. Maya?"

Ronan opened his eyes to find Griff studying him with a knowing look.

"Don't walk away from this one," Griff said softly.

The monitor beside the bed kept its steady rhythm as Ronan considered his response. He had no plans to walk away. But if Maya knew what was good for her, she probably should run. Far and fast.

Problem was, he wasn't strong enough to hope she would.

50

THE WEIGHT OF TRUTH

The Knight Tactical hangar gleamed in the morning sun, housing sleek aircraft worth more than most small countries' GDPs. Ronan leaned against the nose of a modified Bell 429, trying not to think about how this might be the last time they gathered here. Their mission was over. No more team, no more purpose binding them together.

The thought hit harder than he'd expected.

His team—former team now—drifted in one by one, finding their usual spots without discussion. Old habits. Zara hopped up on a work bench, legs swinging. Kenji settled cross-legged on the floor, his back against a tool chest. Izzy and Deke stood near the helicopter's tail, while Axel took up his customary position against the wall, arms crossed. Griff, as usual, hung just outside the open door.

They weren't Knight Tactical. Never had been, really. Just a thrown-together squad that somehow became family. And now ...

But that wasn't why they were here.

"So," Izzy broke the silence, characteristically direct.

"Anyone want to tell me why we're having this reunion at zero-dark-thirty?"

Kenji's dark eyes moved from Griff to Ronan and back again. "Something's been weighing on you both. Since Copenhagen." It wasn't a question.

"An excellent catch there, Doctor." Griff moved to face the group, hands clenched at his sides. His voice stayed steady as he told them about Copenhagen, about the underground lab he and Ronan raided, about the woman strapped to the examination table—young, blonde, looking so much like his sister that for a moment he'd forgotten where he was. About the doctor who'd been using her as his latest test subject. About the shot he'd taken, killing a terrible man, but a civilian non-combatant.

A move the Navy would never condone.

When he finished, the hangar fell silent except for the distant whir of ventilation fans.

Deke moved first, crossing to Griff. "You did what you had to. Combat situation, split-second decision."

Kenji nodded slowly. "That intel was messed up from the start. We shouldn't have been there blind like that."

"Why didn't you tell us?" Izzy's voice was soft, hurt. "We're a team."

"My call," Ronan said. "I ordered Griff to keep quiet. Took responsibility myself. I was CO. Brass was going to end my career no matter what. No reason for Griff to go down in flames, too. I ordered him not to tell anyone."

"What?" Kenji looked like he'd been slapped. A fair reaction. "Why?"

Now, face-to-face with these extraordinary folks, the full weight of his stupidity crashed down on him. He ducked his head. "I figured there was no need to burden you guys. It was my decision. My consequences."

"And mine," Griff added.

Yeah. And that.

"Idiots," Zara muttered, but there was no heat in it. "Both of you. Carrying this alone."

Axel hadn't moved from his position against the tool chest, arms crossed. But his eyes, when they met Ronan's, held understanding rather than judgment. "That makes a stupid kind of sense. Right instincts. Wrong answer."

Ronan clenched his jaw against the wave of emotion building behind his throat. Yeah. For sure. He should have had more faith in his team. His friends. Might have kept him from staying away these past three years.

Painful lesson learned.

Movement at the hangar entrance caught his attention. Christian and Jack stood in the doorway, clearly having caught the tail end of Griff's confession.

"Sir," Ronan started, but Jack waved him off.

"About time this came out," Christian said, his face carefully neutral.

"You knew," Ronan said. It wasn't a question.

Christian's lip quirked slightly. "Had a source close to the action."

The pieces clicked. "The woman on the table. The one we got out."

"She was the little sister of my Annapolis roomie." Christian's voice softened. "Why do you think your squad got called for that mission?"

Ronan stared at him. "You chose us?"

"You guys are the best of the best." Christian grinned. "I mean, after my team, that is."

"Your friend's sister," Griff said, voice rough. "Is she ... ?"

Christian's expression gentled. "She's good. Great, actually. Thanks to you."

The tension in Griff's shoulders eased slightly.

"So what now?" Izzy asked, after Jack and Christian had moved on.

"Now," Ronan said, "we stop carrying secrets that can break us." He looked at his team—his family—and saw nothing but solidarity looking back. "We do better." Not what he meant to say. He waved a hand in the air. "I mean, I do better."

Axel pushed off from the tool chest. "Together," he said simply, and one by one, the others nodded. "Whatever that means, going forward."

"Duh. It means no more disappearing," Izzy said, giving Ronan a sharp look.

He swallowed hard, his throat tight. "Copy that, Petty Officer."

It wasn't perfect. It wasn't fixed. But it was a start.

As the team started to disperse, the admiral's voice rang through the hangar. "Hold up a minute."

They turned to find him striding toward them, looking more relaxed than Ronan had ever seen him.

"Mrs. Knight's organizing a party here tonight. Tradition, after successful missions." His expression turned wry. "And while this isn't technically an order, I feel obligated to warn you that crossing Mrs. Knight would not be ... advisable."

A ripple of nervous laughter moved through the group.

"We'll be here, sir," Ronan assured him.

The admiral nodded and headed out. The others followed, voices echoing off the hangar walls, until only Ronan and Axel remained.

"So," Axel said after a moment. "Maya."

Ronan sighed. "Not you too."

"Look, I know you. You're thinking about all the reasons this can't work, why you should walk away—"

"It's called being realistic."

"It's called being a coward." Christian's voice made them

both jump. For a big guy, he moved like a ghost. "Don't be an idiot." He considered for a moment. "Or at least try being less of an idiot than you already are."

He punctuated this with a slap to Ronan's good shoulder that nearly knocked him sideways.

"Time to put on your big boy pants and take a risk, bro." Christian's grin was wolfish. "Unless you're scared?"

Ronan straightened, rubbing his shoulder. "I hate you both."

"Yeah, yeah." Christian started walking away. "See you tonight. Try not to overthink yourself into a corner before then."

Axel followed, but paused at the hangar door. "He's right. Bossy and insufferable, but right."

Ronan watched them go, their words echoing in his head. He looked up at the helicopter beside him, sleek and dangerous and beautiful.

Maybe it was time to jump without a parachute.

51

TARGET PRACTICE

THE SHARP TANG of gun oil and Pyrodex filled Ronan's nose as he headed for the locker room. His shoulder ached from where Christian had smacked it, their words about Maya still echoing in his head. He spotted Christian lounging against the wall near the weapons vault, the fluorescent lights casting harsh shadows across his half-brother's scarred knuckles.

"Quinn." Christian jerked his chin toward the door. "Walk with me."

Their boots squeaked against the polished floor as Ronan fell into step beside him, matching his lazy pace down the empty corridor. The temperature dropped several degrees as they entered the indoor shooting range—Christian's sanctuary, according to base scuttlebutt. The familiar scents of gunpowder and metal intensified. Christian's callused fingers moved with practiced efficiency as he began field-stripping a Sig, the pieces clicking softly against the wooden bench.

"So," Christian said, not looking up, "you planning to actually shoot something, or just stand there looking pretty?"

The protective earmuffs pressed uncomfortably against

Ronan's temples as he settled into the lane next to his brother. They shot in companionable silence, the synchronized rhythm of their breathing barely audible under the sharp crack of gunfire. The weapon's recoil traveled up Ronan's arms, grounding him in the moment.

"Your grouping's decent," Christian finally offered, the paper target rustling as he examined it. "For an invalid."

"Yeah? Let's see yours."

Christian's target showed a slightly tighter cluster. Maybe. If you squinted.

"Lucky shots," Ronan muttered, catching a whiff of Christian's familiar combination of sage soap and weapon solvent as the man leaned closer.

"Keep telling yourself that." The soft cloth made whisking sounds as Christian cleaned his weapon, each movement precise. "You know, for someone carrying my cross, you're kind of a smartass."

The metal was warm against Ronan's chest where the cross lay hidden under his shirt. His fingers were slightly sweaty as he set his pistol down. "Look, I know I'm not what you expected in a brother. The screw-up Murphy. I can own that."

Christian's hands stilled on the weapon, the silence sudden and heavy. "I never blamed you, you know. For Dad's affair with your mother. For any of it."

"You ... didn't?"

"How could I blame a baby for choices two adults made?" Christian's voice echoed slightly in the concrete range. He reassembled his weapon with quick, metallic clicks. "Though I guess I owe you an apology too. For never reaching out when you were growing up."

"Why didn't you?"

Christian's laugh bounced off the walls, hollow and harsh. "Because I didn't want to deal with the feelings. In case you haven't noticed, we Murphys aren't exactly emotional champions."

The admission loosened something in Ronan's chest. His fingers found the cross at his neck, warm from his skin, its edges smooth from wear. "Hey, do you want this back? I'm going to make it, and I appreciate the gesture—"

"Keep it." Christian's voice was firm, his jaw set. "If you're willing to honor what it represents."

"I am." Ronan's eyes traced the elaborate cross tattooed down Christian's forearm, the black ink stark against his tanned skin. Sweat beaded at Christian's hairline from the range's stuffy air. "Though what I really want is one of those."

Christian blew out a breath that smelled faintly of coffee. "That's a hard no." Then his face cracked into a grin, softening the scar above his eyebrow. "Just kidding, bro."

The words hung between them, warm and genuine for the first time, free of its usual bitter edge.

"When you're ready, I'll take you to my guy. You're good with travelling back to Damascus, right? No. Wait. Hassim emigrated to Jordan, which is awesome. I like Amman way better. You're not on any wanted lists there, right?"

Ronan blinked hard, trying to maintain his hold on the thread of the conversation. "No. No problems." He set his weapon down. "What do you mean, 'ready?' Are you talking an initiation or something?"

"Nah." Christian's fist thumped against his own chest. "When you're ready in here. Like when you finally know for sure you're going to make it through BUD/S and earn your trident. You'll know."

"Sounds reasonable." And way better than the vague hazing he was imagining. They'd exchanged few words, but what had just passed between them felt momentous. He wasn't sure whether the buzzing in his head was from the illness, or this emotional overload. Whatever the cause, it was time for some air. He shuffled his feet. "So we're good?"

Christian set his handgun in its case and zipped it shut. "I'm good if you're good."

"Great."

"Fine."

The overhead lights hummed as Christian shifted, his boots scraping against the floor. "Actually, I'm glad we're talking. The Big Man authorized me to feel you out about something. How would you and your team feel about joining Knight Tactical?"

Ronan's pulse jumped. "Are you serious?"

"Dead serious." Christian's eyes, the same shade of green as their father's, held his steadily.

"I ... I don't know if they'd want to. Izzy and Deke have kids, and the others ... it's been a long time." His fault, completely.

"It's not all or nothing. We'll take whoever wants to come."

Ronan's throat closed. He swallowed hard before asking, "What about Maya?"

Christian's grin turned predatory, his teeth flashing white. "The admiral's extending a personal invitation to the lady right this very minute." His expression hardened, shoulders squaring. "That gonna be a problem?"

Only if she refuses. Ronan's fingers found their way into his pocket, crossing tightly. The childhood gesture made his palms sweat.

"Nope," he said aloud, proud of how steady his voice sounded.

"Good." Christian's hand cracked against his back, the impact stinging through his shirt. "Hockey team'll be hitting the gym Monday after school. Fifteen hundred. Be there."

His footsteps echoed off the walls as he left, leaving

behind the lingering scent of gun oil and sage. Ronan stood alone in the fluorescent glare, possibilities spinning in his head. The cross felt heavy against his chest as he bowed his head, offering up an awkward prayer, acknowledging the unwavering faith he'd witnessed in Christian, in his team, in Maya. He could learn if the Lord was willing to have patience with him. Something flickered in his chest, tiny but warm—a seed of hope to nurture.

And while he was at it, maybe the Lord could help him find the courage to tell Maya how he felt about her. His fingers traced the cross again, and for the first time in years, he felt truly anchored.

52

MAYA END...

Maya paused in the doorway of Tailwinds, momentarily disoriented. The homey café that shared a wall with Lauren Daggett's original DreamBurger location in the tiny Hope Landing Terminal had morphed into something out of a music video. Tables lined the walls, strings of lights crisscrossed the ceiling like a constellation map, and the usually quiet space thumped with bass notes that vibrated through her borrowed heels.

But it was Ethan's DJ station that made her grin. The tech genius had transformed a corner of the café into what looked like mission control for a Mars landing. Screens flickered with pulsing visualizations, RGB lights swept patterns across the makeshift dance floor, and Ethan himself wore what appeared to be a vintage NASA flight suit as he adjusted controls with the same intensity he brought to drone operations.

"Pretty impressive, right?" Star materialized beside her, lemonade in hand. "My husband doesn't do anything halfway."

Maya accepted the glass, taking in the unlikely mix of faces. Tactical operators in casual clothes mingled with kids racing between clusters of adults. A far cry from the sterile NCIS office parties she was used to. She spotted Austin's wife Lauren in animated conversation with Jose near the kitchen, probably discussing the café's journey from her original vision to his current ownership. The smell of carnitas drifted from the kitchen, mixing with perfume and the sweet-sharp bite of craft root beer.

"I still can't believe you let me borrow this. It's beyond cute," Maya said, smoothing the buttery cotton that Star had insisted would be perfect. The deep blue material felt like wearing midnight.

"Honey, that dress was made for you." Star clinked their glasses together. "And wait until you see what happens when Ethan really gets going. These guys may look scary in the field, but give them a dance floor ..." She gestured toward Jack, who was attempting to teach his daughter what appeared to be the robot. Kelli was recording it on her phone, shoulders shaking with laughter.

Maya smiled, but her eyes kept drifting to the door. She told herself she wasn't watching for anyone in particular. She was just ... appreciating the scene. The way the Hope Landing family celebrated. The perfect blend of professional precision and absolute chaos.

Just then, Ethan hit something on his controls and the lights shifted into what had to be his mission-accomplished sequence. The café erupted in cheers as the music swelled.

The cheers hadn't even faded when Izzy, Zara, and Axel descended on Maya like a tactical strike team. Izzy's sequined top caught the shifting lights, Zara had traded her usual tech gear for a striking red sundress, and Axel ... well, Axel still wore combat boots with a wrinkled button down and hiking shorts.

"So what did you decide about Knight Tactical?" Izzy asked without preamble, her direct gaze as unwavering as when she had a target in her scope. "You in or what?"

Maya watched the admiral across the room, his arm wrapped possessively around his wife's waist as they swayed to something slow. Must be nice, that kind of certainty. "I'm still thinking about it."

"What's to think about?" Axel sprawled against the wall. "We're all in. Even that pain-in-the-ass Kenji's signing on. He has med bay envy."

"Everyone?" The word caught in her throat. She didn't need to specify who she was asking about.

"Everyone," Zara confirmed softly. She shot Maya a look that was far too knowing.

Maya's lemonade suddenly needed her complete attention. The thought of working with him every day, planning ops, running missions ... Would the ache in her chest ever dull, or would it just get sharper with proximity?

"Look who's corrupting my daughter now!" Her father's voice carried over the music as Victoria dragged him onto the dance floor. For an old guy, he moved with surprising grace, his laughter younger than Maya had heard it in years.

"Hey." Star nudged her shoulder. "You okay?"

"Fine." Maya managed a smile. "Just ... processing."

Jack's daughter raced past with his wife, strobe lights glinting off the matching plastic tiaras Kelli had somehow been talked into. Their laughter mixed with the bass line as Ethan transitioned into something with more edge. The dance floor filled, tactical operators and support staff moving with the same fluid coordination they brought to missions.

Maya recognized the moment for what it was—a glimpse of what her future could be. A team that functioned like family. Work that mattered. Everything she'd ever wanted in a career.

Everything except ...

The door opened, letting in a burst of cool air. Maya's heart stuttered as she turned, already knowing who it would be.

53

MAYA AGAIN

The Hawaiian shirt should have been ridiculous. It was obviously borrowed—probably from Christian, given the slightly tight shoulders—and clashed spectacularly with Ronan's borrowed board shorts. But somehow the tourist-casual outfit looked like something that belonged on a magazine cover. His dark hair was still damp from a shower, curling slightly at his neck, and his easy stride showed no trace of his recent injuries.

Christian followed right behind him in an equally outrageous outfit.

A matching pair in more ways than one. The resemblance between the two seemed even stronger now. Same mouth. Same gorgeous eyes. Same over-the-top magnetism.

Maya downed the rest of her drink. This was exactly why joining Knight Tactical would be the worst kind of torture.

"Holy tactical beefcake," Izzy muttered, earning an elbow from Zara. "What? I'm just saying what we're all thinking."

Ronan stopped to high-five Jack's toddlers as they blazed past, then got waylaid by Griffin near the makeshift bar. Maya watched him laugh at something the boss said, his whole face lighting up in a way she'd rarely seen during their mission. He looked ... lighter. More at peace.

"So?" Izzy cocked her head, zeroing in on Maya with sniper precision. "You gonna join us at Knight Tactical or what?"

The words stuck in Maya's throat. How could she explain that her dream job had somehow become complicated by a man who'd barely let her past his walls? That the thought of seeing him every day, watching him slowly heal and maybe eventually open his heart to someone else, felt like signing up for daily surgery without anesthesia?

"I ... need to think about it some more."

Izzy and Zara exchanged a look that contained volumes. Then Zara wrapped her in a fierce hug that smelled like gunpowder and expensive perfume. "Men," she said firmly, "are idiots."

"Copy that," Maya managed.

She felt the exact moment Ronan noticed their group. His stride hitched slightly as he approached, and that magnetic pull she'd been fighting since day one kicked in like a riptide. The others melted away with suspicious efficiency, leaving them in their own pocket of space despite the crowded room.

"You look ..." His eyes tracked over her borrowed dress, leaving heat in their wake. "Amazing."

The word hung between them like smoke signals neither of them knew how to read.

The music faded with a deliberate slowness, and Maya watched Deke step onto a chair, his massive frame silhouetted against the twinkling lights. The room hushed without him having to say a word.

"Before we get too deep into celebrating," Deke's deep voice carried easily, touched with the gravel of emotion, "I'd like us to take a moment. For Marcus."

The silence that followed felt sacred. Maya glanced at

Ronan, standing close enough that she could feel the heat of him, yet he somehow remained miles away. His jaw was tight, but his eyes were clear.

"Tank ..." Kenji started, then had to clear his throat. "Tank once told me the meaning of life was good barbecue and better friends. Then he corrected himself and said it was actually proper trigger discipline, but the barbecue thing was a close second." Scattered laughter mixed with sniffs.

Others stepped forward, sharing pieces of Marcus. The way he'd volunteer for the worst watches so younger operators could sleep. His terrible jokes and worse singing and unfailing loyalty.

"He showed up at my door at 3:00 a.m. once," Kenji offered quietly. "Said he knew I was having nightmares about that op in Manila. Brought coffee and sat with me till dawn."

Maya felt tears spill over. She wasn't the only one. Zara was openly crying, Axel's arm around her shoulders. Izzy stared straight ahead, jaw set, fragile as glass. Even Griffin looked suspiciously bright-eyed.

"If you're the praying type," Deke said finally, "now would be the time."

Maya wasn't surprised to see heads bow—these people faced death too often not to have wrestled with faith. But she wasn't prepared for the way Ronan's eyes closed, his lips moving slightly in silent words. There was no hesitation in it, no self-consciousness. Just the simple devotion of a man who'd found his way back to believing in something bigger than himself.

Her heart ached with pride and loss all at once. He'd come so far from the broken man she'd first met, letting down walls brick by careful brick. Learning to trust again, to pray again, to let people in again.

Just ... not her. Not in the way that mattered.

"To Tank." Griffin raised his glass.

"To Tank," the room echoed.

Ethan let the silence hold for a heartbeat longer, then eased into something slow and sweet. Couples gravitated together, seeking comfort in connection. Maya watched Victoria draw her father onto the dance floor, saw the admiral pull his wife closer.

Victoria laughed at something Maya's father said, her head tipping back with unguarded joy. He looked younger somehow, the lines of grief softened by new possibilities. They moved together with the easy confidence of people who knew exactly what they wanted.

Maya's throat tightened. She'd always thought her father would be the one struggling to move forward, to find happiness after loss. Instead, he was dancing with his heart wide open while she—

Ronan's hand touched her elbow, and her skin hummed like a live wire.

"Dance with me?"

It was probably a mistake. But then, her heart had been making mistakes about Ronan Quinn since the beginning.

She turned into his arms, and it felt like she was coming home. His hand settled at her waist, warm through the silk of her dress. She caught the familiar scent of his cologne mixed with leather and gun oil—a combination that should have screamed danger but instead made her feel impossibly safe. Their bodies remembered this dance, falling into rhythm as naturally as breathing.

His heartbeat steady under her palm. The subtle flex of muscle as he guided her through a turn. The slight calluses on his fingers where they intertwined with hers. Every point of contact sent sparks racing along her nerves, and she found herself drawing closer, drawn by the gravitational pull that had always existed between them.

The music wrapped around them like a cocoon, and Maya

let herself forget about everything else—the mission, the danger, the complicated history. For these few precious moments, there was only the dance, only Ronan's arms holding her like she was something precious and breakable and essential all at once. His thumb traced small circles on her back, probably unconsciously, and she had to fight to keep from shivering at the intimate gesture.

As the song ended, she eased back from Ronan's embrace, needing space to breathe. To think.

Turning down her dream job because of a man felt like something out of a bad romance novel. The kind where the heroine sacrificed everything for love and somehow it all worked out in the end.

But this wasn't a romance novel. This was her life, and seeing Ronan every day ... that wasn't sacrifice. That was self-destruction.

"Ronan!" Christian's voice cut through her thoughts. "Blair's dying to hear about that time in Kandahar with the goat."

Ronan's hand dropped from her waist abruptly, like he'd suddenly remembered himself. He took a half-step back, creating a chasm between them that felt wider than the actual space. "I should probably ..." He gestured vaguely toward Christian, leaving the sentence unfinished.

"Right." Maya wrapped her arms around herself, missing his warmth already. "You should ..."

He nodded once, sharp and military-precise, then turned away without another word. No promise of another dance. No lingering look. Just the straight line of his shoulders as he walked away, each step methodical as if he were forcing himself not to rush.

She watched him disappear into the crowd, tall and remote and more untouchable than ever. The music pulsed around her, celebration in full swing, but she barely heard it over the hollow echo in her chest. That's what she got for letting hope creep in—just another reminder that some distances couldn't be bridged, no matter how close you stood.

Maybe she could stick with NCIS and request a transfer. San Diego had openings. Or Pearl Harbor—Hawaii was about as far as you could get without leaving the country entirely. She could start fresh somewhere new, somewhere without ghosts of almost-love haunting every corner.

But she already knew the truth. There was nowhere far enough to escape her own heart.

Star appeared at her elbow with another glass of sparkling lemonade. "You okay, honey?"

Maya accepted the glass, watching the bubbles rise like all her broken dreams. "I will be." She took a slow breath. "I just need to figure out what's next."

The party swirled on around her, full of joy and possibility and future plans. She just had to find the courage to choose her own.

Alone.

54

BEGINNINGS

Ronan slipped out of Tailwinds, needing air that wasn't thick with laughter and possibility. Inside, Blair had just finished telling some story about Christian memorizing her entire coffee order before their first real date—right down to the extra shot and splash of vanilla—and his teammate's besotted expression made something in Ronan's chest ache.

The summer night hit him like a wall of warm velvet. The tarmac stretched black and empty under the stars, its edges bleeding into shadow where the valley walls rose up, sudden and steep. Granite peaks cut jagged lines against the sky, and somewhere in the darkness, cicadas were singing their endless summer song.

He walked until the sounds from Tailwinds faded, until he could pretend he wasn't listening for footsteps behind him. The mountains felt different now—less like the backdrop to another temporary assignment and more like ... home. The thought stopped him cold. When had he started thinking of this place as home?

Since Maya.

He hadn't gotten a chance to ask her about the offer.

She'd been surrounded all night—his mother, the admiral, the endless stream of people wanting to congratulate her on her first op. And when they danced, he couldn't bear to ruin that brief, shining moment. But he'd caught glimpses: her quiet smile, the way she kept tucking her hair behind her ear when she was thinking hard about something. The look on her face when Blair had talked about making a life here, like she was seeing something just out of reach.

If she turned down the job ... if she left ...

He pressed his palms against the hood of the nearest vehicle, letting the residual heat from the engine ground him. The practical part of his brain, the part that had kept him alive through a dozen hot zones, told him to start preparing. To imagine a future here without her, working with Knight Tactical, rebuilding his life.

But standing there under the stars, with the mountains rising like walls around him, he finally admitted what he'd known since she'd ordered him and Axel out of Tank's condo: there was no preparing for a life without Maya. Not anymore.

A burst of laughter from the party carried across the tarmac. He straightened, squaring his shoulders against the night air. He needed to talk to her. About the job, about them, about everything he'd been too careful to say.

Before she walked away thinking he wanted her to.

He just had to figure out how to—

"You planning to hide out here all night, dude?"

Ronan turned to find his team emerging from the shadows, Griffin bringing up the rear. From their expressions, this wasn't a casual check-in.

Well, yikes.

The team spread out in a loose circle, and Ronan caught the faint scent of gunpowder that always seemed to linger on their clothes, mixed with the sharp pine from the surrounding forest. Axel's boots scraped against the tarmac, the sound unnaturally loud in the night air. The asphalt still radiated heat through Ronan's boots, but a cooler breeze had started flowing down from the peaks, carrying with it the metallic hint of snow that never quite melted, even in August.

"So," Deke said, his shadow stretching long under the security lights. "You and Maya."

Ronan's fingers twitched, missing the familiar weight of his rifle. He'd rather be pinned down under heavy fire than have this conversation. "Not now."

"Yeah, actually now." Axel's voice was gravel-soft but immovable. Like the mountains themselves. "Because we're all in on this Knight Tactical thing, and we need you operating at full capacity."

The circle tightened almost imperceptibly. Ronan could feel the pressure of their concern like a physical touch against his skin. These people had saved his life more times than he could count, had trusted him with theirs. The least he could do was listen.

Griffin stepped forward, his presence solid and steady as always. "You're not the only one who's noticed how you are around her."

"And how's that?" The words came out rougher than he intended.

"Whole," Zara said simply. She'd materialized silently at Ronan's four o'clock. "Trust me on this one. I wrote the book on watching happiness walk away because I was too stubborn to reach for it."

He clenched his jaw. The metal of his watch was warm against his wrist. He focused on that sensation, trying to ground himself. "It's not that simple."

"Actually," Axel said, "it really is." His boot scuffed against the tarmac as he shifted. "You love her. She loves you. The rest is just details."

The words hit Ronan like a physical blow. He'd been so careful not to think them, not to admit them even to himself. But here they were, laid bare under the stadium lights, as obvious to his team as the mountains against the sky.

Deke's massive hand landed on his shoulder, warm and anchoring. "You've spent your whole life running toward the fight, Quinn. Maybe it's time to stop running from this one."

The truth of it settled into his bones, as undeniable as gravity. They were right. God help him, they were all right.

"And now," Axel said, a familiar gleam in his eye, "we're going to help you fix it."

Ronan caught the quick glances between his teammates, the slight nods. "What are you—"

The crunch of gravel turned him around. Maya was walking toward them, her silhouette unmistakable even in shadow. His heart slammed against his ribs.

By the time he looked back, his team had melted away like smoke, leaving him alone with all the words he'd never said and the woman he couldn't lose.

The night breeze brushed his arms, electric and alive with possibility and terror in equal measure.

Maya stopped a few feet away, close enough that he could catch the faint citrus scent of her shampoo on the night breeze. The security lights caught the planes of her face, the uncertain set of her mouth. Behind her, the mountains rose black against the star-scattered sky, and Ronan thought of all the times he'd mapped escape routes, planned extraction points. How automatic it had become to look for ways out.

Not this time.

"Your team," she said, her voice holding a mix of exasperation and affection, "is about as subtle as a breaching charge."

"Subtlety was never our strong suit." His voice came out rougher than he intended. "We prefer the direct approach."

"Is that what this is?"

"Maya." Her name felt like a prayer on his tongue. "I need to ask you something."

She took a half step closer, and he caught the whisper of her dress against her skin. "I need to tell you something first."

His heart stumbled. "Okay."

"I'm staying." The words fell between them like stones into still water. "I accepted the position with Knight Tactical."

The relief hit him so hard his hands shook. He curled them into fists at his sides, fighting the urge to reach for her. "Why?"

"Because it's everything I've trained for. Everything I want to do." She paused, and he watched her gather her courage. "And because you're here."

The last of his careful walls crumbled. "I was going to ask you to stay."

"Just for the job?"

"For the job." He moved closer, drawn by the gravity of her. By all the possibilities spinning out before them. "For this place. For me." His fingers found her wrist, traced the delicate bones there. Her pulse raced under his touch. "But mostly, for you."

She turned her hand in his, their calluses catching. "That's a lot."

"Too much?"

"No." Her free hand came up to rest against his chest, and he wondered if she could feel his heart thundering beneath her palm. "But fair warning—I'm going to need my own office. And a really good coffee maker."

A laugh broke free from his chest, unexpected and real. "Anything else?"

"Yes." Her fingers curled into his shirt. "I'm going to need you to kiss me now. Before your team decides to help with that too."

Ronan's hand slid into her hair, tilting her face up to his. "That," he said against her mouth, "I can definitely handle."

He kissed her like a man coming home, like a soldier laying down his weapons, like every dream he'd never let himself want. She tasted of coffee and promise and tomorrow, and when she smiled against his lips, he felt the last piece of his world slide into place.

Somewhere in the darkness, he heard the distinctive slap of a high-five and Axel's badly whispered, "Finally." But with Maya warm in his arms and the mountain night wrapping around them like a blanket, he couldn't bring himself to care.

For the first time in his life, he was exactly where he needed to be.

∼

I HOPE you enjoyed Ronan and Maya's story. Writing a sequel to the original Hope Landing series has been on my mind for a long time. I'm thrilled to be able to revisit old friends…and share a whole new found-family of heroes with you!

The action continues in DEADLY HOPE as Axel, struggling with his worsening PTSD, finds himself protecting the first woman to touch his heart since…forever. Unfortunately for him, Olivia Kane is also the first professional to crack the battered armor holding him together.

In the meantime, here's to Faith, Family and Friends—
All the best, Edie
Click HERE to order DEADLY HOPE.

∼

LOST HOPE

HE CAME FOR A THERAPY SESSION. He left with a mission.

After months of pushing from his team, and the higher ups at Knight Tactical, Axel Reinhardt, a battle-scarred former SEAL, is forced to seek help for his PTSD. Walking into Olivia Kane's office is the hardest thing he's ever done. But it's nothing compared to what happens next.

Olivia, a dedicated trauma therapist, is ready to help Axel confront his demons until a violent attack turns her safe space into a war zone.

Now, Axel must protect the woman who was supposed to be healing him. Can he overcome his own trauma to keep her safe? Or will the secrets of her brother's past destroy them both?

Faith under fire. Love on the line.

Meet the new SEALs in town. Hope Landing: Where every mission echoes with danger. Faith lights the way. And love is the ultimate rescue mission.

Click HERE to order DEADLY HOPE.

WHAT READERS ARE SAYING about Edie James—

Fast-paced and emotionally gripping!

Edie James delivers another heart-pounding story in *Lost Hope*! I started this book and couldn't put it down until the last page. Maya and Ronan's partnership is electric—full of tension, action, and trust-building moments that kept me hooked. The return of Knight Tactical through Christian Murphy was a fantastic bonus for fans of Edie's previous series, but new readers will easily dive in too. The plot twists were masterfully done, and the ending left me desperate for the next book. Highly recommend!

--Nadia G. Amazon Customer

What a thrilling start to the Hope Landing New Recruits series!

Oh, WOW! *Lost Hope* is a spectacular beginning to Edie James' new series. The chemistry between Maya and Ronan is off the charts, and the suspense had me on the edge of my seat. I loved the mix of action, mystery, and romance—plus the deeper layers of family and redemption that gave the story so much heart. I can't wait to see where Maya and Ronan's journey goes in book two. A must-read!

--Sandy S. Amazon Customer

Edie James does it again—another late-night read!

I stayed up way too late finishing *Lost Hope* because I just couldn't stop turning the pages! Maya's determination and Ronan's edge make for such a compelling duo. The stakes are high, the twists are shocking, and the subtle weaving of faith into the story adds so much depth. I loved seeing Knight Tactical characters make an appearance, but the focus on Ronan and Maya's journey was perfection. Edie, PLEASE write faster—I need book two now!

--Beth C. Amazon Customer

FREE SERIES STARTER!

Start the HOPE LANDING series FREE. Click HERE to join my newsletter and download HARD LANDING free.

**Two wary souls get a second chance at love
If a killer doesn't find them first.**

When a stalker turns to murder, pilot Kelli Spencer needs protection. What she doesn't need is her old love Jack Reese returning to stir things up, but the former Navy SEAL and his team of protection specialists are the best of the best. Trust him with her life? If she has to. Her heart? No way.

The last time Jack left, he made it clear married life held no appeal. Ten years later, he wastes no time letting her know he hasn't changed. Not that she'd be fool enough to hope.

As the commander of Knight Tactical, Jack jumps at the chance to protect Kelli and take down a killer, but as soon as she's safe, he plans to shake the dust of the small mountain town off his feet again...until he realizes he never should have left the first time.

Can he convince Kelli to give him another chance, or will a devious killer destroy his plans for a happily ever after?

Danger. Family. Faith. Meet the SEALs of Hope Landing. Born to protect. Destined for love.

Welcome to Hope Landing, where the former SEALs of Knight Tactical Protection battle danger and tests of faith on the road to lasting love. A series of clean, inspirational action adventure romances, each guaranteed to lift your heart.

I LOVE hearing from readers! Connect with me at Edie@EdieJamesBooks.com

Made in the USA
Columbia, SC
19 September 2025